ALSO BY VICTORIA GLENDINNING

Rebecca West: A Life (1987)

Vita: The Life of Vita Sackville-West (1983)

Edith Sitwell: A Unicorn Among Lions (1981)

Elizabeth Bowen (1978)

A Suppressed Cry (1969)

THE GROWN-UPS

THE

GROWN-UPS

Victoria Glendinning

ALFRED A. KNOPF

New York 1990

THIS IS A BORZOI BOOK
PUBLISHED BY ALFRED A. KNOPF, INC.

Copyright © 1989 by Victoria Glendinning
All rights reserved under International and Pan-American
Copyright Conventions. Published in the United States
by Alfred A. Knopf, Inc., New York.
Distributed by Random House, Inc., New York.
Originally published in Great Britain by Hutchinson,
an imprint of Century Hutchinson Ltd., London, in 1989.

Library of Congress Cataloging-in-Publication Data
Glendinning, Victoria.
The grown-ups / by Victoria Glendinning. — 1st ed.
p.   cm.
ISBN-0-394-57947-X
I. Title.
PR6057.L43G7   1990
813'.54—dc20   89-45300   CIP

Manufactured in the United States of America
First American Edition

For Ann Crawshaw

THE GROWN-UPS

1

THERE'S MORE TO LOVE than fucking.

Clara didn't say that aloud, not to Martha.

Leo had been dead a week. The two of them were picking over a pile of newspaper cuttings and Clara was remembering walking on Clapham Common with Leo on a windy day, years ago. They both walked self-consciously, arms swinging at their sides, Clara's fingers stiff with longing and indecision. If she put her hand in his, there could be a shock, an explosion, an illumination—or just nothing, no connection, embarrassment. She didn't risk it. Leo snapped the lead on to Mungo's collar, and they went back to the house, and to Martha.

Clara turned up the obituary from *The Times:*

DR. LEO ULM

Philosopher, author and television personality

Dr. Leo Ulm, D.Phil., FRSL, who died in the early hours of October 16, his fifty-ninth birthday, was a gifted scholar and a natural communicator who emerged with the new generation of bright young academics in the 1960s and became increasingly prominent in the forefront of intellectual life both in Britain and abroad until the onset of illness earlier this year.

He was born in Manchester in 1928, the only son of Camelot Ulm, a textile wholesaler . . .

Clara skipped the long middle bit about his education, his books, his charm, his career in TV and his university posts, and read the very end:

In 1954 he married Charlotte Bench-Markham, only daughter of Brigadier F. R. O. Bench-Markham of Belwood in East Sussex. There was one son of the marriage, which was dissolved in 1975. The same year he married Martha Pardo, the illustrator, who survives him.

"I never knew Charlotte's name had been Bench-Markham," said Clara.

"So what?" said Martha. "There was no need for you to know, was there?"

"One knows hundreds of things one doesn't need to know. Including some things that one would rather not know."

No one ever knows the whole story. Well, that's obvious. The outside story puts pressure on the inside story. Inside the inside story, distorted, are more stories. The people on the inside know a few small things, mostly about themselves. The people on the outside know a few big things, from which they draw wrong conclusions.

So no one knows what's going on.

Nothing is going on at all, not in that sense. Things happen all the time, evenly, everywhere, the way the rain patters on the lake at Belwood. In order to keep sane, each person focuses on a few drops and joins them with a line, like in a dot-to-dot colouring book. The pattern this makes is called a story. Once upon a time . . .

You probably know these people already. They are the flotsam of 1980s Britain. Flotsam, because they are floating, just. Jetsam is what gets thrown overboard, to be washed up no one cares where.

You will know their famous friend Leo Ulm anyway, because you saw him on television. Didn't you think he was attractive? Most people, men and women, were drawn to him by his tension, his vitality, his lopsided smile. That air of uncertainty was irresistible in someone so popular and successful.

He always had a genius for publicity. He was first in the news just after the war, an unknown boy from Manchester doing his National Service, when he rescued a fellow lieutenant from drowning in the Rhine. In the 1960s he was the flower children's favourite thinker. They read his books and quoted them at each other. He became seriously famous again just recently because of that television programme.

His private life was a bit odd. Wasn't there something about an immensely rich first wife who went mad? A son who was handicapped or something? No, it was an accident, with fireworks.

Friends of friends said that there was something peculiar about the way Leo Ulm died, on the night of the hurricane in October 1987. But nothing ever came out.

Leo was a great lover of women. That's the story, anyway. When he married as his second wife a girl less than half his age, the tabloids made the most of it. "TEACHER'S PET" was a typical headline—untrue, because Martha Pardo had never been Leo's pupil.

Clara Cook was one of Martha's two best friends. (Alice, who married Leo's son, was the other.) Drawn into Leo's orbit, Clara too became obsessed with him. She might not have said that she was in love with him exactly. Clara had never been loved, or so she believed. She was therefore wary of doing too much loving.

There are people who think they are loved, though they aren't. They are merely figures in the landscape. Habit and good manners—other people's—make up the lack. Clara's situation was preferable to that sort of fool's paradise.

That was what Clara told herself. She had to work hard to see anything positive about her life and the sort of person she was, after she lost her job. Arundel & Carton, the publishing house where she had been an editor for five years, had been bought by a conglomerate with interests in the construction industry and a hotel chain. Why they wanted Arundel & Carton it was hard to imagine. There were jokes in the trade about the new proprietors turning the firm into another pair of hotels, since the names were so suitable, as were the ample premises in Covent Garden.

In the fallout Clara was made redundant, in the nicest possible way. She minded very much, though she tried to hide her misery from Martha and Alice. Clara was proud. With the job she lost the comfortable structure of her days, most of her self-respect, and her play-group. "Come in and see us," said her colleagues as she cleared her desk on the last day.

But she did not and knew she would not. She had watched former Arundel & Carton people calling into the office, glanced at blankly by the new intake. The visitors would lean on the old friends' desks, ready for a chat and a giggle, but it didn't really work. The scandals and the running jokes were new and incomprehensible, loyalties were realigned, and it was all just too complicated to share with the old-timer. No one even tried. You could tell, or Clara could, that the ones sitting at their desks were longing to get on with their work. "We must have lunch." No date specified. Clara did not want that.

In view of her youth and, the new chairman said, the fact that she would undoubtedly be snapped up by another publishing firm within a month, the handshake had been less than golden. Even so, it was better than nothing.

Clara had not "signed on." She made one inconclusive visit to her local Department of Health and Social Security office in a black cliff of a building at the top of the Holloway Road called Archway Tower. There she was given an appointment for an interview the following week. She did not go for the interview, and so was getting no dole.

She had not yet been offered another job and was too proud, or lazy, to look for one with proper strenuousness. She should have been telephoning everyone she knew, letting it be known that she was on the market. Instead, she had gone to ground to lick her wound. She read a lot. She wasn't going out with anyone special. Because she was not seen around, she wasn't asked out much. She was in baulk.

Then Clara, nearly thirty, redundant and unattached, fell unexpectedly for Harry Ashe, whom she met at a performance of *Der Rosenkavalier* at the Coliseum. Both alone, they were sitting next to each other in the upper circle. In the first interval they went for a drink together. Clara said:

"It's so silly, a girl playing a boy dressing up as a girl. All that first bit rolling on the bed is just a lesbian superdrama."

"It's a convention, and an excuse for a lot of luscious caterwauling," he'd replied. "Anyway, love makes nonsense of gender—the two sexes keep changing places and behaving like the one they're not."

"I don't know much about opera, and even less about love."

In the second interval they wandered out into St. Martin's Lane, shivered, and took refuge in the Salisbury pub on the other side of the road. They didn't go back for the last act.

Six months later, Clara no longer dreamed of the unattainable Leo, or not every night. She did not know how her unlikely passion for Harry would develop. She hoped that "in love" would become love and last for ever. Love Divine All Loves Excelling, as in the hymn.

She didn't risk letting Harry know how hopeful she was, though she was beginning to let herself believe that Harry loved her. But it's different for men.

Well, isn't it?

Clara wished she could inhabit a man's body just for an hour, and know what it was like to carry around that awkwardly positioned and demanding spare part. A third party, as in Third Party, Fire and Theft. Or like the sports equipment that cluttered her brother's sock-stinking bedroom in adolescence. Cricket bat. Tennis racket. Fencing foil. Billiard cue.

There was a billiard table at Belwood—on the upstairs landing, which was as big as a big room, with corridors running off it, and the stairhead curling down towards the hall. Belwood is the country house that Leo's first wife Charlotte had inherited; it was Leo's first marital home. Afterwards their son

Ferdie lived there, with Alice. The billiard table, like the Italian oil-paintings of romantic forested landscapes that covered the landing walls, had been acquired by Charlotte's father. It had shiny bulbous legs and worn leather cushioning round the edge.

Just before Leo's last trip to America, Clara was staying with Alice and Ferdie at Belwood. Everyone had gone to bed. Clara lay in the spare room listening to the owls. Suddenly the front door banged and there was a shout in the hall, and footsteps coming up the stairs. Clara jumped out of bed and emerged from the mouth of her corridor on to the wide moonlit landing at the same time as Alice appeared on the other side. Both in long pale nightdresses, barefoot, hands to their throats, they stared.

It was Leo, in high spirits, white-blond hair gleaming, glasses askew, a little drunk. He had been speaking at a dinner at Sussex University. He wanted a bed for the night.

"But first, I think, a game of snooker. Which of you will play?"

Alice had to make up a bed for him, so it fell to Clara to play with him.

It was the first time she had Leo's undivided attention. It made her dizzy. He had snapped on the lights, taken off his dinner jacket and arranged the red balls in their triangle before she told him that she had never played before.

"I'll teach you."

He seized a cue from where they stood against the wall and handed another to Clara. He rubbed the point of his cue round and round in a cube of blue chalk. Turning away from her to the table, he cradled the tip of the cue on his hand, pushing it backwards and forwards with nervous anticipation, his right elbow pistoning.

"Now, darling Clara. To obtain points, you have to pot an object ball with the cue ball. The cue ball is the white ball. But to attempt a colour you must first have potted a red. The sequence thus goes, red, colour, red, colour, and so on. The colours all have different values. Red is one, yellow is two, green three, brown four, blue five, pink six, black seven. They all have special places on the table—look where I've put them."

Clara turned the paper-covered chalk cube in her sweating hands. "King of Them All," it said on one face. And, on another, "Tweeten, Chicago, Ill."

"If during the game a colour is potted but can't be put back on its own spot, because another ball is there already, it goes on the highest available spot—that is, the vacant spot of the ball with the highest value, black then pink and then blue and so on. Let's begin. It's practically impossible to get a red in from the break, so you want to do a safety shot—just clip one of the reds and bring the white ball back to the edge. I'll go first and show you."

A mist of stupidity rose in Clara's brain. When she was thirteen they had tried to teach her bridge, sitting around a table after supper—herself, her father, her brother, Aunt Margaret ("since we've got a four").

Her father was paying one of his rare weekend visits. Aunt Margaret made a considerable fuss setting up the card table on its silly legs, finding the special cloth to put on it ("I know I put it somewhere"), fetching pencils and pads. Her brother knew how to play. Bridge was fashionable at his school. He and his friends played in the Sixth Form Unit on Wednesday afternoons.

Clara could not learn. Bridge made her cough. She always coughed when she was nervous. Aunt Margaret took the view that if she explained the conventions and the rules of bidding to Clara in a patient voice all over again from the beginning every time she made a mistake, it would eventually sink in.

Her brother got bored, looked at his watch, began humming. Her father became exasperated.

"But it's only a game!" said Clara, exasperated herself. "What does it matter? You're going on as if it was *important*."

"It's a game," said her father. "It's not *only* a game. That's like saying a ten-pound note is only a ten-pound note. It depends on what you do with it. There's no *only* about it."

"If a thing's worth doing at all, it's worth doing well," said Aunt Margaret with confidence. "Push your hair out of your eyes. And stop coughing. You don't have a cough."

"Well, I don't think it is worth doing," said Clara.

Her brother, with a turn of his wrist, sent the cards fanning out across the table in a perfect arc. He was showing off. Her father rose from the table and made for the door.

"It may not be worth doing, my girl," he said, "but it's all there is. It's all there is. And now if you'll excuse me I have some calls to make."

And off he went to telephone Brazil.

Clara didn't see the point of the shot Leo had just made, but he seemed very satisfied with it. She took the cue, leaned over the table and struck the white ball in the direction of a cluster of reds. It reached them, just.

"Ah, you kissed it!" said Leo. "Now watch what I do. I'm going to put a heavy screw on the white ball, so that it spins back."

He did whatever he did, and it must have been whatever he meant to do, for he cheered himself enthusiastically and moved around the table knocking different balls into the corner pockets.

"Reds stay off the table when they're potted," he said. "Did I tell you that already? Now your go. Your turn to 'visit the table.' That's the proper way to say it. Every game has its language."

He stood back, and Clara, bent over her cue, became paralysed with nervousness at the thought of Leo looking at her behind under the thin cotton nightdress. She missed the red ball she was aiming at.

"Foul shot!" shouted Leo. "You lose four points."

Part of Clara's trouble was that her spectacles were on the table in her bedroom, and she couldn't see what she was doing. She played so many foul shots of different kinds that she put down her cue and said she'd rather watch. So Leo turned back his cuffs to bare his sinewy wrists and played solo, stalking round the table, lying over it, taking solemn aim with his left hand spread on the green table, giving little trial shoves to the cue as it rested on the curve between his fingers and his twitching, waisted thumb, issuing a fluent running commentary on what he was planning to do, lunging and withdrawing, jabbing and sliding and flicking the cue, and then *crack* and a great shout from Leo. Again and again the coloured balls clicked and collided and spilled apart, ricocheted, rolled, lolled, clustered, dropped into pockets, fell silent, and Clara leaned against the top of the stairs out of range of the stabbing back end of his cue and watched him in a daze. Being near Leo affected her so shockingly that Harry and her new life with him faded into water-colour.

Then Alice came out of her room again, and complained that Ferdie could not sleep with all this going on and they would wake up the whole house. Clara looked at lovely thoroughbred Alice, whom she always envied, and saw that she was jealous. Alice idolized Leo, but Leo had married Martha. Marrying poor Ferdie, Clara understood for the first time as she faced Alice over the billiard table, was as close to Leo as she could get. Alice had looked wonderful at her wedding, great eyes, dark hair under white lace. Leo had looked at her that day, and hungrily. His lovely daughter-in-law.

Soon after the snooker game Clara and Harry were at the opera together again, but under very different circumstances. The crimson and gold interior of the Royal Opera House looked like a massive tiered birthday cake. There should have been candles instead of red-shaded lamps in the crooked gilt sconces. They were hearing *The Marriage of Figaro*, and they were sitting not in the upper circle but in the Royal Box.

2

IT WAS LEO ULM'S TREAT. Leo had friends in high places. One of these (female) was on the board of directors at Covent Garden. She had given him the use of the box for tonight as a present.

But Leo was in the United States, recording television interviews in New York, then going on to Washington for a conference. His young wife Martha took the evening over. She invited Clara and Harry, Leo's son Ferdie and Alice, and Anthony Arklow-Holland to make up the numbers. None of them was accustomed to such privilege and luxury. Except perhaps Anthony. He was a mystery.

In the private ante-room supper was waiting as if by magic: the first two courses before the performance, the pudding and cheese during the interval. There was champagne. They were all much more impressed and thrilled than they would have admitted and so pretended, in self-irony, to be even more impressed and thrilled than they secretly were.

"It's a good thing Leo isn't here, really," said Martha, with rare disloyalty. "He'd be quite capable of reminding me that one must not talk during the performance."

"I won't mind if you talk to me," said Anthony. Martha was looking bright-eyed and pretty. Anthony was his usual dapper self. Harry was his usual dishevelled self. Ferdie was his usual gloomy self. Both he and Alice were less animated than the others, Alice because Leo's absence stripped the evening of glamour for her and Ferdie because he was Ferdie.

From the privacy of their dining-room they moved into the dimmer, dark-red intimacy of the Royal Box. It was a deceptive intimacy. From the box's open mouth they looked out, down, across and up to thousands of faces, and thousands of faces looked down, up and across at them.

"It's a pity that none of us could pass as the Princess of Wales," said Alice. "I feel like a false tooth. And I can tell I am going to get a crick in my neck." The box was at right angles to the stage.

Against one wall, in the shadows, was a chaise-longue. Anthony pounced on it. He reclined in an exaggeratedly languorous pose.

"You know what this is? It's what Edward VII used to lie on with his lady friends when he got bored with the opera. He got bored with the opera quite soon after the overture."

"How do you *know*?" asked Alice.

"Because one of his former ladies told me. One of my Old Bats."

"She must be very old. Edward VII died in about 1913."

"Nineteen ten actually. She was ninety-something when she told me. She said the couch was still in here. I couldn't believe it."

"Who was she? You can't *half* tell a story, Anthony—it's very irritating."

"I promised I'd never tell anyone. She married a very grand bishop afterwards."

None of the others knew any bishops, dead or alive, grand or otherwise, so it was no good guessing or pretending to rack their brains.

This was a typical outcome of conversations with Anthony Arklow-Holland.

Because Ferdie could not see, it was important to have no sound-muffling obstacles between him and the music. He, Clara and Alice sat in the front of the box, with Martha, Anthony and Harry behind.

Clara was stirred and elated by the music of the last act. Unable to touch Harry, behind her, she took Ferdie's bony hand in her own. He did not take it away. His skin was cool.

After a while her warmth and his coolness proved negotiable. Their hands became the same temperature, like a pair.

There was a commotion in the front stalls, just behind the conductor's podium. Clara craned to see. A man went running up the aisle towards the back exit. The music did not falter.

"What's happening?" whispered Ferdie.

"Nothing, it's all right."

The man returned with a uniformed nurse. The person who had been taken ill, or died, was in the middle of the row. There was a lot of creaking and thudding of seats in the half-dark. An evening that is a great night out for me, thought Clara, will be remembered by these people as the beginning of a nightmare. If only we knew what was going to happen to us, and when. It's not as if we behave as if there were no tomorrow. We behave as if there were an unlimited supply of tomorrows.

On the stage the assorted pairs of lovers were lining up and belting out the final swooping ensemble. Harry leaned over and touched Clara's shoulder. She turned and smiled at him; and said to Alice, through the clapping:

"Do you realize that all the loveliest, most heartrending love songs in Mozart operas are false love songs, pretending, meant to deceive?"

"Anyone who's ever noticed anything has noticed that," said Alice. "Does that tell you something about Mozart or something about love?"

Driving her home after the opera, Harry asked Clara to marry him. She was astonished.

When they met for lunch the day after the opera, Clara and Harry did not talk at once about marrying—or not marrying. They discussed Harry's need for a new pair of trousers.

"Just so long as you don't get cavalry twill," said Clara. "I just can't stand it."

"I was thinking of cavalry twill, as it happens. Smart and hard-wearing."

"It represents everything I've dreaded since I was fifteen. That dreadful fawn ridged stiffness. I liked boys who wore wrecked jeans for best and dirty pink velvet the rest of the time."

"I'm not a boy any longer, and I have to have something practical for the office, and I don't want to wear a suit."

"Lay off the cavalry twill anyway, or I certainly won't marry you. What's the point of us getting married, really? It won't stop you leaving me, or me leaving you, if things didn't work out. It might not even save us from AIDS."

They had a sad little talk about AIDS, about friends, and friends of friends and, tentatively, about themselves. But it was superficial, an exchange of tokens which was evidence of the will to frankness but not frankness itself. Each was sitting within a thicket of spines, peering out, thought Clara. She must try to get inside him, to see what he saw and be what he was. She would clamber into his body, forcing herself between the barricades of his skeleton, pushing aside branches, lianas and trip-wires, skirting the big soft obstacles, to the very centre of him. But there was nothing there, there was no place in the middle of a male where you could huddle down. It was hopeless.

He was talking about being gay, which he was not, but could have been.

"It's so much easier."

That caught her attention. "How on earth is it *easier?*"

"When you are very young what you want is sex. Girls make you serve time for it. They dole it out as a reward for good behaviour. They make you feel guilty, they make you hypocritical. So much time gets wasted. My first girlfriend, at school, expected me to go round the shops with her on Saturday afternoons, looking at clothes that she didn't even buy. With another boy, you'd just have sex, and then watch *Match of the Day.*"

"But lots of the gays I know are more sentimental and clinging than most women. And there've always been lots of girls who just want to get laid. Surely?"

"Maybe I just had bad luck."

"And if that's all you want why on earth do you want us to get married?"

"You're being stupid. I was talking about when I was very young. Sixteen. Nothing to do with now. I want to make a whole world, now. With you."

Clara picked at her pasta. Harry poured the Chianti, brand-name Machiavelli. Harry was not at all Machiavellian.

"It's not that I'm so crazy to be married either, for the sake of being married. I just think we would be good at it, we would make it work, we would be happy together."

"Look what happens to married people. Look at Leo and Martha even, not one of the great romances of the century I don't think."

"Leo's not ordinary. Leo's a special case. I'm not a bit like Leo."

"No, you're not . . . ," said Clara, trying to make it sound like a compliment.

"Would you go to bed with Leo if he asked you?"

"He wouldn't ask me. I'm Martha's best friend."

"Damn it, I meant to bring *Private Eye* to show you."

"I've seen it, OK? And do you think, just for once, we could have a conversation without mentioning Leo at all?"

"I doubt it," said Harry. "Anyway, it was you that brought him up."

"It was Martha I was really thinking about. And marriage in general, not just her and Leo."

Over the coffee she tried to explain her doubts and confusions. To Harry, she seemed to be talking about power and the balance of power; and they kept coming back to the Ulms.

"It will all change for them, anyway," said Harry, "because of Leo being so much older. A time will come when he will be dependent on her instead of vice versa. She'll come into her own then."

"I'm not so sure," said Clara, stirring and stirring. "She'll just be his keeper then, when he's an old lion. She'll be the minder. Then when he dies she'll be the curator of his legend.

She'll soon find out, when she's the widow, who her real friends are. The people who were only interested in Leo will drop her. Anthony may drop her for a start."

"You're horribly cynical."

"On second thoughts Anthony won't drop her. She'll still be Mrs. Leo Ulm—she'll have control over his copyrights and all his papers."

"I love you very much and I intend to marry you," said Harry, signalling for the bill, "but sometimes you chill me to the bone. You're too sharp about everyone. You may as well tell me what Alice's views are now. I presume you mull over all this with her, as you do everything else."

At least Harry knew Alice and Martha. There is nothing worse than being with someone who talks all the time about people you don't know. Voices in other rooms, glamorous and unlikeable. What is one to do about this? If you are going to a party given by old friends where you will know most of the people, and you are taking with you someone who knows none of them, you fill him in on the essentials on the way there. There's no point telling him which ones to like and which ones to dislike; he'll make up his own mind.

You have to talk fast. Briefly, the thing about Clara, Martha and Alice was that they went to the same school. It was a single-sex boarding-school in Wiltshire. Alice came from the sort of family whose daughters went to schools like Redbrook House as a matter of course, as the sons went to Marlborough or Rugby. Clara was only there because her Aunt Margaret was the under-matron and infiltrated her bright niece in at reduced fees—which she paid herself out of her salary, since Clara's mother was dead and her father irresponsible though socially pretentious.

Martha Pardo came from Selby in Yorkshire, where her parents kept a pub. The Pardos sent their daughter to Redbrook House in order to give her every advantage. They were disappointed that she did not lose her Yorkshire accent, baffled when she became an artist, and washed their hands of her when she married a divorced philosopher the same age as her father. Though they liked his being famous, and on television—not that they had the time to sit down and watch *Homo Sapiens.*

Martha was popular at Redbrook House because she was a kind girl. Clara and Alice were both sharp-tongued. They made enemies. Martha was devoted to Clara and Alice. In their early twenties, before their lives and loves diverged, the three of them shared a top flat off Mornington Crescent in north London, behind Euston Station. It was a rough area. Their neighbours were whores and DHSS bed-and-breakfasts. They lost touch with everyone else from school.

Alice said that vicarages all over the English shires were harbouring old Redbrook House girls, transformed into vicars' wives at no cost to the taxpayer. Redbrook House was a very religious school. At their Mornington Crescent parties the girls entertained their visitors with esoteric hymns sung in plangent close harmony:

> *My song is love unknown,*
> *My Saviour's love to me,*
> *Love to the loveless shown*
> *That they might lovely be.*

So cruel, said Alice. The loveless remain unlovely, which was why they were loveless in the first place. My Saviour's love should be prosecuted under the Trades Descriptions Act.

The three still saw each other all the time. They rarely met as a trio. When they did they talked about work, or politics, or other people. No one of them would disclose a personal secret to the other two together. Three is an awkward number.

But Clara saw Martha. Martha saw Alice. Alice saw Clara. Any two of them exchanged shockingly candid confidences and confessions. And any two of them discussed, with the sort of background knowledge that in any other field would be called scholarship, the latest confidences and confessions of the absent third. An eavesdropping outsider might consider these conversations uncharitable, if not spiteful. But Harry Ashe knew better than to criticize Alice or Martha to Clara, whatever outrageous stories she told him about them.

Maybe Harry was right to be wary of Clara's friends.

"Clara does not need Harry," Alice remarked to Martha. "She needs a bisexual Armenian. Something really difficult."

"That's rather extreme," said Martha. "I wouldn't want a bisexual Armenian, would you?"

"I was speaking figuratively," said Alice. "Leo is absolutely a bisexual Armenian. So is Ferdie, sort of. A *mild* bisexual Armenian."

As Harry was signing the credit card docket at the end of lunch, Clara said:

"Alice says marriage is a context for life, not life itself."

"Does she indeed?"

"But to tell the truth, though I see Alice all the time, I don't have a clue about her relationship with Ferdie."

"It's a funny situation, really."

(He meant that one of Clara's best friends was married to the celebrated Leo Ulm, and the other was married to Leo's completely uncelebrated son Ferdie, the child of his first marriage to poor Charlotte.

Alice met Ferdie through Martha and Leo, Harry supposed.)

Clara and Harry emerged into the Strand. The rain had stopped. The puddles in the gutter shone. They kissed on the pavement. It was a happy kiss.

"I'll be round about seven then," said Clara.

They would eat at his place tonight because he was the better cook. Also, he had to feed his house-plants.

Alice said that if a committee of feminists designed a blueprint for a totally acceptable male they would come up with Harry Ashe. Harry was generous, gentle, capable, and able to talk about what he felt. He was a good listener. He was not vain or a bully.

Alice's comment should have pleased Clara, or at least amused her, but it irritated her. So, far from seeming a tribute, Alice's remarks had the effect of making Harry out to be somehow ridiculous.

Clara had not yet been taken down to Southampton to meet Harry's mum. But she had met Harry's *Amomum cardamomum*, which was at least as important. When she first visited his flat in Marsham Street she was not prepared for the vegetal life that shared his home. Two leafy climbing plants, so tall they hit the ceiling, swayed towards her as they went in.

"*Monstera deliciosa*. And *Philodendron crassinervum*," said Harry formally, by way of introduction.

"How do you do," said Clara. The plants twitched in the draught as Harry closed the door.

Right up against the window three glass shelves were fixed, crammed with small pots full of cactus plants of different shapes and sizes. Cheaper than net curtains, thought Clara. And different. Harry drew her over to them.

"*Astrophytum myriostigma*," he said. "And Obregonia, Wiggininsia . . . this one is *Mammillaria elegans*—and Epostoa, Greenoria, Frailea."

He pressed a switch by the fireplace, and the inside of the hearth lit up.

"I've put a fluorescent strip in the chimney. So that these ones get enough light . . . Dracaena, Tradescantia, Episcia." The fireplace was a thicket of whippy, stripy foliage.

Clara sat on the edge of a leaf-patterned settee, trying to avoid a *Fatsia japonica* on a table behind her. It was fingering her neck.

"I never knew your friends had to share you with all these green creatures," she called to Harry, who was opening a bottle in the kitchen.

But, as she discovered on a subsequent visit, there were no plants in the bedroom.

The other thing about Harry was that he really was the man from the Pru. He worked in the Prudential's red castellated headquarters at Holborn Circus. Clara watched his thin lanky figure legging it up Chancery Lane, his carroty head bobbing about above everyone else's. Having no office to return to herself, she walked down the Strand to Trafalgar Square to get a bus home. She bought the *London Daily News* to read on the bus. She didn't feel in the mood for the life of Napoleon, which she had in her carrier bag. Her heart bumped slightly when she saw that the television column in the paper was all about Leo. It was wholly flattering. He would be very pleased.

Clara's Aunt Margaret said that there were only three types of human face: horse, bird and bun. According to Aunt Margaret, Clara and her two female friends encapsulated humanity. Martha's face was a bun, round and smooth, with widely spaced eyes. Alice was a dark horse (in all senses), with a flying black mane and expressive eyes that she used dramatically, showing a lot of white. Clara couldn't see herself at all, but she had to concede she was a bird, since everyone said *yes,* and laughed.

Of the three girls, only Clara remained faithful to north London, where they once all lived together. Her present flat was off the Holloway Road. When on her own, she lived on eggs, bread, tomatoes and apples. She was tired of scraping scrambled egg off the bottom of saucepans; passing the Reject Shop in the Tottenham Court Road after her lunch with Harry, she jumped off the bus, went in and bought a heavy non-stick pan.

It was still in her carrier bag when she was coming home late, in the dark, from her evening at Harry's place.

Turning into her road, she saw a scuffle going on. It was worse than a scuffle; it was a fight. Someone was being beaten up.

She had always wondered how she would react in a situation like this. She was appalled when she read in the papers how witnesses hurried by, preferring to let someone be murdered rather than get involved and risk their own skins.

When she saw as she approached that the victim was a woman, her resolve hardened.

The battling pair moved like a single animal out of the shadows and into the ring of light under a street lamp. The woman cringed and whimpered, not even trying to defend herself. Her attacker was punching and punching her head and face and breast in a grunting frenzy. Neither had noticed Clara.

The attacker swung round, presenting Clara with a hunched-up back in a dark jacket. Clara fumbled in her bag for the life of Napoleon, which was good and heavy. Instead, her fingers found the handle of the new saucepan. She pulled it out of its paper bag, raised it high and brought it down as hard as she could on the back of the attacker's head.

There was a moment's freeze, as if they were all playing statues. The street lamp glinted on the bottom of the saucepan, and on the price ticket stuck on just off-centre: £4.99.

Slowly the person whom Clara had hit turned round to face her, rubbing the back of his head.

Rubbing the back of her head. The assailant was another woman. The three looked at one another speechlessly.

The woman who had been doing the punching took the arm of the one who had been punched. Shoulder to shoulder they pushed past Clara back towards the main road. Clara looked after them for a moment, then turned and walked on down the street towards her own house, the saucepan still swinging from her right hand. There were no cars passing. She heard her own footsteps and, receding, the muddled, irregular steps of the other two fading gradually. She did not know what to think. About anything.

3

✳✳✳✳✳

"WHAT IS WORSE than living with a man who makes you unhappy?" Charlotte asked herself, and answered herself: "Not living with him."

The tree by the lake was almost bare. A few leaves hung on, motionless, vertical. They were brilliant ovals of rose and gold in the autumn sunlight. If rain fell after dark they would be gone by morning.

"We have come to the parting of the ways," said Charlotte. She talked to herself all the time now. Her death was growing inside her like a fungus in a cave. It had begun to sprout in the soft darkness on the day her husband Leo Ulm had left her for a younger and more attractive woman. Recently, since she had realized she was going mad, it had grown faster.

Everything had speeded up. Before Charlotte knew it spring had come round again. She still spent hours, whatever the season, staring out over the lake. The pattern was set after Leo left. She could not believe that he would not suddenly realize that he had made a crazy mistake. She waited for him to come back. Waiting is a full-time occupation. For months she did nothing but wait, tense and expectant, listening and watching for his car, leaping to answer the telephone, not going out in case it should ring. Sometimes she saw him in the evenings walking on the misty far side of the lake, and her heart leapt in relief. It was only a mirage, part of the trouble in her mind.

At first she had written letters to him. She was so used to

telling him everything, she did not feel anything had happened unless he too knew of it. She could not believe that he would not need to know what was going on in the neighbourhood. She hurried to write to him when she heard that the Old Rectory in the village was changing hands; Mrs. Parks had gone into a home in Hove and the house had been bought by a young couple called Bollard. She could not believe he would not want to know that the big branch of the cedar tree, the one that threatened the greenhouse, had broken off with a dreadful crash, bringing the greenhouse down with it. She could not believe that he wanted to divorce Belwood, the house in which she had been brought up and in which he had taken so much pleasure, even if he wanted to divorce her. But Leo did not need her, nor Belwood any more. Nor her money. He did not answer her letters.

She had been staking the delphiniums at Belwood when he walked across the lawn, his hands in his pockets, and told her he was leaving, and why, and with whom.

"I'm sorry," he said.

There was before, and there was after. After was for ever.

She had not been able to finish staking the delphiniums. Only the clump she had already done stood upright that wet and windy June. The rest slumped and sprawled, the luminous blues that she adored extinguished by weeds in the neglected border.

Every spring the ducks on the lake at Belwood hatched out squads of fluffy ducklings. Some were yellow, most were brown. Within hours these babies were churning around in the water, leaving arrowhead wakes. They paddled in flotillas, in circles, in zigzags. They made piercing sounds when they lost their mothers. They knew what they were for, which was everything and nothing. Life for life's sake.

For most of them life is short, reflected Charlotte. As the lake becomes crowded the drakes get nervous. When a duckling swims too close, a drake turns his head and breaks the soft neck of his baby or someone else's with a single twist of his beak. That's that. Snuffed out. Rats and cats prey on the ducklings, who have no means and consequently no idea of defending themselves. Ducks are not emotional. What happens happens. Out of fifty fragile portions of life only three may survive.

A drake is not a gentle lover. He pushes his mate under the water in the act of copulation. Watching from the window one would say it was rape. Once released the duck scoots off to join her female friends at the water's edge, grumbling, composing herself, shrugging, recovering.

As she watched them Charlotte thought about Ferdie, her son and Leo's. Ferdie now lived at Belwood, the big house on the far side of the lake where she had been first daughter and then wife. She was twice wife.

What? She had married again, in spite of being so obsessed with Leo? In spite of being stricken, terminally, with grief?

She married Andy McAndrew in 1977 in desperation, as someone who has cut an artery staunches the blood with whatever comes to hand. It was not yet time to die, even though the fungus was growing inside her. Being married to Andy had not stopped her thinking about Leo, but it had stopped her endless waiting for his return.

Andy was fifteen years older than Charlotte. When Andy died, and Ferdie announced that he was going to get married, it seemed only sensible for Charlotte to move out of Belwood and make it over to her son and his Alice. She also made over the money, keeping only Andy's pension for herself. Managing the money became Ferdie's job; it was the only job he had. Ferdie's finest hour came daily, when he rang his brokers to discuss the management of the portfolio. Ferdie referred ironically, but with pleasure, to his "invisible assets." Ferdie was completely blind.

Charlotte did not move far. The cottage on the other side of the lake had been a staff cottage in her parents' time, and had stood empty for years. She had always liked the look of it, and moved in with relief.

But once she was on her own there the watching and waiting had begun again.

What is worse than living with a man who makes you unhappy? Not living with him. That went for both her husbands.

The sun was going. The glow had gone out of the trees. Rose and gold faded to dullness. In the big house, an indefinite mass against the incoming darkness, a light came on upstairs. Her room, then Ferdie's room when he was a child, now her granddaughter Agnes's. It was the only light in the long double row of tall windows. Ferdie and Alice were in London. They had a house in Fulham. Alice had wanted a house in London, and Ferdie sold the Middle Wood to buy it. Charlotte did not know what they did in London; she vaguely imagined they went to parties.

It was not perhaps a good idea to leave a seven-year-old child alone so much, with only Christa to look after her. Before Christa, Ingela. Before Ingela, Dominique. When Alice could not get back to Belwood for the weekend she would summon Christa and Agnes to London. Charlotte knew when this happened if only because she had to run the pair of them to the station in Lewes.

Charlotte left the window in order to look up "death" in the dictionary. She was curious to know how they would put it. Death is the act or fact of dying, she read. It is also the state of being dead.

"Those are two very different things," she said to the dictionary. "And the difference between them is the whole point, so far as I am concerned."

She was date-stamped with the day of her death but she couldn't read the code. Charlotte's second husband died on 15 July 1982. Again, there was before and after. Would she have behaved any differently if she had known about 15 July 1982?

When Ferdie was a little boy, long before the dreadful accident that blinded him (3 November 1964, unforgettably), she watched him running down the grassy slope from the house towards the lake. She stood at the garden door, beside the Wellington boots, the hanging mackintoshes and the long box that held the croquet mallets, and thought: Just by bringing him into the world I have condemned him to death. Snuffed out, everyone, sooner or later.

The boots, the mackintoshes and the croquet box were still there, much as they had been in her childhood. But Leo had gone and Andy had died. The plastic pig that Charlotte had picked up out of the grass by the lake would last longer in the world than Agnes who had dropped it. The pig was in the pocket of Charlotte's long blue cardigan. She fingered it.

The ducks quacked at Charlotte from the lake, ruffling the black water as they surged towards her, hoping for bread before bed. It was cold. Charlotte, her arms crossed, walked round the side of the cottage to get some logs. There were hardly any left—she should have ordered another load. She took up as many as she could in her arms. They were the bottom of the heap; they had been lying against the damp ground for so long that a colony of woodlice was established on their undersides.

Charlotte saw the woodlice rushing around in panic when she dumped her load on the brick hearth of her living-room. Disgusted, she brushed bark, splinters and woodlice off the front of her cardigan. She picked up three of the logs, heaved them into the fireplace, shoved in three firelighters and applied a match.

The flames rose and the woodlice began to evacuate their homes in the wood. In orderly lines they hurried down the mountainsides of those parts of log still out of the fire, down the slopes of old soft ash and on to the hearth. There they took to the roads, scurrying along the runnels between the bricks of the fireplace and dropping on to the rug when they reached the end. Charlotte snatched up the hearthbrush and sent the refugees flying back into the ashy foothills. Most of the woodlice righted themselves at once and set off again down the brick roads. Again, Charlotte swept them back into the ashes. Some succumbed, some did not.

After ten minutes, with the fire roaring high, brave individuals were still setting out from the hot ashes, ash-covered themselves, to start again on the trek towards safety. Charlotte dealt with these champion woodlice one at a time, on a personal basis. "It's massacre," she said to an obstinate survivor, sending him flying to his death with a swipe of her brush. "It's massacre, but I can't help it."

There were new snail-trails every morning on the green carpet in her little dining-room. In the damp weather, toadstools sprouted overnight where the carpet met the wall. Cobwebs blotted with bluebottles hung in the corners of the windows. Night after night, skittering spiders waited for her on the bottom of the bath.

After her bath, later that evening, when the gongs started ringing in her head, Charlotte forced herself to take the test. It would have been more sensible not to, as she told herself every night; but it always seemed better to know than not to know. If she did not go through with it, the gongs would not stop. If she did go through with it, she was feeding the madness. The results of the test were always the same. The only decision she had to take was whether to open the front door or the back door.

Charlotte stood in her dressing-gown and slippers at her closed back door. Beyond it lay her quiet garden: herbs on either side of the flagged path, a small lawn, a sundial, overgrown bushes of Roseraie de l'Haye and Maiden's Blush, clumps of hellebore against the hedge. All now hidden by the night.

Charlotte opened the back door.

The scorching sun dazzled her and hurt her eyes. She was prickling with sweat and her mouth was dry as she inhaled the flying dust from the track. Her shoulders ached with the weight of the sack. She kept her eyes on the wheels of the cart in front of her. It made such a noise on the dusty stones that she had to stoop to hear Ferdie, who was dragging at her left arm, crying, "I can't see. I'm tired. Where are we going?" Agnes, clinging to her other hand, was too quiet. Glancing down, Charlotte saw that she was deathly pale under the dirt. The little girl crumpled up on the road. Charlotte hitched the sack higher on her back, picked Agnes up on her right arm. She had seen, as she half turned, the long hot road behind her, crawling with incomplete families like her own, all bleached grey under the harsh sun. "Why are we going on?" wailed Ferdie. "Are we nearly there? When can we go home?" Charlotte said flatly, "We can't go home. Something bad happened. No one can go home." Ahead the road stretched on to nowhere. A car passed them in second gear, throwing up dust and stones in their faces. Charlotte felt sick. Her back hurt. The dead weight of Agnes, whose head lolled over her shoulder and on the sack, became unbearable. "We'll have a rest," she said to Ferdie, and dragged him over to the scorched grass beside the track. The verge was littered with sick, exhausted people, no longer caring. Stepping across them, Charlotte thought it was like trying to find a space on a crowded Mediterranean beach. She hallucinated within her hallucination and saw blue water, white waves breaking. She had no water and no food. Charlotte lay down, her head on the sack, and held the two children in her arms. Her aching eyes closed. She heard the tramp and shuffle of those who passed on the road.

Charlotte slammed the back door.

"Ferdie is a grown man," she said to her reflection in the kitchen mirror. "He is thirty-two. He is alive and well and comfortable in Fulham. And Agnes is safe in her own bed up at the house."

She knew that what she saw out of the back door was part of her madness. It was not hindsight. It was not foresight. It was just sight—unwanted, tormenting knowledge about something real.

Agnes lay in her yellow and white bedroom in Belwood House, with Christa the au pair girl within call. Beyond the self-contained apartment in which they lived—playroom, Agnes's room, Christa's room, kitchenette and bathroom—a corridor lined with water-colours and carpeted with haircord stretched away until it reached the big landing, where the billiard table stood, and the dark oil-paintings hung, and the carpet became misty-blue Wilton.

The blue carpet was a river in Agnes's imagination, flowing smoothly round the stairhead and cascading down the wide curling staircase, pale by day in the white light from a tall window, deeper blue in the evening when the lights in the stairwell were on. Whenever Agnes ran down the stairs she was a canoe shooting the rapids. Mostly she and Christa used the back stairs, a clattering wooden tower that led down into the big kitchen.

For a child of seven, she fell asleep very late. While her grandmother was opening the back door of her cottage, Agnes too was busy. No one knew about this game—not her mother, not Christa. When Agnes judged that Christa was safely settled in her own room—she could hear the television—it was all right to begin.

This was the game. Agnes got out of bed, took off her nightdress and, shivering already, lay on her back on the floor, all bare, her arms straight by her sides. She was a Poor Girl lying on a stony pavement. It was night, and rain was falling. People walking by splashed mud and icy water over her. Then someone stopped beside her and said, "Poor Girl, you must be very very cold. Here is something for you to wear." (Agnes groped for her nightie on the bed, pulled it on and lay down on the floor again.)

It was better, not being all bare, but it was still horribly cold and wet. Then another kind person stopped and said, "Poor Girl, the pavement must be so hard. Here is a cushion for your head." (Agnes reached for her pillow, and lay down again on the floor.)

It was quite luxurious, the softness under her head, keeping her hair out of the gutter. But the rain turned to snow, and it was colder than ever. Footsteps clicked by on the pavement—until at last a kind voice said, "Poor Girl, you are all covered with snow. Take this." (Agnes pulled her duvet off the bed and put it over herself.)

That was much better. Who would mind sleeping on the street if they had such warm covering? Agnes, who had been genuinely cold, and whose feet were icy, began to warm up. But the story was not quite over. The end was the best part.

A kind gentleman passing by stopped and said, "Poor Girl, I cannot bear to think of you sleeping out on a night like this. Come home with me." He took her to his lovely house and put her in a real bed. He got in beside her and put his arms around her.

Here Agnes jumped up, remade her bed and climbed into it. How comfy, what softness and safety, what a piece of luck. The Poor Girl never dreamt of such bliss. Agnes wriggled deeper under the duvet, and slept.

She used to call this game "Poor Girl." Then one day her mother came in while she was playing it—luckily she was at the pillow stage, and not all bare—and asked her what on earth she was doing. Agnes did not want to tell her. She said she was playing Fulham. Something to do with hard pavements, which there were in Fulham but not at Belwood. Her mother had not understood, which was what Agnes intended. But now, just as a precaution, she called it "playing Fulham" even to herself.

Away down the passage, an imperfect moon shone through the high window on to the glittering stair-rail, the billiard table and the blue carpet, leaching their unreliable colours to silver-grey. Christa, having judged that Agnes must be asleep, had long ago left her room (with the television on) and run down the drive to the trees by the gate, where her boyfriend Clancy was waiting for her. Clancy was a student at the University of Sussex. They went to lie down in the long damp grass under the trees.

It began to rain. Christa and Clancy got wet. So did Agnes's dot-to-dot colouring book, left outside on the terrace.

4

※:※:※:※:※

WHILE LEO WAS IN AMERICA, Ferdie and Alice asked Clara down to Belwood for the weekend. Alice wanted to talk to Clara. She thought Clara ought to be putting all her energies into looking for a new job. She was afraid Clara might marry Harry Ashe just because she couldn't think what else to do.

Clara went down on Saturday. She took with her a paperback of *War and Peace* to read on the train. She had got to chapter eight. If Alice could have prescribed her reading, she could hardly have chosen better.

"Marry as late as possible," Clara read, "when you're no good for anything else. Or else everything good and noble in you will be lost. You will be submerged by triviality."

She stopped reading and stared unseeingly out of the filthy window. I am submerged by triviality as it is. What is there in me that is good and noble? Not a lot. Perhaps I'll just sit in the flat reading my way through Grandfather's books like a hoover until I've read them all. Then what? Then I shall be old.

Alice met her at Lewes. Back at the house, Clara was turned out on to the terrace like a pudding out of a pudding-basin to talk to Ferdie while Alice went off to put the weekend shopping away.

"The garden looks wonderful," Clara said, and then wondered whether this was tactless. But it did look wonderful, and Ferdie must surely be pleased to know it. She put her hand over his—they were sitting side by side on wrought-iron chairs, much cushioned—and was reassured by his light pressure.

"The cherry tree is good this year," he answered, shifting his hand so that his palm lay upwards. "It's all right, I know what it looks like. I saw till I was nine, you know. I remember everything."

"You must remember everything as so big. You would think you were living in a doll's world if—if you suddenly saw again."

Clara looked at the flowering cherry. Leo and Charlotte had planted it when they first married. In its maturity, in bloom, it was an Amazon of a tree, its black arms supporting massed cascades of whiteness.

"Before the accident, I climbed the cherry tree. Can you see a fork quite low down? It was always an easy tree to climb. It's much taller now, I suppose, but Agnes can just about do the first bit already—you just have to give her a leg up. On this day I climbed it, I'd done it lots of times before but for some reason my foot slipped and I simply fell out of the tree. I landed on my back and I was completely winded. Can you remember what that feels like?"

"Did you hurt yourself?"

"No, not really, children don't. It was just that all the breath was knocked out of my body. I lay there waiting to begin breathing again, with my eyes shut. And then I opened my eyes, and looked straight up into all those flowers, all that white, with the wind moving it about and the sky blue behind. I didn't even know to call it beautiful. I just looked and looked, till my breath was back. I don't suppose I'd ever have seen anything lovelier than that."

Alice stood at the garden door, listening. Glancing at her, Clara knew what Alice felt about her husband. She liked him. She loved him. And she was bored stiff by him.

Agnes came pushing past her mother to say hello to Clara. She trotted a brown and white plastic cow along the metal arm of Clara's chair: click-click, click-click.

"How's school?" Clara asked her.

Her eyes bent on the cow, Agnes cocked her head to one side. "Well—it's all right, I suppose."

"Have you decided yet what you're going to be when you're grown up?"

Agnes breathed deeply and smiled at her shoes. She leaned against Clara's chair and swung backwards and forwards on the arm. She turned her eyes up to Clara and breathed deeply again. It seemed that a statement of great moment was about to be made.

Clara was flattered that Agnes had taken her banal enquiry so seriously. Agnes was adept at not hearing questions that seemed to her stupid.

"Hurry up, darling," said Alice from the door, wanting to hear what her daughter would say. "Clara can't wait all day for you."

Agnes beamed. "I'm going to be—a grown-up!" she announced triumphantly, delighted with her answer—and then laughed, because everyone else did.

"Who do you like best at school?" Clara pursued her advantage, feeling as much a success as Agnes.

"Well—I like Tracy best."

"What do you like specially about Tracy?"

Agnes turned the cow over and inspected its udders. "Well—I like her feet."

"Her feet?"

Agnes sighed theatrically. She did not have the skill to explain how she admired the way the silky pink of Tracy's soles crept up round the edges of her feet and merged with the matt brown-black of her heels and ankles.

"From the back," she managed. "It looks pretty. And she plays with me. And she has corn-rows."

Agnes began to laugh again, seeing her father raise his eyebrows.

"Daddy doesn't know what corn-rows is."

"You tell him, then," said Alice.

This was nearly as difficult as Tracy's feet, for Agnes.

"It's when your hair's all in lots and lots of tiny thin plaits, not just the long part at the back, the plaits are all over, from where your hair starts right to the ends. Tracy doesn't even undo them at night, not till it gets all messy, then her mummy does it again. I want to have corn-rows like Tracy but Mummy says not."

Clara flipped Agnes's straight blond hair. "If you had corn-rows it would really look like corn," she said. "I saw a fair-haired girl on a bus in London with her hair done like that. It looked like lines of specially long ears of wheat stuck on. Peculiar, but pretty."

"Ears?" said Agnes, screwing up her face. "Hair isn't *ears*."

"It's an expression," explained Clara. "Ears of wheat."

"That's silly," said Agnes. And, to her mother: "Can Tracy come round today? Please?"

"No, not today. Perhaps next week. The Bollards are coming today. You'll be able to play with Patience."

Agnes had gone. The cow was left on the white table, on its side, legs stiffly extended.

Tom and Helen Bollard lived in the village, in the Old Rectory—Edwardian bow windows, conservatory, cedar trees, swings, doll's pram up-ended on the lawn, tricycles in the drive, Transformers and Lego scattered all over the front hall, pin-board on the kitchen wall covered with children's drawings, postcards, reminders about dentist's appointments, dancing classes, swimming lessons, pony club, PTA meetings and birthday parties. He was a wine merchant and she was the mother of their children.

"Five of them, all under ten," said Helen Bollard, in answer to Clara's polite questioning.

"Goodness," said Clara; and then, for something to say: "What are their names?"

"Damian, Patience, Fred, Hatty and Polly. They are awfully nice, though I say it myself, but noisy. But once you've got two you may as well go on and have more. I've never regretted it. I said to Tom, we've got all the gear, we may as well use it. High chair, playpen, that kind of thing."

Helen Bollard talked as if she were being interviewed. She

had said all this before, many times. It was her subject. She was smilingly indulgent about the necessity of explaining everything again. Obviously people could not help being interested.

Her front teeth stuck out. She was not a pretty woman, nor an ugly one, and to Clara she seemed neither clever nor particularly stupid.

"Of course I do get tired, particularly at the weekends, Tom loves asking his important clients down for the weekend, and men never realize, do they, how extra people means extra work. It was a big decision, us moving down to the country, but I've never regretted it."

Helen Bollard, it became apparent, never regretted anything. Every expensively mundane acquisition was a triumph. Her washing-machine, her microwave, her dining-room carpet, her perm, her last year's family holiday in the Dordogne, her fitted kitchen, they were all profoundly hers, and had proved really good value.

Clara, veering between awe and contempt, wondered if any unspoken regrets lay buried beneath this domestic imperialism. Helen Bollard, secure in the knowledge that no one's life was richer or more fascinating than her own, asked Clara nothing about herself. Which was as well, since Clara felt more full of vague regrets than a corpse is of worms.

At the other end of the room Tom Bollard, Ferdie and Alice were discussing the problem of the gypsy encampment on the edge of the village.

"The trouble is, frankly they're dirty," she heard Tom say. "They'll be bringing lice into the village school."

Clara, a Londoner to her chewed finger-ends, thought how very local was local life in the country. She was ashamed of thinking it, knowing that envy was no small part of what she felt. These nice people shared a context as stable as a padded coffin.

"The thing is," Tom was saying, "they're better off than we are. They don't need anyone's help. Going round in bloody Rolls-Royces. They aren't real gypsies, not Romanies. Spongers off the welfare state. Irish, I wouldn't wonder."

Christa the au pair girl was deputed to look after Damian, Patience, Fred, Hatty and Polly—with Agnes's cooperation. Polly, who was still learning to walk, sat down on the playroom floor upstairs and howled for her mother.

"She won't stop now she's started," Patience informed Christa. She spoke with the air of an experienced mechanic explaining the idiosyncrasies of an engine to an amateur.

Christa carried the bawling toddler downstairs to the drawing-room and to Helen Bollard, who put out her arms for Polly without pausing in her flow of talk—". . . it really does prove it's all in the genes, how Damian and Fred have turned out so different, though we've treated them all, boys and girls, exactly the same, I said to Tom I can't think where Fred gets his artistic streak from, he said something amazing the other day when we took them all, except this little monster of course, to that art show in Lewes, local artists, will you have time? No, I suppose not, you must miss so much being shut up in London all the time, I must say we've never regretted getting out, anyway young Fred looked at this picture of flowers in a blue jug, and he said . . ."—settled Polly deeper in her lap, absently stroking the wispy colourless hair, cradling the fat red face between hand and bosom, comforting the child with the expertise of long practice.

Polly shuddered, gasped and fell silent. She put one thumb in her mouth and rubbed a fold of her mother's pink jumper between the thumb and fingers of her other hand. She gazed at Clara with round eyes. She was in such a safe place that if Clara had been a witch or a dragon Polly would have stared at her with the same unconcern.

After half an hour and some more sherry the drawing-room door crashed open, knocking over a dried-flower arrangement in a tall jug on the floor, and in came Damian, Patience and Fred, who clustered round their mother. Polly pulled at their hair and seemed very pleased to see them. They were, as Helen Bollard had said, noisy.

"Are we going now?"

"When are we going home?"

"Can we go home now, Mum?"

Agnes stood in the doorway watching. She righted the jug of dried flowers, awkwardly. They still did not look quite right. Clara thought Agnes looked pale and not happy. Entertaining the Bollard children was probably no joke.

Agnes was mesmerized by the Bollard children. She did not like them but she wanted them to like her. Helen Bollard, when she met Alice or Christa in the village, was always warmly urging that one or other of them should bring Agnes round to play. Helen regarded Agnes with compassion because she was an only child and, by Bollard standards, neglected.

Alice politely evaded all suggestions that she, with Agnes in tow, should spend any of her precious weekend time at the Old Rectory. During the week Christa occasionally went over with Agnes after school, but Christa was not keen on this arrangement either. Helen Bollard always took the opportunity to make an expedition into Lewes, to stock up at Safeway (the organic foods counter) and The Gourmet, leaving Christa in charge of all six children. Agnes would not go to the Bollards at all unless Christa came too. Alone with the Bollards at the Old Rectory Agnes felt abandoned in perpetuity to the mother's relentless kindness and the children's relentless cruelty.

Agnes's friend among the Bollards was alleged to be Patience because they were in the same class at school. They were not friends at all. They avoided one another effortlessly both in class and in the playground. On Agnes's first day Patience, who had been primed by her mother, came and sat beside her on the bench at break. Agnes was sitting waiting for break to be over.

Patience said, "Will you be my best friend?"

"Yes," said Agnes. "All right."

Patience skipped off.

Agnes worried a little, being unsure of the rights, duties and responsibilities of being a best friend. She need not have worried. Patience never spoke to her again.

The person Patience loved was her elder brother Damian.

She and Fred, two years younger, directed their energies towards pleasing Damian so that he would play with them. This left only Polly, who was too young to play, and Hatty. Agnes Ulm got left with Hatty when she played with the Bollards. This was humiliating because Hatty was only three. Agnes trailed behind the elder trio being as discouraging to Hatty as she dared. The lordly elder trio were in turn as unkind to Agnes as they dared.

While the grown-ups and tearful Polly were in the drawing-room at Belwood with the sherry, Hatty sat upstairs watching television with Christa. All the other children went into the garden. Since they were on Agnes's territory the Bollards could not exclude her as brutally as they normally would. Instead they played at taking tests. Damian gave the orders.

"You've all got to find some things and bring them here to me. This is my camp. Fred, you've got to find a slug or a snail or a big beetle. Agnes, you've got to bring me a worm. Patience's got to see that you both do it."

Damian's camp was on the terrace. From the playroom window above, Christa shouted to them not to go down to the lake. The sloping lawn was already in darkness. The terrace was lit by bulkhead lights on the side of the house. Fred and Agnes scuttled away into the dusky shrubberies and squatted down, searching and scrabbling among leaf-mould, earth and stones. Patience stalked up and down between them like a prison guard. Damian sat illuminated on the terrace in one of the metal chairs, arms folded, staring grandly out into the twilight.

Agnes found a worm without difficulty but it broke when she pulled it out of the earth. She wanted to take it to Damian, to be the first, but she suspected he would be unimpressed by half a worm. She persevered and, taking more care, extracted a second, entire worm from the soil. With the worm in the palm of her hand she emerged from darkness into light and offered the worm to Damian.

"I don't want it," he said, after a critical inspection. "Put it down just there."

He indicated a spot on the terrace with the toe of his Clarks sandal. Agnes laid her worm down. She kept looking at it in case it wriggled away. She felt pleased. She was successful and obedient. Fred was still searching in outer darkness. It was exciting but embarrassing to be waiting there alone with Damian. Agnes sat down on the flagged terrace at his feet, with a keen expression on her face to show him how alert and co-operative she was. All the time she kept an eye on her worm.

Fred and Patience returned to the terrace. Fred had found a snail.

"Put it down by the worm," said Damian. "No, not so close. Over there. That's right. Now stamp on it."

Fred stamped on the snail. He was not a hefty child and he was wearing rubber flip-flops. The snail survived the stamping, intact.

"Get a stone," ordered Damian.

Fred crushed the snail's shell, and the snail, with a stone.

"Now you," said Damian to Agnes. "Eat the worm."

Even Patience looked impressed by this. The three Bollards looked at Agnes to see what she would do.

"I can't, that's awful . . ."

"If you don't we won't play with you, we won't talk to you, we will hate you."

Agnes ate the worm.

As they made their way back to the grown-ups in the drawing-room, Agnes, betraying Tracy, whispered to Patience:

"Am I really your best friend now?"

"Course not, silly."

It took the Bollards a long time to take their leave. Tom Bollard had to be prised away from the adult conversation—"Come on, Daddy, we're going"—and one of Polly's socks had to be retrieved, by Agnes, from the upstairs playroom. Quantities of jumpers and anoraks had to be fitted on to the right parts of the right children.

Finally they streamed out into the night. Polly was plonked in the pram parked in the porch, and strapped in. Clara stood silent, a spectator, not knowing what to do to help. She was struck by how long the simplest things took, with the Bollards. Helen twanged a row of pink plastic ducks strung on elastic across the hood of the pram and said, turning to Clara:

"Rather LMC, I'm afraid, but Poll does love thcm so."

Clara did not know what she meant. LMC. It sounded like a college. Or a disease.

"What?"

"The plastic ducks on the pram. Rather LMC. Lower middle class!"

"Oh goodness," said Clara. "I'd no idea." She couldn't resist adding, "I suppose one can't be too careful." Enraptured by this exchange, she looked forward to telling Alice afterwards.

Helen Bollard turned amid the waist-high cloud of mouse-brown heads to smile her radiant toothy goodbye. Tom exuded tolerance and helpfulness, weighed down by toys and equipment surplus to immediate requirements.

The home team, exhausted, turned their minds to supper. They laid out everything they might want on the dining-room table, sat down, and talked about the Bollards. Clara tried to describe to Ferdie exactly what Helen Bollard looked like, remaining just on the charitable side of honesty.

"My mother says that women with buck teeth are never without a man," observed Ferdie. "Buck teeth are apparently irresistible."

"They are a very happy family, anyway," said Clara. She believed this to be true. She was overwhelmed by the Bollards' golden stink of fertility, domesticity, intimacy, self-sufficiency.

"Happy," said Alice, pouring herself mineral water. "Happy. No. They are complacent. And ruthless. I get bubbles of irritation in my stomach whenever I am with them for more than half an hour. They're saying all the time, Mummy see me jump."

"How can they be saying, Mummy see me jump, when they are so much the mummy and daddy?" Clara asked her. "I never saw such a parental pair in my life."

"They're still saying, Mummy see me jump. To everyone.

They are saying, Look how likeable we are, look at all the people who want to come and stay with us at weekends. Look how I can cater for twelve people every Sunday and remain serene, Helen is saying, look what an earth mother I am, how able, what a provider."

"And what's Tom saying? Does he get a word in edgeways?"

"He's the deep bass continuo. Tom is saying, Look with what tender gravity I answer my children's questions, on the backhand as it were while sorting out the wellies and grating carrots for another healthy feed. Look how beautifully we manage in our lovely country home on not *that* much money, though between you and me the business is doing pretty well, he says. Look how right all our values are. It doesn't count though if no one sees. There have to be witnesses. Mummy see me jump. Their real terror is of being left alone with one another. Babes in the wood. God knows what will happen to that pair when the children grow up and leave home."

"Everyone needs witnesses," said Ferdie. "An unwitnessed life is terrifying. It might as well be a death. God looked at his creation and saw that it was good. Genesis."

"Darling," said Alice, "you're being embarrassing. Don't try and teach your grandmother to suck eggs. Leo has written a book about precisely that. *Unseen Peacocks* . . . It's no good us trying to think this out for ourselves—philosophers have been at it since year one. Though I don't agree with you that God saying it was good made it good. Tom and Helen aren't particularly good anyway. Helen's a greedy, self-conscious, self-indulgent, conceited woman without brains or beauty. Tom has no brains or beauty either, and precious little talent and no charm. He's probably grossly inadequate in most ways."

"He's not a bad wine merchant," said Ferdie mildly. He and Clara were drinking claret presented by Tom Bollard, imported by his firm. He raised his glass. "Here's to you, Tom."

Alice was not to be deflected. She snorted.

"Helen has only done what any rabbit can do—have lots of babies and stay around to rear them. It doesn't make her into a mixture of the Virgin Mary and Catherine the Great, which is how she carries on."

"Fear," said Ferdie, his blind eyes rolling upwards in his long pale face.

"Fear of what?" asked Alice sharply.

"Helen's fear that she is freakish and dull, that she might not be able to do anything, not even what any rabbit can do. Tom's fear that he is freakish and dull, that no one could love him or respect him. They've made a whole sustaining world for each other and they see and say that it is good. They go on about it because they want to share the goodness."

"It isn't good," said Alice. "It's very boring and rather disgusting."

"Presumably," said Ferdie, "that's exactly what the serpent was getting Adam and Eve to see in the Garden of Eden. You are too hard, darling. You'd be discontented in Paradise. You are the Angel of Destruction."

His head was bent low over his plate and Clara could not tell whether or not he was laughing.

There was something about the dining-room at Belwood that made people quarrelsome. No meal eaten in it these days was quite up to its pretensions. There was too much space. Voices came out brittle. The room had not been redecorated since Charlotte and Leo had been first married. Cream paint was now sour yellow. It had chipped, revealing the older dark-brown paint underneath. The lighting was bad. Yet the room itself was lovely in its proportions. If you had not known where you were, you would have guessed that you were in an unsuccessful private boarding-school in a once beautiful house. Ferdie's invisible assets stretched to living at Belwood, but not to maintaining and improving Belwood. To him it hardly mattered. Most of the rooms in the house had decayed gracefully. Only the dining-room had the jangling, tinny quality and the power to unnerve.

"OK, so we'll change the subject," said Alice abruptly. "Let's talk about Clara."

This was not reassuring to Clara. Not with Alice in such an abrasive mood.

"What's the situation with you and Harry?"

"He wants us to get married. I don't know . . ."

There was a silence. Then Ferdie said, gently:

"No one should marry unless they absolutely have to. I don't mean just because they've got pregnant or something. No one should marry unless they think they would die if they didn't marry that particular person."

Clara had her second revelation of the day. She saw, gratefully, that Ferdie liked her a lot. She relaxed. Alice did not.

"That's a ridiculously romantic view. There are lots of reasons for getting married. But Ferdie's right, Clara, you ought to think very carefully."

"And feel carefully," said Ferdie. "Let the pendulum swing a bit and see where it settles. It's no good opting out by saying divorce is easy these days. It's not easy, it tears flesh apart. Look at my poor mum. Anyone who says it's easy is lying in their teeth."

"I think that's true," said Alice, studying her fingernails. "Especially for women."

Briefly, Alice and Ferdie were two locomotives running smoothly behind one another on the same railway line. They might have reached that point from different positions but they were coupled, a couple.

"Of course it's nothing to do with us," said Alice, "except that we're fond of you. I think you should get a new job first. Be yourself again, your real self, and then see how it goes with Harry. You don't have to get another job in publishing—you could learn computing. You were always good at maths."

"I'm not sure whether that's got anything to do with computer programming."

Clara was irritated. It was two against one. She found Ferdie and Alice easier to be with when each could be talked to separately. She addressed Alice:

"It's all right for *you*. And anyway, you don't have a job yourself any more."

"I just can't bear it when you say, 'It's all right for you.' What in hell's name do you mean? You've always said that, ever since I've known you. Do you really imagine I have no problems, do you think I can manage everything, do you think

I'm always all right? Because I'm not. I'm not at all all right."
Alice's voice broke.

Clara could not explain what she meant by "It's all right for
you" without praising Alice, and she did not feel generous
enough to do that. She meant that Alice had style, and confidence, and resilience and intelligence, and the right accent,
and a good figure, and Ferdie, and Belwood, and Agnes. Alice
led a charmed life and she liked you to acknowledge it. But as
soon as her easy success became a cause of dislike or even
reproach she laid claim to terrible sorrows and anxieties, more
terrible than anyone else's.

Clara sighed. It was all so familiar. In their first term at
Redbrook House, both she and Alice had been seriously home-
sick. Clara pent up her tears until she could get to a lavatory,
and then let them flow in secret behind a locked door, her
sobs muffled by the singing of water-pipes. She watched the
clock for the end of classes, unsure whether she would be able
to hold back the tide of tears until after the bell. Because no
one must know.

She emerged from the lavatory to see Alice weeping in the
cloakroom among the coats and berets and hockey-sticks, the
centre of a ring of concern. Big girls queued up to put their
arms round Alice's thin, heaving shoulders. Little girls thrust
sweets at her on their open palms, pushing in under the overhanging busts of the big ones. The games teacher, who was
pretty, led Alice by the hand out into the sunny garden. Clara,
unnoticed, was left alone in the dank cloakroom with her for-
titude. Even in grief, Alice was successful. Clara no longer felt
like telling Alice the story about Helen Bollard and LMC.
She did not want to offer Alice this morsel on the palm of
her hand.

"Anyway," said Alice, refilling her glass with Perrier, "I do
have a job now, of a sort. I'm working for my dear old father-
in-law. For Leo."

Clara was surprised. "I didn't know that!" she exclaimed,
revealing more curiosity, and more of herself, than she intended.

"Oh, it's not much. Very part-time. Just typing up his notes while he's in America, and doing some elementary research in the Senate House Library. Anthropology mostly. I'm not sure what it's all in aid of, but it's pretty interesting."

It looked as if Alice was blushing, but in the dim mustardy light Clara could not be certain. Glancing at Ferdie, she saw that he had not known about this either. Alice was releasing the information in front of a third person so as to inhibit his reaction. But Clara was too old a friend to be much of a buffer.

"The funny thing is," said Ferdie slowly, "that this is as new to me as it is to Clara. Well, well, well. How come you didn't talk to me about this, darling?"

"I knew you'd be difficult about it. Obviously. You wouldn't mind me working for anyone else. But you're always so awful about your old dad."

"Well, I know him. Damn it." Ferdie's voice rose to a sort of howl. "Does he have to have everything—everything he wants?"

Alice took a deep breath. "Now you're being silly. But yes, within reason, yes he does. He's special. He's not just a private person like the rest of us. You're too jealous and mean and small-minded to accept it, to face up to it, to rejoice in the fact that your father's a great man."

"Balls, bullshit." Ferdie's face was twisted as if he were being eaten. "And, even if he were, would it mean I had to lend him my *wife?*"

Alice set her glass down too hard. The stem broke and a pool of Perrier crept over the table and slid over the edge into her lap. She jumped up, wiping at her skirt with a napkin.

"Ferdie, you understand nothing, you see nothing," she said as she mopped and dabbed. Her chair fell backwards with a crack.

Then there was silence. Clara was not about to break it. She should not be present when Alice and Ferdie were behaving like this.

Nevertheless, it was interesting. Like being at a play.

"Has she gone?" asked Ferdie anxiously into the silence. Strange that he could not tell.

"No," said Alice coldly. "But I'm going. Clara, will you do the coffee? The cups are by the Aga, the little black ones."

Alice went upstairs, took off her wet frock and put on a dressing-gown. Through her open bedroom door she heard a thin calling. Agnes, awakened by the loud voices downstairs. She would not go. Christa was in, and would hear. Christa was paid—not very much—to hear Agnes.

Clara did not make the coffee. She stayed in the dining-room with Ferdie.

"It is all the most utter bullshit, isn't it? About my father? About him being a great man?"

Clara poured more red wine for them both. "There *are* great men," she said tentatively, "if you mean men who have power over other people and control their lives."

"My father doesn't have that sort of power."

"But he might have another sort of power, over people's minds, because of what he writes and says. And there are such things as nice men, and good men, but they don't usually have power over people's lives."

"I suppose that Christians think that Jesus combined all the sorts of greatness, power and not-power."

"But that's all a muddle, don't you think? The king of heaven, the sacrificial lamb, having it both ways."

"That's why it's so attractive."

"Nice men, good men," Clara tried again, "don't have power, so they are never great in the world's sense. They are people like—"

"Like Harry?"

"Like Harry."

"And what about another sort of power, people like Mozart and Shakespeare?"

"They are geniuses. It's got nothing to do with what they're like as people. Do you think?"

They drank their wine. Clara said:

"What about being great just in a single context, like the village elder. Or the Victorian husband and father whose word was law. Everyone at the office might see through him, but at home he was a great man. To his wife."

"Nice for the wife, was it, to believe that she was married to a great man? ... Is that what Alice would have liked, do you think?"

"Alice isn't servile. She's a hero-worshipper—it's not quite the same thing. It's done from afar. At school she used to get crushes on people."

"So what's left?"

"Love," said Clara, "and that comes and goes."

The only true love is between a person and an animal. Clara was thinking of Martha and her dog Mungo. An unbreached contract of devotion, whatever the vices of either party. You never hear of anyone divorcing his middle-aged dog, do you? Poor Charlotte.

No, I know it's not quite the same.

Desperate, Clara burst into song:

> "He's honest and faithful right up to the end,
> That wonderful, wonderful, four-legged friend."

"Very good," said Ferdie. "Let's have some more wine."

She poured. It was the end of the last bottle. The last visible bottle.

"OK, something else," said Ferdie. "Just for you, this is. What about great women? What does it mean if you say someone's a great woman?"

"If a man's saying it, like you just did, then it doesn't seem to have anything to do with power. It has to do with her personal qualities, or her usefulness. A man can say 'a great woman' in a hearty, condescending way which would still leave him on top."

"Responsibility without power. Unless it's Elizabeth the First or Mrs. Thatcher."

Clara grimaced, and was relieved that Ferdie could not see. Her antipathy to Mrs. Thatcher was political. But it was not just political, and the impurity of her hostility was something she was too wine-muddled to analyse. Talking to Ferdie alone was like talking in the dark. It was, for him, talking in the dark. He imposed the desultoriness of conversations in bed, touching on large matters in small ways. It was like sharing a bed with a friend who was not a lover. Clara was tired, and would have liked to be in bed. But the evening was not over yet.

5

�֎✖✖✖✖✖

CLARA ALWAYS FELT TIRED, cold and hungry when she stayed in other people's houses. She felt tired because of having to concentrate on an alien routine, judging whether she should be around, ready to talk and to help, or whether she should get out of the way for a bit. It was like map-reading, for hours and hours. She felt cold because she did not know where it was that she took refuge from the day; she was a dog without a basket. Her hunger was the most irrational of all, since people provide better and bigger meals when they have visitors than when they are alone. Her hunger was the opportunist hunger of an animal in unfamiliar territory who is not certain of the availability of prey. You do not, even in a friend's house, have access to the fridge as of right.

When the wine was finished, Clara was overcome by tiredness. She felt grey inside and out. Alice's footsteps were heard in the hall. Clara, remembering Alice's remarks about maths, said inconsequentially:

"Greatness is just an empty set."

"And nature abhors a vacuum." Ferdie turned his body and put out a hand so that Alice would have to take it as she came back into the room. She stood beside him and stroked his hair.

"Come on you two," she said. "We're going swimming. In the lake. A midnight bathe."

"But won't it be freezing? Besides, I haven't got anything to put on."

"You don't need anything. Ferdie can't see you and I've seen you before."

The bathe was absolutely horrible. The water was icy, and the stones at the bottom of the lake hurt Clara's feet. As she came out, her legs gave way under her and she fell down heavily on the muddy wet grass. Too much wine, she supposed. Alice, who had drunk nothing, pranced and flitted ahead back to the lighted house, her body flickering white in the glow from the terrace. Ferdie had refused to go into the water at all, though he had gone so far as to undress and put on a bathrobe, and walked down with them.

In the kitchen Clara shuddered and shivered, wrapped in a towel. Her teeth chattered. Ferdie, depressed, sat on a hard chair, his elbows on his bony knees. The robe fell open round his legs. His long testicles hung glumly into space, swinging slightly as he half turned to follow the sound of Alice's movements round the room. She, still naked, riddling and stoking the Aga for the night, was in high spirits.

"We could play Blind Man's Buff! Would you like that, Ferdie? With Clara and me, with no clothes on?"

"No, thank you," said Clara, as firmly as she could, between shudders. "No more games. No more anything."

"Spoilsport."

Clara went up to bed. After about half an hour she stopped shivering and her body relaxed. Ferdie and Alice were still downstairs. She heard their voices. They were not quarrelling, nor playing horrible games. They sounded like any other married couple.

Some time in the small hours Clara woke and lay listening to the wind in the trees and the hollow laughter of owls. She got up and went along the passage to the bathroom. On her way back she met Ferdie, naked, on the same errand. They stood together for a moment in the passage, two chilly ghosts, their arms around one another without lust. For Clara, it was like embracing a cardboard cut-out. They went their separate ways.

* * *

Clara liked Ferdie's mother. She liked the way Charlotte looked. (Might I look like that when I am her age?) Charlotte's cardigan hung oddly short at the back because of the pronounced forward stoop of her shoulders. Her skirts folded baggily round her body because she spent so much time on her knees, doing the gardening. This ruins soft tweed. Her grey hair was cut short, and grew in an upward tuft over her forehead. She looked like an old, long-legged bird.

On Sunday morning Clara walked from Belwood House down the mown field that ought to be a lawn, and took the left-hand path round the lake to the cottage. Everyone going from one house to the other had to make a choice. Both the left-hand and the right-hand path circled half the lake's circumference, joining up at the other side. Clara liked the left-hand path best because it was flanked by a copse of silver birches. In May, there were seas of bluebells under the birches.

Charlotte herself preferred the other way round, because she liked crossing the low brick bridge over the stream that fed the lake. Though she hardly ever went up to the big house now. Both ways had advantages. One had to choose. "You can't have this *and* that, as my father used to say," Charlotte said to Clara as she poured boiling water into a yellow teapot.

That was more or less what Clara had come to talk about: whether it was possible to have this and that. Specifically, in a marriage. She was unnerved by the disapproval of Ferdie and Alice. She wanted to talk to someone—not them—about her own doubts, which were fed by all the biographies she was reading. She did not know what to make of the evidence of her own eyes. She had seen the Bollards. Nearly everyone she knew was now married, or else living with someone.

Charlotte, she felt, was above the battle, being a widow, twice married and old enough to be her mother. Clara's trouble was motherlessness. Having decided to confide in Charlotte, Clara invested her with wisdom. Whatever Charlotte said she would take seriously.

"Getting married doesn't really change anything," said

Charlotte. "If you're fond of him now, you'll be fond of him when you're married. What changes you is having a child. You think you are going to go on just as before, but you don't, you can't. That's the real change, having a child."

This was not what Clara wanted to hear about. It surely wasn't true of Alice, only of someone like Helen Bollard. She found what Charlotte said both irrelevant and hard to believe. Charlotte did not leave it there.

"One does love the baby so. You can't imagine how much, before it happens. It's the only real loving, the only real happiness, the only real miracle."

Clara was embarrassed, drawing her own conclusions about what this implied about Charlotte's relationships with men, and knowing how infrequently Ferdie made his way round the lake nowadays to see Charlotte. Ferdie was kind to everyone, but his mother's unhappiness terrified him. (Besides, Alice saw so much of Martha, Leo's second wife.) Ferdie had been shocked by his mother's grief twice: when he lost his sight, and when she lost Leo. The mother was more afraid of the dark than the son. Ferdie adored Alice because she was not a blame-thrower or a tragedy queen. Even when she was chillingly foul to him, as she often was, she did not make him feel guilty. Alice did not see him (or anyone else) as having enough influence on her life to be responsible for her frustrations. This, to Ferdie, was a great relief.

Clara tried again. "What worries me," she said to Charlotte, "is whether one is forced into a role—the wife."

"Not nowadays, surely? Not for people of your generation. Married women have jobs and their own friends, don't they? Marriage isn't a profession or a career."

"But don't most men still expect you to take responsibility for everything boring? Like seeing that there's a stock of loo-paper and so on? I've heard a husband say to a wife"—she was thinking of Leo and Martha, but it would be tactless to mention them—" 'Where do you keep the salt?' As if she kept it, personally, in some special place. Why couldn't he say, 'Where do we keep the salt?' or just, 'Where's the salt?' "

"I don't think that sort of detail is very important really, do you?"

"Well it might be, to me. I feel it's the sort of thing that might drive me crazy."

"I expect it depends on what sort of person you are." Charlotte was retreating into cliché. "I've known childlike women married to men who'd know much more than their wives about the practicalities of domestic life. I was very inexperienced when I married Leo. I had everything to learn."

"But why should you have to learn?"

"Because learning anything is worthwhile. Nothing is wasted. Someone has to see that life goes on, that the clothes get washed, that the dinner appears on the table. In my day that was the woman's job. No question. Of course I had help, for me it was more a matter of administration. But if you married your Harry and got a job again you could be like that too. I don't see anything difficult about hiring domestic help. It's providing a job for someone who needs it. If you're not a natural nest-builder, you're not. But everyone seems to manage in their different ways."

"And what happens? How do you go on and on and on? What happens to love, to *in* love?"

Charlotte took the lid off the yellow teapot and fiddled with it. She tried to put it back on again and failed because she was fitting the square-cut side of the lid against the round edge of the teapot. She felt in her cardigan pocket for her glasses and produced the glasses and a pink plastic pig. She stood the pig on its feet beside the teapot, put on her glasses, scrutinized the teapot lid, turned it in her fingers and fitted it correctly on the teapot.

Clara thought she had gone too far and given offence to Charlotte. After all, Leo had stopped loving her. "It doesn't really matter," she said. "It's just that I read such depressing things in books, and I look at the married people I know, and I wonder."

Charlotte took refuge again in platitudes. She did not like the gross littleness of Clara's preoccupations. There were more important things to think about. Cruelty, massacre, despair, evil at the gates. She said:

"Perhaps love and shared history and comfort take over from *in* love for most people. *In* love can be carried by one. A marriage that doesn't break up is so long that almost anything, everything, must happen. There are so many phases."

She wanted Clara to stop this and go, or else change the subject. She was fond of Clara and was afraid that she might begin to tell her things from the gross littleness of her own life, things she had never told anyone. The conversation that they were not having, but might, pressed for admittance.

For example—she might have told Clara that a failed, terminated first marriage goes on existing like an amputated limb; that it was of Leo she thought when she woke in the night, not Andy.

She'd met Andy McAndrew, a retired major, in the flower tent at the County Show. He was a quiet, conscientious person, and had merged into the life of Belwood after they married with no friction, taking his place on local committees as if he had always been the consort of Belwood's heiress. He was not to know that to her he was just a life-saving device, the reinforced steel joist that prevents a load-bearing wall from collapsing.

The odd thing was that after some years of undemanding middle-aged marriage Andy had fallen in love with his wife in his old age. He left little notes in the bedroom for her to find, the sort of love-notes he had sent her by post—once or twice—before they were married. She was touched, then mystified. It was terrible to realize, as fantasy turned into nightmare, that his mind was going.

As Andy grew frailer and less involved in the farms and forestry he spent more time in the house. He began to question her telephone calls and read the letters on her desk. He paid her extravagant compliments in front of other people.

"I am married to the most beautiful woman in the world," he said apropos of nothing to the newly married Bollards at dinner.

"How wonderful," breathed toothy Helen Bollard to Charlotte over the coffee. "How wonderful to have your husband so much in love with you after all these years."

It had not been all that many years, though Helen Bollard was not to know that, being new to the area. And it was not wonderful at all. The reinforced steel joist was crumbling. Andy had a bad heart attack, which frightened Charlotte very much, especially as in the aftermath he became perversely consumed with physical desire. Night after night he turned to her. Because he was her husband and she was fond of him she did not feel she should say no. Her revulsion filled her with remorse. How could she be so ungiving, so cold-blooded, so mean-spirited?

It was years after his death, one day when she was dividing the roots of peonies, that she wondered whether her guilt was not displaced, and whether her love had not been stronger than Andy's. If he had loved her, would he not have known that she was being tortured? If she had not loved him, could she have amiably endured something against which every cell in her protested? These late couplings had little to do with their deep feelings about one another, perhaps.

The divided peonies had not thrived. Peonies dislike being disturbed. She knew that perfectly well, but thought, in her expertise, that she might be able to fool them.

There was worse to come. The day when she came in from the garden and Andy looked up from the newspaper and said:

"Who are you?"

"I'm Charlotte," she replied cheerfully, thinking he was being facetious. "And who may you be?"

"You're not my wife," he said. "You're not a woman at all."

He thought she was a man, an intruder. That was what he said she was. It was not a figure of speech and there was nothing wrong with his eyesight. He meant it. He looked at her and he saw a strange and threatening man. As a girl, gawky Charlotte had been afraid of being thought unfeminine. She thought Leo had left her because she was not womanly enough. It was as if Andy was seeing through her to her fears, which were maybe his fears too all along.

She left the room. When she came back ten minutes later with two cups of coffee he knew her perfectly well and began to tell her about something he had read in the paper. But every now and then after that he would not know her and she would be this frightening man.

In the last year of Andy's life—which was only apparent as the last year of his life after he died; until then, it was just the year it was—he had stopped getting dressed in the mornings and wandered about all day in his dressing-gown and pyjamas. If visitors were expected Charlotte went upstairs with him and persuaded him to dress, as if he were a child.

Most of the housework at Belwood was done then, as it still was, by Irene. She was the niece of Mrs. Cross, who had worked for Charlotte's parents. Charlotte had known Irene and all her family since she was a child. Irene was doing the dining-room when Charlotte, crossing the hall, saw Andy standing at the dining-room door in his pyjamas. He said:

"Come over here, Irene, I want to show you something."

Irene turned off the hoover, straightened up and obligingly went over to Mr. McAndrew—who grasped her wrist and pulled her hand down into his pyjamas. Irene snatched her hand away, giggling, her face flooded with scarlet.

Charlotte said to her husband, "Come along, Andy, it's time to get dressed now."

He came upstairs with her as if nothing had happened and was put out by her anger.

"I'm sorry, Irene," Charlotte said later in the kitchen. "Mr. McAndrew just wasn't himself today. It's his age. Please don't hold it against him."

"That's all right," said Irene, not looking up from the sink. Charlotte knew Irene would not keep the story to herself and was too proud to beg her to. Her heart bled for Andy's reputation in the village. He would mind so much. Except now he did not mind anything. Charlotte loved Andy but she hated this false Andy.

Since his death, which happened in the night while they both slept, the real Andy had been restored to her. But it was of Leo that she still thought with longing.

She used Andy's old pyjamas as cleaning-rags. The dressing-gown, which was a good one, was dry-cleaned and passed on to Irene's husband, who ran the garage down on the main road.

Clara's questions brought back what Charlotte wanted to forget and yet longed to tell. She resisted.

"More important than being in love, in the long run," she said finally to Clara, "is respecting each other. Minding what the other one feels. Wanting to know what the other one thinks, finding that interesting and important."

"Reckoning each other, do you mean?"

"Contempt is the killer." Charlotte felt contempt for herself. The death growing inside her shimmied and shrilled like a shebeen queen.

Clara thanked Charlotte for the tea and went away unsatisfied. Charlotte had talked like a woman's page advice column. She was not the magic mother that Clara wanted.

Charlotte poured herself a half-cup of dregs. She wept a little. She turned on the television news and watched scenes of violence. In another country buildings burned and children screamed. In her own country men in suits discussed the massive lethal capability of the nuclear warheads stockpiled by the great and the lesser powers as if they were talking about a game of bridge. A woman of about her own age, in a hospital bed, related how she had been mugged and raped in her front garden when returning from an evening at her daughter's. There was a shot of the front garden, with its privet hedge, dustbins, chequered tile path and milk bottles. Charlotte smelt apocalypse. She was going queer as Andy had, but in her own way. She guarded this secret and kept a watch on her tongue.

Clara went back to London straight after lunch that Sunday, resisting Alice's pleas that she stay on another night and drive up with her and Ferdie on Monday morning. Clara had had enough of Belwood, and of the Ulms, for the moment.

She took a cab home from Victoria. But she could not stay

in the flat. She went straight out again, and walked the north London streets for hours. As evening came on she found herself on an inner-city high street that was unfamiliar to her. She had been walking immersed in her thoughts, hardly seeing which way she went. But she was as tired of her own thoughts now as she was of the Ulms; she put on her glasses and looked at everything as she strolled on down the Sunday-quiet street.

Old black women with bad legs and big bags. Black men, brown men and grey men. They passed her on the pavement or stood staring into shop windows, or just stood. A man in a woolly hat on a corner stood and trembled. He had not moved when she looked back. A woman on the next corner, ratty fur round her neck, was addressing an invisible multitude at the top of her voice in a language that Clara could not identify. All the shops were shuttered except for an Indian grocery and newsagent. The closed shops had metal grilles across their windows and doors, secured by padlocks. There was a Citizens' Advice Bureau with notices in the window: "Women— Would *You* Like a Free Medical Check Up?" A few doors down, a notice stuck on with a drawing-pin: "Association of Single Parents. Due to Lack of Funds we can no longer operate a drop-in service. Please telephone or write." The pavements and gutters were littered with drifting newspapers, milk cartons, plastic bags, chip papers, chocolate wrappers, pieces of card-board, paper bags, dog-shit. In a café so small that there was no room for anything but a counter and a narrow shelf along one wall, a man sat on a stool drinking something from a cardboard cup. Outside the café Clara had to walk in the road to avoid black plastic rubbish sacks slumped against and on top of one another. They had holes ripped in their sides from which the contents spilled. Rain and time had reduced the rubbish to a fetid mush.

On the doorstep of a bank sat two men and a woman, alco-holics. Their clothes were a mixture of new and old—so new that Clara could see the hands of the social worker still on them, so old that colour, texture and shape had degenerated into mere matter. Cider bottles and beer cans lay at their feet along with a patient dog. Immersed in some fierce, incomprehensible quarrel, the three automatically passed a can between them as they shouted and threatened one another.

Shall I be like that one day? It could happen. If my redundancy money runs out, and I go on the dole. If the dole runs out, and I go on whatever social security I can get. If I lose my flat because I can't pay the mortgage. It could happen. It wouldn't happen suddenly. It would happen little by little. The day I realize it is months since I had a bath, or saw Alice and Martha. The day I no longer think it's odd to pick things over in litter bins. The day I no longer mind sitting down on the pavement when I feel tired. The day I steal something from a shop because I can't pay for it. The day I take alcohol instead of food. The night I sleep rough for the first time. The day the unthinkable seems routine. Who will know or care? By that time, not even I. Perhaps Leo would say one evening, in that bookish, richly warm Clapham sitting-room, "Whatever happened to Clara?" And Alice would say something shrewd that puts the Clara situation in a nutshell, so that no more need be said. Alice might grieve, but she would step fastidiously over the mess that Clara had made of her life. Martha would grieve, and wonder. But Martha had her hands full with Leo.

Clara had reached a bridge over the canal. She went down the steps to the canal walk. Here it was even quieter. And more interesting. She walked along, liking the barges painted in primary colours that were moored to great rings in the canal edge. The waterway was hemmed in by tall buildings—old warehouses of sooty-gold London brick with haphazard fantasies of heavy ironwork, great pipes, ducts, chutes, outside staircases, barricades on the oddly placed windows. Buddleia burst out of the brick cliffs twenty feet up.

On the other side of the canal the warehouses were interspersed with frivolous new buildings trimmed with blue and yellow paint, coloured pineapple-shapes in a row on the pediments against the evening sky. She passed under a low brick-vaulted bridge and came out at a lock, a series of locks, the massive wooden beams and iron fixings of their machinery speaking their weight. A detour through a cobbled yard—then a gleaming pool in the canal, another turn, another bridge, more changes. Gardens on the other side, with willows and moored rowing-boats. Then no more buildings, and high green above both banks. Clara, already elated, saw three elephants lumbering among the green on the farther bank and thought she was hallucinating—until she realized that the canal was now driving its way through Regent's Park Zoo.

The canal walk did for Clara what her friends and bosomy Sussex and Charlotte could not. She turned back after sating herself on the sight of the elephants. Empowered, she walked slowly, inhabiting her skin, her clothes, her London. She walked slowly, her happiness enlarged by her knowledge that what she was feeling was happiness.

I can walk like a lover even when I am alone.

Back in the lee of Victorian warehouses, she stopped and looked down into the water. The canal was not idyllic as it swung greasily eastwards. Clara gazed down into a log-jam of beer cans, soggy cigarette packets, broken bottles, newspaper and chunks of white polystyrene, swinging loosely together in a shifting swirl of scum. She saw it all clearly and with a concentration that was something like love. She held her breath, trying to strap her elation down so that it would not escape, so that she could tame it and ride it later.

She would never go back into publishing—God, how dreary. She would do something quite different, something to do with old London and the flowering weeds springing from filthy walls, something to do with the new London of painted pine-apples against the sky. You can't take inspirational daydreams literally, but hers was the right shape and colour to lift her like a balloon. She did not know what "it" was yet. It would come to her or she would come to it. The important thing was to be open-eyed and open-hearted.

A man with a dog whistled at her as she climbed the steps back to the road two at a time. She waved at him and ran away down the Sunday evening high street until she came to a tube station, and went home. She had not thought of Harry once since she started walking. She longed to see him now, the way that a workman might long to try out a new tool on an old process.

It was nearly dark. There would be setbacks.

6

❋❋❋❋❋

LEO ULM, THE SOCIAL PHILOSOPHER, did not even notice the young Frenchwoman on the first evening of the conference. Most of the British delegation arrived in Washington in mid-afternoon, local time. The inaugural reception and dinner at the Library of Congress began at an hour when transatlantic travellers' internal clocks were telling them that it was bedtime. Leo should have been in better nick than his compatriots. But he had been up very late in New York the night before and had still not adjusted to the new timetable. He was just as exhausted as everyone else.

Leo filled in the time between his arrival and the hour for the party by making himself at home in his room at the hotel. Leo liked hotel rooms, on the assumption that he was not paying for them. He approved of his neat marble bathroom. The bath itself was a bit small, but then Americans prefer showers. It was not at all like home.

Leo and Martha's big bathroom in Clapham was strenuously lived in. Martha never put the top back on the toothpaste tube. (Charlotte hadn't either. Perhaps no woman did.) He saw in his mind's eye Martha's tights hanging disjointedly over the broken basket-chair. Dust and talcum powder dulled the top of the chest of drawers, where disposable razors—used, undisposed of and admittedly his own—lay in angular drifts among damp magazine, aspirin bottles, clogged hairbrushes and pots of old cold cream.

Leo turned his attention to his hotel bedroom. Country-house chintz and dark reproduction furniture. Two armchairs. He ordered a Scotch on the rocks from room service, having failed to find the personal bar concealed in the period furniture. He turned on the television.

Sipping his Scotch, lying on the bed, with mounting incredulity he watched *The Newlywed Game.* The quiz-master's bland indecency made Leo's European scalp crawl with horror.

"In your private romantic moments, what does your wife do most of—grunting, groaning or griping?"

The contestants took this in their stride. A correct answer—correct, that is, in the giggling spouse's estimation—was rewarded with hilarity and an uninhibited embrace. An incorrect answer was greeted with a playful slap and bellows of rueful laughter. The young couples were then invited to expand on these supremely intimate matters, and did so with a cheery wisecracking ease that staggered Leo until he remembered that they must all have been viewers of *The Newlywed Game* for years and were accurately mimicking an established art form. Leo watched very little television, unless he was on it himself. This was the most terrible programme he had ever seen. He could not stop watching it—and comparing the responses to the indecent questions with his own experience.

Charlotte had often wept, silently, clinging to him. Martha, when it was good, laughed aloud. Or used to.

When the programme was over Leo took a look at the fat folder of information left in his room by the conference organizers. Two ballpoint pens and some good stationery were noted by him and approved. The folder contained the timetable for each day of the conference, abstracts of the main papers to be given, a list of the participants with brief biographies, and an ominous note that "Participants are required to attend every session." Oh. Riffling through the pages, Leo decided that he might give the West Germans a miss. He had heard old Steinheil's paper before and he had never even heard of the younger members on the panel. He checked that he himself was not on until the last day. He could relax for the moment.

He lay in the too small tub, relaxing. Leo was not at home with showers. He never seemed to get the pressure or the temperature quite right. He found it hard to arrange himself so that he was not blinded by the water. He never knew what to do about his hair. He found showers particularly unsatisfactory when it came to rinsing the soapsuds from his private parts, or rather from the underparts of his private parts. How was it to be done, without a really excessive amount of slapping, slooshing or contortion? Grunting, groaning or griping? He lay in the tub.

The Scotch, which was three times larger than any double in any English hotel, had gone straight to his head. He wanted to go to sleep. He longed to get into the bed, but struggled into a clean shirt and a dark suit, polished his glasses with his discarded shirt, combed his pale floppy hair and prepared to face his peers.

It wasn't really an ordeal. Leo Ulm was famous and he knew it. Heads turned in the hotel lobby as he emerged from the lift to join the distinguished but diffident group waiting for transport. Was it his imagination or did he hear a murmur of "Ulm . . . Ulm . . . Ulm . . . ," like a mantra? It was surely not his imagination. Intoxicated, he stepped forward and fell unintentionally into the arms of old Steinheil (and, God help us, Frau Steinheil). He shook hands with them, with Perez Llanes from Caracas, with Pietro Condorsi from Milan, with the fat Austrian lady who was a Russian expert and whose name he could never remember, even though she had been a colleague of his for a semester at Amherst in 1974. At least she assured him it was 1974, as she skilfully converted his try at a statutory handshake into a prolonged three-cheek embrace.

On the way to the reception, in a limousine in a convoy of limousines, like a Mafia funeral, Leo's eye was caught by a car-sticker: EAT MORE GOAT. They stopped at red lights beside an orange concrete building, a squat one-storey affair no bigger than a pigsty. A door at one end said BADLANDS. A door at the other end said BADLANDS ANNEX. Leo spent a lot of time in the United States but forgot in between visits that it was a foreign country. It was getting more foreign, or he was getting mossier and more European. He had reached the age when he saw nothing as itself; everyone and everything reminded him of someone or something he had seen before. Washington reminded him of Leningrad.

The spaced-out feeling, the result of whisky followed by white wine on top of exhaustion, grew worse in the vast marble halls of the Library of Congress. Leo's head swam. Voices in six languages assaulted his brain. He kept close to Dr. Black, a fellow member of the British contingent, a thin, opinionated woman from Leicester. He did not care for her. She had sat next to him in the plane from New York, and depressed him with her spiky darkness and her talk about not getting a professional chair "because I am a woman." You hardly are one, darling, so far as I am concerned, he wanted to say, but did not—being a courteous man and furthermore uninvolved in her problems. It was either Dr. Black or the in-flight movie—*The Color of Money*—so he talked desultorily to the unrewarding and unrewarded Dr. Black until they both fell asleep.

He stood beside her now for comfort. With her height and her shoulder-stoop she had the outline of a lamp-post. He would have liked to lean against her. Mungo, Martha's dog, would probably have raised his leg against her. She reminded Leo of Charlotte.

His eyes went out of focus, then homed in on a small patch of swirl-patterned marble untenanted, for the moment, by feet. If he had been one degree drunker he would have made for that silky space and curled up on it like a dog. Again Leo thought of Mungo. He disliked Mungo but Martha did not know that. When, descending shakily from the upper level of the library, he saw banisters and railings ornamented with cascades of over-lifesize marble babies, he thought he was seeing things. He did not like babies either. (Martha knew that.)

It was not until the second evening that he noticed Emmeline Bernay. The reception that night was in the Phillips Collection, just opposite the hotel. The delegates wandered through the rooms with glasses of the now habitual white wine in their hands, congratulating themselves and each other on being able to see such marvellous paintings in such privileged circumstances. Although he had slept badly the night before, Leo was now in fine form, adrenaline running in his veins along with another massive pre-party Scotch, ready for some social excitement to offset the irritation of the day's proceedings.

The Italians had behaved badly. Instructed, like everyone else, to limit their interventions to ten minutes, they had all produced elaborately moulded clouds of rhetoric which took over half an hour to billow forth. Some of the clouds contained hailstones of content; most did not. It had taken both the morning and the afternoon sessions to get through their contributions. The whole timetable was thrown off course. The Americans, as hosts, selflessly agreed to merge with the Canadians' session so as not to curtail the time allotted to any other delegation. Everyone was pleased about this except the Canadians. The Italians were perceived by everyone as being beyond criticism or control, like forces of nature. That was certainly how they saw themselves.

Pietro Condorsi was standing in front of a large, pinkish painting by Degas, his hand caressing the sculptured grey waves on the back of his head.

"It is agreeable," he said in Italianate French, "to see at last a Degas of the first class."

The woman beside him said sharply, in the French of France, "There are no Degas of the second class."

Leo, who thought he probably agreed with this, shot a look at her. He looked again. She was small and slim and fairly young, with blond hair cut very short, neat pale features and a lot of gold chains round her neck. She was wearing loose trousers of thin yellow silk. She looked as out of place in that company as a canary among crows.

Leo moved in. He did what he always did when an unknown woman at a party attracted him. It never failed. He went and stood close to her, looked at her and smiled. And said nothing at all, while she looked at him, as she had to, and answered his smile.

"You are right about Degas," he finally said, in English. He wished his French was trustworthy, but it was not.

They agreed that they had not met before. She told him her name.

"I am Leo Ulm," he said, offering her his right hand.

"I know—oh, I *know*," said Emmeline Bernay, changing her glass from one hand to another so as to take his. He held her hand for a moment.

He went on standing beside her, without making conversation. He was staking his claim. She did not move away.

Is it for this that distinguished men go to conferences in faraway places? Professional contacts, flattering recognition, the exchange of ideas are all very well. But the hope of an Emmeline, for a Leo Ulm, was the real draw. He had no idea of this until it happened.

If Leo's wife Martha knew why men go to conferences in faraway places she did not mention what she knew to him, because it was safer (for her) that he remained ignorant of his intentions. She comforted herself with the belief, born of experience, that physically attractive people are more thin on the ground at academic conferences than they are at, say, race meetings or on Greek islands. Because she was attractive herself Martha was a sexual snob. She forgot that the thudding arrow struck indiscriminately, and that available people wore their availability like haloes and gravitated to one another like sleepwalkers. Sometimes, like Leo and Emmeline maybe, they were taken by surprise. That only showed how little their waking selves knew about the sleepwalker within. "Le coeur a ses raisons que la raison connaît pas," as Emmeline might have said had she been a more banal girl. It had nothing much to do with the heart anyway. Not Leo's heart.

In spite of Martha's belief in the deadliness of academe, Leo (even at fifty-eight) and Emmeline were both attractive in a recherché sort of way. In the ensuing forty-eight hours they became considerably more attractive. Both acquired a glossy patina. Their plumage grew brighter, their eyes glittered. If Leo had been a drake his neck would have been a wicked glistening green. During the informal breaks and lunches they were both outstandingly animated and vital. Dun-coloured professors found them both wonderful company and asked them for their home telephone numbers. They did not stand silently together with their glasses of white wine any more because proximity gave them electric shocks. Leo Ulm and Emmeline Bernay were living in one another's gaze and that for the moment was all they could handle. They were conducting their courtship ritual.

They preened in one another's gaze and that was as close, yet, as they could decently get. They were separated during the conference by the seating plan. The British were placed behind the French and to one side. It was like being in church. Leo could look at Emmeline's straight back, and sometimes her neat three-quarters profile. Every now and then she would look casually over her left shoulder. He dropped his eyes when she did that. Babel was all around them and Babel meant gossip. Nor did he follow her out when she left the hall, as everyone did during the long sessions—to take a cup of coffee from the urn set up outside, or go to the lavatory. He sat tense until she returned, ambling up the central aisle, relapsing gracefully into her chair, whispering some smiling remark to her left-hand neighbour and casting a reassuring glance at Leo's self-consciously bent head.

When it was the French delegation's turn to be on the platform Leo was able to watch Emmeline legitimately and continuously. He was high on his own hopping hormones as well as on sleeplessness and unaccustomed amounts of alcohol. He half closed his eyes and absorbed her colours, gestures and intonations as she addressed the conference.

Her confidence took him aback. He was sufficiently *ancien régime*, as he would put it, to be astonished and put out by a pretty woman who was also authoritative. Emmeline was talking about the relation between modern literary theory and the social and ideological changes in France since 1968. Leo's French was not good enough to follow her; but the flat male voice of the simultaneous translation in his ear was so jarring that he removed the earpiece, turned down the sound and just listened to her voice. Desire flickered and flared.

When he heard her mention his own name his heart bumped. Then he realized she was quoting, in English, lines from *Royal Essence* that he could not remember having written. It sounded fine. She must have read the whole book. It wasn't the bit that Umberto Eco had quoted in the *Theory of Semiotics*, which it would have been easy to lift. As Emmeline finished reading the extract, faces turned to him in friendly acknowledgement. He half lifted a hand, palm spread, in deprecation. Bliss flooded his heart.

All over Washington, every evening at dinner-time, well-dressed people cluster in hallways and drawing-rooms tearing open envelopes so small that Leo's granddaughter Agnes would have thought they were designed for dolls' tea-parties.

"Someone with a fine italic hand," remarked Leo to an uncomprehending Brazilian, "must earn a fortune in this town simply by writing out two thousand names a night."

Each evening, every delegate was handed a minuscule envelope of thick cream paper with his or her name beautifully handwritten in black ink. Inside each envelope was a card on which the same hand had inscribed a single digit. This referred to a numbered table. The place at the table had the relevant name on yet another card. There was no escape and no cheating. No one sat next to the same person more than once during the conference. An arcane system of hierarchy and diplomacy, native to the city, was in operation.

Tonight the conference was divided up into several small, prestigious dinner-parties given by society hostesses in Georgetown. Leo was feeling nervous and aggressive.

"In my country 'hostess' is not a profession. Or, if it is, it's not a respectable one. Maybe it's not so respectable here either," he said to the Brazilian while looking round desperately for Emmeline. For all he knew she was at some rival dinner-party. This was getting to be too much like an obstacle race. No, there she was in her yellow silk trousers, milling round with two dozen others in Mrs. Otto Flassinger's transcendent entrance hall. She made straight for him.

"Où étais-tu?" she said, anxiety in her face and in her voice.

"I went to the gallery, and I slept a bit," he answered. She looked for the envelope with her name on it on the silver tray on the hall table. They opened their envelopes together. Different table numbers. Well.

Leo found himself sitting on the right of his hostess, which was the place of honour. He behaved as beautifully as he could. He looked at her a lot, he smiled at her, he did his best, and he began to enjoy himself. Mrs. Flassinger was a handsome blonde a little past her prime, dressed as for a ball in aquamarine gauze, with diamonds. She was well informed, articulate and kind.

"Wonderful!" she said, often and appreciatively.

Leo became aware that she was outwardly more glamorous and inwardly more humble than any of her London counterparts that he had come across. Nor, in London, would the dinner be so good.

On his other side was Frau Steinheil. This was harder. This was duty. They talked gravely about her children—one a dentist, the other a vet—and about her difficulties in getting Hansi to take a proper holiday. Leo gathered that conferences were the nearest thing to a holiday that this plain, devoted woman ever got. Leo bent a benevolent gaze upon her and thought about Emmeline, who was out of sight round the angle of the L-shaped room.

The wine was as good as the food. What impels even a rich woman, Leo wondered, to extend this sort of hospitality to strangers, who are possibly ungrateful and most of whom she will never see again? He turned to Mrs. Flassinger again when the dessert came round. She spoke of the importance of international conferences such as this one, and thus partly answered his unspoken question. He did not say that he could not consider such events really important. That begged too many questions about what was important, and to whom. He asked her what she found so specially important about this one.

"The bringing together," she said radiantly, "the cultural leaders, the experts, the thinking people, from all over the world!" Leo did not remind her that there was only one black man present, and that the one black man spoke with an Oxford accent. He did not mention the scores of small unpopular nations and the two or three large unpopular ones which were not represented. All the delegates, who had come by invitation, were people who knew (more or less) how to behave at a Georgetown dinner-party. They were what the French delegates would have called *sortable*. Leo ate a morsel from the monumental wedge of chocolate cake on his plate and looked at Mrs. Flassinger sideways and smiled.

Mrs. Flassinger laughed, becoming the lively middle-aged woman she was under the aquamarine flounces and the cultural reverence.

"Come on, it's fun, isn't it?" she said, leaning towards him and displaying a sympathetic leathery cleavage. "How else is someone like me going to get to meet someone like you?"

From then on they were friends. She told him about Mr. Flassinger, who was away on business, diversifying, and about her summer place in Maine. She asked him about his books— "What are they really *about?*"—and he told her, in a way he knew would amuse and intrigue her. He promised to send her *In the Beginning* as soon as he got back to England. She said "Wonderful!" a good deal more, and they agreed that *fun* was the only reason why anyone did anything—it was just that some people get their fun in ways that would be purgatory to other people. Leo told her about his reactions to *The Newly-wed Game*. "Just fun!" said Mrs. Flassinger, shrugging bare shoulders which had the patina of antique polished wood.

Fun at the Flassingers' was contingent on everyone behaving properly. In Washington, dinner-parties break up early by Leo's ramshackle London standards. By eleven o'clock there was a drift, not discouraged by Mrs. Flassinger, towards the door. Frau Steinheil took it upon herself to round up the stragglers with a quiet word. The stragglers included Emmeline, trapped by the earnest Brazilian behind a potted tree. Leo was not disturbed by this. She had to pass the time somehow.

The limousines disgorged the dinner guests at their hotel. No one, not even Leo and Emmeline, wanted to go to bed yet. The group flowed with one mind into the hotel bar. It was already crowded. Leo and Emmeline, who did not intend to be separated, made for a vacant table in an alcove. There were two other chairs at the table. Emmeline waved at her Brazilian, but he did not notice. Leo called to the Steinheils, shambling like linked hippos through the half-darkness, but they did not hear. Leo and Emmeline were divided from the herd. So really it was decided for them.

Now it begins. They both knew it. Leo ordered the inevitable white wine. The waiter, misunderstanding, brought only a single glass.

"We will share it," said Emmeline, her eyes very large and shiny.

As they sat close together, sharing the wine, the voltage passing between them became hard to tolerate. Hand shuddered towards hand and touched and withdrew as if burnt. Each of them was moth and each was candle. Leo was finding it hard to breathe or to speak. His brain closed down, apart from a single busy piece of programming which was about himself and Emmeline.

"What are we going to do?" he asked her. It was a genuine question.

"We will go for a walk."

He had not expected that. He looked at his watch, tilting the face towards the dim lamp. After 11:30. His brain made a last sortie. He had promised Martha he would telephone some time today. He was a bit late. At home it would be almost dawn.

"Yes, if you like. But I must go up to my room for a moment."

He called Martha on the telephone in his bedroom. He heard

the repeated double ring, and imagined her hearing it through her dreams.

"Hello?" said Martha, as clearly as if she were in the next room.

"Darling. You OK?"

Clutching his crumpled air ticket, he read off to her his flight number and time of arrival.

"Would you like me to meet you at Heathrow?"

"Don't bother. I can easily get the tube."

"No, no, I'll meet you, it's no trouble, I'd like to. It will be good for me to have to get up early, anyway. Are you having a nice time?"

"Not bad. A bit too much of the Steinheils—you remember?"

"God, do I. Poor you. I hope you aren't getting too exhausted. It must be pretty late at night for you there now. Have you read your paper yet?"

And so on. You can write it yourself. A supportive marital conversation. Leo felt much the better for it. He had a quick pee in his marble bathroom, brushed his teeth and descended to Emmeline. She was sitting in the lobby trying to look casual as the clotted residue of the evening's dinner-parties stumbled past her to the elevator and, one must suppose, their virtuous beds.

Once out in the dark on Massachusetts Avenue, Leo and Emmeline stopped trying not to touch each other. The flames licked higher, and lower. Dizzy, they wandered aimlessly, turning right at every intersection. Hardly knowing what he was saying, since all his remaining intelligence was concentrated on the messages passing between her fingers and his, he talked to her about Mitterrand (whom he had met) and Chirac (whom he hadn't), and discovered that he and she were not likely to agree on politics. This was not to be a meeting of minds.

After they had walked past the same all-night supermarket for the third time he pushed her against a wall and kissed her. All this told him was that kissing was not enough.

"You are better than your politics," he said to her solemnly.

They walked back to the hotel very fast. They separated at the door. He said goodnight to the hall porter. Five seconds later she said goodnight to the hall porter. They entered the elevator. Emmeline told him the number of her room.

"I'll give you five minutes," he said.

7

✳✳✳✳✳

EMMELINE OPENED THE DOOR to him wearing a short nightdress, her face very bright above its high-buttoned neck. She turned and jumped back into her bed, smiling, watching him as he closed the door. Leo sat on the edge of the bed with his back to her and began to take off his clothes. As he unbuttoned his shirt, looking at the carpet, he said her name for the first time.

"Emmeline."

"Léo," she answered, in a thoughtful, amused way. He turned, saw her lying curled in the bed, and felt awkward.

"Do you mind moving over to the other side?" he asked her.

At home he always slept with Martha on his left. It always worried him to have to do everything the other way round. Like right-hand drive on a car. When he and Martha hired a car in Naples he had sliced the wing of a yellow Fiat within seconds of leaving the parking lot, forgetting where the bulk of his own machine was in relation to himself. This had led to a lot of unpleasantness and spoilt the holiday.

Without comment, Emmeline moved over. He lay down on her warmth. As he pulled the sheet up over them both—it was hot in the room and there was no blanket on the bed—he knew already that there were going to be no distressing difficulties. With this anxiety out of the way he turned to her in excitement. Her grey eyes, inches from his own, disconcerted him.

"Are you not going to take off your glasses?" she asked.

Unwillingly he removed his glasses, leaned away from her and put them on the bedside table. He felt at a disadvantage without his glasses, and normally took them off only for sleep. Martha always let him keep them on.

"Do you mind if we turn the light off?"

"Comme tu veux."

She turned off the bedside lamp on her side of the bed.

Then everything was all right. It was more than all right. Leo drowned in sensation. There was no awkwardness, no difficulty. Peeled of her nightdress in the dark, Emmeline seemed as small and perfect as a child. He did not want this pleasure ever to stop. He broke from her and turned the light on again. He wanted to look at her now.

Her body was not as beautiful as he had been imagining. Bodies never were. She had borne a child: her stomach was streaked, her breasts used. Her torso was spattered with small moles. He suppressed his disappointment. In his mind he had been violating a virgin, though her responses were not those of a virgin.

He returned to the business of pleasure. Emmeline was experienced. He did not like to ask her for what he wanted. There was the language difficulty—she might not understand. He need not have worried. She was ahead of him all the time.

Surreptitiously Leo put out his right hand, fumbled on the table and retrieved his glasses. With them safely settled on his nose and hooked behind his ears, he relaxed and looked down at the top of Emmeline's head, liking the way her short hair grew in a whorl at the crown. She was lovely. What she was doing was lovely.

Not yet, not yet . . . He pulled her up towards him and turned her over. She was as cooperative as a schoolgirl trying to set a record rally at table tennis. Everything was possible and easy. Leo launched himself into his final flight.

"Darling. Darling. Darling." He hardly knew who she was. He knew who he was; he was Leo Ulm and all was well.

Emmeline said something in French that he could not follow.

"Tu es belle," said Leo. It was the best that he could manage, linguistically.

She said, in English, that there was a box of tissues on his bedside table. He located the box. They made use of the tissues.

Emmeline turned off the light again. Leo lay on his back listening to his breath returning to normal. She lay against him and caressed his feet with her own.

"Do you think the feet are érotique?"

Leo considered. At that moment he had not the strength to find anything erotic. Maybe there was something one did with the feet which he did not know about. She was, after all, French.

"I think feet are sort of friendly," he said at last, remembering how unfriendly Martha's could be when he accidentally slashed her ankles with his toenails.

AIDS was a space-age anxiety so far as Leo personally was concerned. He worried much more about traditional hazards such as pregnancy. He recalled the possible result of the activities of the past hour and formulated in his mind a sentence that would be easily understood and neither prissy nor alarming.

"I hope we haven't made a little baby," he said, with a false laugh. "Are you all right? I mean do you . . . have you . . . ?"

Emmeline laughed too, in a way that reassured him not one little bit.

"But I should so much like a Léo-baby with a crooked smile and who wears his spectacles in bed."

He had no time to analyse the implications of this because she began to move against him in a way that activated his machinery for a second time.

"This is crazy. This is *rape,*" said Leo, to excite himself still more. The word "rape" fizzed and exploded in his brain as he abandoned himself to its red message.

"We know each other very well now," said Emmeline as she returned from the bathroom.

"We don't know each other at all."

She climbed back into bed and settled herself against his shoulder. "So tell me."

Leo began to talk, lying on his back, his eyes closed. Once he started talking he could not stop. His voice rumbled on and on in the Washington night while the air-conditioning machinery roared softly outside the window.

He talked until the darkness turned to greyness and birds began to sing in the trees on Massachusetts Avenue.

Emmeline interrupted him every now and then, wanting a clarification or not understanding a word or a phrase. He answered her queries rapidly, anxious not to lose the flow of his thoughts about himself. He told her things he had never told Charlotte or Martha—anxieties, failures, triumphs, mistakes, strengths, weaknesses. He risked himself with her, talking about himself, more absolutely than when they had made love.

When at last his voice came to a stop, Emmeline said:

"And tomorrow night I will tell you my life. My stories."

Leo was not charmed by this thought. He did not want to spend his last evening in America listening to girlish confidences.

Then, to his surprise, Emmeline suggested that he should return to his own room and get some sleep. Leo believed women set great store on the aftermath of sex, and felt let down if the man left the bed before it was strictly necessary. In the long-ago days when he was deceiving Charlotte to sleep with Martha, Martha's eternal grievance had been that he could never spend a whole night with her.

He looked at his watch. It was 5:30.

"Would you mind?"

"Not at all."

"Perhaps it would be the sensible thing."

"I am a very sensible girl."

Leo got up, dragged on his clothes and left.

In London, it was mid-morning. Martha, after her interrupted night, lazed on the double bed. Mungo had his hairy head on

Leo's pillow. Mungo was asleep. Martha was not. She was trying to suppress the wish that she did not have to go to Heathrow the next day to collect Leo. She had offered, insisted even.
She felt all the same that he had exacted that offer, that insis-
tence. Leo set great store on the outward signs of devotion.

Leo was a demanding husband. Martha watched Clara and
Harry with interest. They did not live in one another's pockets. They came and went in one another's lives without elaborate explanations. Neither seemed to know or to need
grievances and resentments. They extorted nothing from one
another. But then they were not married; and Leo, who was a
uxorious man, would say that such ease and casualness meant
that Harry and Clara did not really love each other.

This suggested that love, for Leo, was not love unless it
included a certain amount of punishment as well as intensity.
The way Clara and Harry went on would not suit Leo at all.
When Martha and he were first together he confessed to her
that he hated to come home to an empty house. This seemed
to her touching at the time. Later she found it inconvenient,
and troubling. Maybe it originated in some buried insecurity.
She respected Leo's sensitivity but felt that it did not extend
beyond himself.

"If you can't bear coming back to an empty house," she said,
"then someone else has to come back to an empty house. What
about that person? Wouldn't it worry you, if you think like
that, that it might be just as awful for her as for you?" For of
course that person would be a her.

"But she wouldn't have gone anywhere. She would already
be there. Ideally, I mean."

"So I'm never to go out?"

"Now you're being silly."

It transpired, on further questioning, that the women in
Leo's life very rarely had gone out. Charlotte had never left
Belwood unless she had to. "Charlotte will never go anywhere
with me" had been Leo's chief complaint against her when he
was looking for a justification for leaving her.

Second wives do well to listen to the criticisms men make

of their first wives. There is a covert satisfaction squirming beneath the complaint. Charlotte might have seemed to be failing Leo socially and as a companion; seeing her in that light certainly made Leo feel better about the way he claimed his own freedom, which enabled him to see Martha. (And Martha was not the first, as she well knew.) But the homebody waiting beside the fire satisfied an older, deeper yearning.

Martha thought about these things often as she sat in silence doing her own work, and as she went about her household tasks.

When the women in Leo's earlier life did go out, it was thoroughly discussed beforehand and the hour of their return stated and adhered to. "I'm going to Wythenshawe for the day to see Miriam Rosen. I'll be back in time to see you get your tea." Leo's father had never had to say, "Where's your mother?" In Leo's childhood before the war, bread, groceries, meat and fish were all delivered by tradesmen on the same day and at virtually the same hour every week. If anything extra was needed one of the maids slipped out for it. The uneventful regularity of life was interrupted only by birth, marriage or death—and there were established routines for coping even with these.

Leo's parents were middle-aged when he was born, and traditional in their habits. They preserved the domestic rituals of their own parents, which made Leo not so much a pre-war child as an Edwardian one. He told Martha that his immigrant grandfather, when he became prosperous, had required his whole family and his staff of cook, nurse, parlourmaid, housemaid and bootboy to be out on the steps to welcome him when he came home from warehouse or office in the evening. If they were not all there to greet his return he was disappointed to the point of tearfulness. Leo seemed to think his grandfather's behaviour was a sufficient explanation for his own milder idiosyncrasy.

This tableau of the Manchester household hailing the master's homecoming caught Martha's imagination. It conjured up an arrangement for a formal photograph to mark a special occasion, not a daily occurrence. She wondered whether Leo as a child might have seen such a photograph and invented a story to fit it, a story which he grew up to believe. He actually had a faded photograph of his grandparents' house. There were no people at all in the brownish-grey print, just dark shrubs crowding the front steps, and what looked like a handcart up-ended on the gravel sweep. Maybe no one ever watched for grandfather's return. Maybe he dreaded the dark approach to the forbidding house on winter evenings. Maybe the welcoming party had been grandfather's fantasy, and had become Leo's.

Martha painted a careful picture, from the photograph, of the house as Leo's grandfather dreamed of seeing it as he hurried home to Moss Side full of hope. Grandmother stood in the open doorway, a shawled baby in her arms, the glow of gaslight behind her. A fat cook, a pretty nursemaid, a thin parlourmaid and a stunted child of a housemaid were ranged down the steps, one below another, their hands on the balustrade. The bootboy, in a flat cap too big for him, stood grinning on the gravel. He was holding a rake, and the handcart was piled high with fallen leaves. Martha preserved the sepia fog of the photograph by making it an autumn evening. In the foreground uncollected leaves lay scattered; the sooty evergreens pressing up against the house were spotted with scarlet berries.

Martha was pleased with her picture. She thought it would please Leo, and soothe the ghost of his grandfather. Leo was ambivalent about it. The picture was, accordingly, given only ironic status in the Clapham house and hung in the bathroom.

Leo was billed to read his paper to the conference at nine o'clock the next morning. He woke in his own room at twenty minutes to nine feeling terrible. At one minute to nine he was in the conference hall and making his way up to the dais, where the chairman of the session and the British scholars who were to take part in the discussion afterwards were already settled with their papers and their glasses of water.

Leo passed Emmeline sitting at the edge of a row. She looked as fresh as a leaf. She met his bleary eyes, he raised an eyebrow, and took away with him up to the platform the cup of coffee that Emmeline had on the desk in front of her. He heard an American voice behind him remarking: "What cheek. What a boor. Why couldn't he have gotten his own coffee?" Leo knew if he did not have a cup of coffee he would faint. He felt barely capable of speaking, let alone speaking well.

His spirits revived as he half listened to the chairman's extremely flattering introductory speech, and the applause that followed. He looked once at Emmeline, who gave him a secret smile, and plunged in.

It was only a matter of reading aloud. He stumbled once or twice, and sometimes had no idea what he was reading, losing track not only of the argument but of his own voice. All he had to do was to keep on and on until he got to the end.

He kept on and on until the end. The applause was polite. It was less prolonged than the applause before he had spoken.

During the discussion, in which he took very little part except when he was asked a direct question, he fell asleep once or twice.

I am getting too old for the sort of thing that happened last night. Or for so *much* of the sort of thing that happened last night.

Emmeline was animated as the session broke up. She was chatting cheerfully to the people around her. What vampires women are, he thought.

As the day wore on Leo felt better. It was the last day of the conference and the celebratory mood was infectious. Sipping white wine—pure acid now to his overworked gut—after the afternoon session, he said to Emmeline:

"I think you and I will have a quiet dinner out somewhere this evening." He hoped thereby to get the talking part over before he was too exhausted for anything else.

"But we can't—there is a dinner arranged, for everyone together. We must be there."

Leo moaned. He had had enough ceremonial meals.

This last one was the longest and grandest of all, with speeches of satisfaction and self-congratulation from the organizers, and speeches designed to amuse from the certified wits of the intellectual community. Industrialists and congressmen who had supported the conference had to have their say. When finally people pushed back their chairs there was an orgy of kissing and leave-taking; the delegates would be dispersing to all corners of the globe at the crack of dawn. Leo saw the Austrian woman embracing one of the Russian delegates. He looked like Groucho Marx. His eyes rolled wildly, his mouth and moustache compromised by Western lips.

"Glasnost! Perestroika!" trilled the Austrian, having unclamped him.

The Bulgarians, who would be reporting back on the demeanour of the Eastern Bloc contingent, looked sour.

"Glasnost!" cried the Austrian woman, waving her arms at the Bulgarians.

"Goodbye," said the Russian.

Leo saw the Brazilian sneaking up to Emmeline. Probably proposing a glass of white wine in the bar. Leo moved fast and was at her side before she could reply to the Brazilian. He put a hand under her arm and guided her swiftly through the double doors of the dining-room, smiling and nodding genially to right and left. He wanted Emmeline to come to his room tonight. He did not like padding around hotels in the small hours; you never knew whom you might meet, and the word would get around.

But no, she insisted they meet in her room, as before.

In his own room, giving her a chance to prepare for him, he lost his enthusiasm for a second instalment of sexual adventure. He had had almost no sleep the night before. His bed looked very inviting. He considered getting into it, turning out the light and forgetting all about the assignation.

But that would not work—she knew his room number; she would just ring him up.

Emmeline was not undressed and in her bed waiting for him. She was fully clothed; all she had taken off were her gold chains, which lay coiled on the television set.

"I ordered from room service for us."

Leo was put out. It was his place to order drinks, not hers. "What did you ask for?"

"A bottle of Sancerre."

Still more white wine. The waiter brought the wine on a tray with two glasses and a rose in a silver vase. Leo gave him a dollar, feeling cross. He would have given his eye-teeth for a large Scotch.

He opened and poured the wine. She sat on the end of the bed and he sat in the armchair beside it. His feet hurt. He took his shoes off and rested his legs on the bed, not touching her.

As she had said, she wanted to talk. She asked him about himself again, but only as a prelude to telling him about herself. She talked eagerly, half in French and half in English; she glowed, as if she were giving him a present that she knew he wanted.

She told him about her family home in Normandy, the farm which had belonged to her grandparents and where she had been brought up. An ancient fortified farm, with a dovecote and orchards. She explained that it belonged to an uncle now, and she only saw this place that meant so much to her for a week in every year, in the summer, when she visited her uncle. She told him about her school life and her student life. She told him about the courses she was teaching at the moment. She told him about the courses she would like to be teaching. She told him about her first lover, who had been an older man, a friend of the family who was a professor at the Collège de France and who let her down badly. She told him about her four-year-old son—no, no, the professor wasn't the father, someone else . . . She told him about her domestic difficulties, trying to look after him and do her work and see her friends, and about the prejudice in her home village against unmarried mothers, even nowadays. She told him—but it does not matter what she told him, in that it did not matter to Leo.

At first, watching her bright face and graceful gestures, he had taken some pleasure in sitting there with her, anticipating greater pleasure to come. But she became garrulous in her desire to hand him her life-story on a plate, or so it seemed to him. In desperation, he drank the Sancerre. He grew more and more bored and sleepy. He became so bored and so sleepy that he forgot to be polite. He interrupted an anecdote of her childhood, something about a meal eaten in a wine cellar. He interrupted pompously, because he did not know how else to do it.

"Tonight I will not assault your virtue. I will let you sleep in peace. We both have an early start tomorrow."

She stopped short. Her face was stricken. She leaned forward, hugging her knees, her eyes searching his face.

She made him feel guilty, but he did not know why he felt guilty. It was too late to backtrack anyway. He was already tying his shoelaces, already standing up. She still sat on the end of the bed, white-faced, looking up at him.

"I expect we'll meet again," said Leo. "Somewhere. In the nature of things."

She still stared, still said nothing.

"You don't regret what happened, do you? It was good for you, too, wasn't it?"

"Oh no, not regret!"

Touched by the intensity in her voice, and by something else, he found a piece of paper in his pocket and scribbled his Clapham address on it. Not the telephone number. He gave it to her.

"There you are—in case you ever come to London."

She tore the paper in half and on the blank piece wrote her own address, and passed it to him.

"Thank you." He was standing over her now. He bent and lifted the stricken face with his hand. He kissed her forehead. "There," he said. "It's not so bad, is it?"

"Yes, it is bad." Emmeline looked up at him. "It is very bad, but I can support it." She corrected herself: "I can *bear* it."

Leo turned to go. As he passed the television set his eye was caught by the glint of her gold chains. He lifted one of them on a finger and let it fall rippling back on the heap.

"Will you take one? From me, for a present?"

"Are they real gold?"

"Of course they are real gold."

"Then no, I can't take it."

It was then that he saw her room key lying beside the chains. He picked it up quickly and put it in his pocket as he turned to her at the door.

"I'm sorry," he said as he went. "I'm sorry. I'm sorry."

Lying in his neat bed in his own room, Leo asked himself why he had stolen her key, and found no answer. It lay at eye-level on his bedside table and he stared at it.

He must have been mad to walk out on her like that, to throw away the opportunity of another night with her.

He lay tense with irresolution. Then he got up, dressed again and for the second time that night made his way along the carpeted corridors, past the elaborate flower arrangements on pier-tables. He had been frantic with sexual purpose when he left his room. By the time he got to her door, purpose and desire had drained away. He went so far as to fit her key in the lock. He did not turn it. Careful not to make a noise, he removed the key again and, grasping it so tight that it cut into his hand, almost ran back to his room. He put Emmeline's key in his pocket, found his own, shut his door firmly once he was inside, tore off his clothes and went back to bed. He turned off the light and thought some simple thoughts.

He thought of Martha. He had resisted temptation. Nothing had happened. He was safe. He thought about tomorrow, which was already today. He was flying back to New York to lunch with a pleasant viola-playing professor of sociology who was arranging a visiting professorship for him at Columbia. Then he was catching the evening plane to London. London. Daffodils in the parks and traffic jams on Battersea Bridge. Leo slept.

At Dulles Airport, Leo came across Emmeline's room key in his pocket when he was groping for his ticket at the check-in.

8

Leo Ulm, the social philosopher, was home again. The lion was back in his cage. The lion was tired, and a little disappointed—not in the conference, but in his homecoming.

In Washington people really had turned in the hotel foyer as he passed, murmuring, "Ulm . . . Ulm . . . Ulm . . ." He had not imagined it. At the parties and receptions, academics and tycoons really had hovered around him, waiting for an introduction. Limousines had carried him like a baby from A to B. Doormen had opened doors. The college president who introduced his paper had been reverential.

It was true he had not read his paper very well. But no one noticed, or if they did they never said anything to him about it, that his paper was not new but an update of an update of a lecture he gave for the first but not the last time at LSE in 1967, and subsequently published in the *British Journal of Phenomenological Research.*

He was right that no one had noticed. The reasons why nobody remarked on the antiquity of his contribution were, first, that the distinguished non-academics present had neither the time nor the skill to read anything outside their immediate areas of professional concern; and, second, that Leo Ulm was no longer much read by young academics. Old academics wouldn't be able to remember what they had read and what they had not. Leo's most famous books were *In the Beginning* (Routledge & Kegan Paul, 1965) and *Royal Essence* (Weidenfeld

& Nicolson, 1971). These were still on the reading lists. They were mentioned and quoted in student essays and dissertations. The extracts quoted were always the same ones. This was because they were copied from other dissertations and textbooks. For over twenty years the authors of books and learned articles in the field had been building on each other's work, and no one now could have identified the lone pedant who originally quarried *In the Beginning* and *Royal Essence* for the famous paragraphs which ensured the appearance of "Ulm, Leo" in the index of scholarly works—generally between the entries for "Truth" and "Undetermination."

Leo would be the first to concede that he had spread himself too thin. He had not specialized. There were few branches of philosophy and the social sciences which he had not explored, taking from each whatever he needed to shore up his current obsessions. His detractors said that it was not so much a question of branches, for Leo Ulm, as of twigs. His work was twiggy. His admirers described his writing as þoetic, allusive, free-ranging, a contribution not only to the history of knowledge and culture but to culture itself, and to literature. But by the late 1980s it bore the same relation to the history of ideas as the Italian table-centre of painted pottery grapes and pears bore to the Cox's Orange Pippin which Martha gave him for his homecoming lunch, to go with the Stilton.

They had bought the ceramic table-centre in Positano, where their bedroom had been a simple white cube almost filled by the double bed. One whole wall was window, the long white curtains blowing out, veiling and unveiling the blue of the Mediterranean.

Leo did not know that he was no longer much read. Martha suspected it but would have died rather than enlighten him.

Leo had been encouraged by Washington. The comfort, the good manners, the praise, the publicity, had satisfied a hunger that gnawed at him continuously in London. And then there had been Emmeline. On the flight home, released from the low-grade grievance that was his habitual state of mind, he felt weightless. He was so relaxed that his head swam.

He had a window seat. He looked out into blueness, and on

to the cloud layer beneath. He imagined himself out there, bouncing and somersaulting on the clouds. They would be soft as cotton wool, buoyant as a trampoline, so deep he could never fall through, so limitless he could never fall off. He bounced and rolled and dived in the clean, billowy clouds.

The steward was offering him a glass of champagne. Yes, yes, that would be very nice.

Martha met him at Heathrow with the car. It was breakfast-time in England. Martha's face had the pastiness of someone who has got up too early. She had been unable to park near the arrivals building, and he followed her sturdy figure for miles, his suitcase banging against his legs, the champagne recurring as bile in his throat, before she located the dirty blue Ford and they got away.

It was impossible in the dank British dawn to convey to her anything of the glory from which he came. Martha, concentrating on the traffic, was content to drive in silence once she had ascertained that, yes, Leo had had a good time and, yes, his paper had gone down pretty well. No, the other conference papers had not been particularly exciting. (Leo couldn't be bothered to tell her about them.) The conference had been too broad in scope, he told her, "everything from Plato to NATO." Not his own joke, but she did not know that and shot him an appreciative smile.

Big hairy Mungo in the back of the car slobbered into Leo's right ear. Leo put up with it. He felt it would be graceless to tell Mungo to bugger off so soon after his return. Depression began to rise within him.

Martha served up some gobbets of home news. Anthony might look in this evening, if Leo was not too tired; he was longing to hear about the trip. The man had come about the faulty electric point in the sitting-room, and said the whole circuit ought to be rewired. Christa had had her hair dyed blond and done in spikes; Alice had discovered she had a boy-friend, a student at Sussex.

Leo barely responded to these fragments. He was pleased

that Anthony Arklow-Holland was coming—the beloved disciple—though he did not say so. He felt a flicker of interest—the visceral equivalent of a raised eyebrow—at the idea of Christa becoming a spiky blonde. He did not admit the subject of the rewiring very far into his consciousness, since it was uninteresting and must involve spending money.

He was already sulking by the time that Martha reached the Hammersmith flyover. He would not have said that he was sulking. He would have said that he felt a little melancholy, and he would have made the statement sound like a reproach. Martha, who had been married to him for a long time, knew better than to enquire how he felt.

By lunchtime it was as if he had never been away. They had their customary picnic at the sitting-room table, pushing books, newspapers and Martha's drawings out of the way. Ham, lettuce, mayonnaise, bread, the Stilton and the apple. Leo identified a telephone bill stuck between two pears in the ceramic fruit arrangement.

Afterwards he sat alone in his usual chair to the left of the fireplace. Crammed bookshelves loomed behind his chair. There were more books—including his own—in the alcove on his left, close to hand. The Ulms had never bought many pictures; they collected antique rugs and carpets. The floor was a patchwork of overlapping designs and textures. Kilims hung on the walls in the spaces between bookcases and windows. The air was dense with merging colours, and with Mungo's hairs, ash from the fireplace, dust from the books, pollen from the overblown flowers (Leo, who knew nothing about flowers, could not have named them) in a jug on the mantelpiece. He was fresh from the shining surfaces, the pale chintz fabrics and the unspeckled mirrors of his Washington room; he breathed in the fallout from over ten years of luxurious growth and decay and, in spite of himself, was not displeased by it.

A pad and pen lay in their usual place at his right hand, on a low table. He wanted to write a note to his daughter-in-law Alice, who had rung him so sweetly just before he left to wish him good luck, assuring him—correctly, as it turned out—that he would be a star.

But he was tired. He leant his head against the cushion behind him, closed his eyes and thought about women. His relaxed right hand lay over his fly—not to stimulate but to comfort and reassure. There we are. Everything where it should be.

In the plane, as he bounced on the clouds, he had begun to write a poem. He wrote a lot of poetry when he was young. Some of it lay buried in the pages of 1960s magazines stacked in the attic.

He sat forward, picked up the pad and the pen and wrote down the lines that had come to him when he was between two continents.

> *The man that said that women had no souls*
> *Was speaking truth, but not the truth he knew.*

Leo had got no further than that on the aeroplane and he got no further now. He crossed out the first "that" and substituted "who." He replaced pad and pen on the table, leant back and closed his eyes again. Women's bodies. The differences.

Martha and Clara and Alice. The women he knew best. And Christa, whom he saw quite often simply because she worked for Alice. Looking after the child. Martha would lose her figure if she had a child—she'd get that thick waistless look. Walking behind women in the street, weighed down by shopping bags, their long broad bottoms beginning at armpit level and extending like the Sussex Downs to their knees. Clara, now, she could probably have half a dozen children and it would make no difference. If she was pregnant she would look like a snake that had swallowed a rabbit whole. Or a baby.

The point about Martha, thought Leo, was that she did not have a modern shape. Short-legged and short-necked. No-neck monster, his mother would have said, who equated height and slimness with English good breeding. Martha was stubby, like Leo himself and both his parents. He was comforted in adolescence when he learned that Napoleon, Marx, Beethoven, Mozart and Churchill were all short men. Little bulls, like the Pope. In loose trousers and that green sweater Martha looked dumpy. No one would look at Martha twice these days when she was with Clara or Alice.

Clara, long and thin. In her nightie, trying to play snooker. The way she threw herself down on the sofa when she came into a room, legs and arms flying out at angles, the tulip-head floating and swaying on its stem. Her repertoire of poses and postures, her grace. Leo thought Clara was very attractive. She wore her silly clothes with an air. When she talked her hands were birds. Did she know the effect she made? Leo thought not. Martha said that Clara was not at all sure of herself. Nor of anyone else. She had been gauche when Leo first met her—over ten years ago, it must be. Not so gauche now.

Does Clara really like me? Does she admire me?

What would she look like with her clothes off? Nothing at all. Leo shifted into an even more comfortable position. Nearly as bad as that Washington woman, all diamonds and false eyelashes and big hair, but thin, like pictures of Auschwitz victims, ate nothing, waste of her own marvellous dinner, just pushed it around on her plate. Knobby collar-bones, claw-hands and all those rings. Good solid bosom, surprising. Face getting all the help it could buy, skin taut under the tan. Kind eyes, big white teeth. Capped. European women had crooked yellow teeth but at least you knew whose they were. Emmeline's teeth were OK. Not yellow. Silver fillings at the back. Martha had good teeth. Clean, cat-mouthed Martha. But Mrs. Flassinger had been so encouraging. "Wonderful." Whatever he said, she said, "Wonderful." He had felt wonderful. He had been wonderful, that night with Emmeline. Proud to be himself. She'd read all his books, too. Knew them inside out. He got very little feedback of that kind as a rule. But then you couldn't even use the word "intellectual" in London without raising a snigger. Why hadn't his grandparents chosen Paris as a home instead of Manchester? Because they understood only cloth and dealing in cloth and thought Manchester was the centre of the textile world. Which it no longer was, even in their day. Foreign competition.

His family was in his mind more than usual because of the

things he had told Emmeline. The pathos of Grandfather, who believed in the glory of the Austro-Hungarian Empire and knew its history, its politics, its palaces, seeing that world of velvet and sharp steel as the earth's centre and the British Empire as a parish-pump commercial enterprise run by stringy North Europeans who did not understand ceremonial, honour, *Realpolitik* or the concept of empire. Queen Victoria was a dowdy little businesswoman, a third-rate riposte to the Empress Maria Theresa. Poor Grandfather thought he was doing Britain a favour by settling here. He talked to his Manchester colleagues as if he were a grand duke among barbarians. Grandfather never understood that the English found Central Europe and its strutting pomps something to make jokes about, and its courts musical-comedy imitations of the real thing, which went on at Windsor and on Horse Guards Parade. Grandmother suspected, because she picked up quite a lot. That came from listening. Grandfather talked all the time and never listened. Grandmother idolized him and silently watched him making a fool of himself in front of the supercilious, ignorant English.

The one thing—apart from English tailoring—that Grandfather admired about his adopted country was the idea of the English gentleman. But he got that wrong too. He thought it was really all to do with breeding, like Lipizzaner horses. He never cottoned on to the fact that being an English gentleman had nothing to do with any spiritual or even physical qualities but was a matter of codes and signals concerning accent, clothes and, above all, references. These were easily learned or acquired, at a price. The price was the fees of a public school. Grandfather would have been incredulous if he had been told that neither he nor his son nor his grandson was a gentleman; he would have been offended, not realizing that "gentleman," for the English, was a purely technical term when used by the initiated. Grandfather was courteous, honourable, clean, cultured and innocent. Leo wished that he had been less innocent. Neither Leo's father nor Leo had been sent to a public school. Leo was educated at Manchester Grammar School. It was a great school. But as he grew older Leo minded more, not less, about his exclusion from the elite tribe. He would have liked to have had a public school education if only so as to be able to condemn it with comfort.

Comfort. Women's breasts. Alice's disturbed him most at the moment. He was not sure whether or not he was thinking incestuous thoughts. If he had a Book of Common Prayer to hand he would consult the Table of Kindred and Affinity. Alice as a bride, unforgettable. Alice sitting cross-legged, swaying backwards and forwards while she listened to him. Like pears sliding under that blue silk thing she wore last time. Must have cost a mint. She had got better-looking recently— excited, perhaps, about her work for him. Living with poor Ferdie couldn't be much fun, though everyone was so loyal. But Alice hadn't seemed much, to Leo, when he first got to know the girls.

The best friends. A hurdle. Confronting Martha's friends had made him feel old, older than he felt now. There were advantages in marrying a younger woman. Poor old Steinheil, in Washington, lugging round that grey mountain of a wife.

To be fair, Steinheil seemed devoted to her. How was that done? How do men continue to dote on women who are no longer attractive or amusing?

Martha had been the one, then. She put Clara and Alice in the shade, the night she brought them round to see him. Martha's breasts, low-slung and heavy, unfashionable. The very first time he ever saw her she was nineteen, she was wearing a dark-red dress, soft woollen stuff (Grandfather would have fingered it speculatively) with long sleeves and a deep V-neckline. The devastating cleft, shocking, beneath a face as clear and young as a madonna's. No make-up, straight brown hair hanging round her ears. Her tiny waist, another shock, a miracle of engineering between those great curves. Short legs, so that the full red skirt, which would come just below the knee on someone like Clara, covered everything but her neat ankles.

The first sight of Martha was a major experience for Leo. He couldn't take his eyes off her. He annotated her, constructed and deconstructed her, decoded her as if she were a text. He believed up till then that beauty was not a significant concept. This was what he taught his students; it was what he had been taught himself. Suddenly aesthetics and ethics became of consuming interest to him. He wrote *Unseen Peacocks* because of Martha. In his seminars, when he talked about penetrating phenomena, he knew that the phenomenon he wished to penetrate was Martha. He used to teach his students to attend not so much to art itself as to the kind of things we say about art. His subject was the ways that ideas change. But if truth is relative then the statement "truth is relative" must itself be unstable. Martha is absolute beauty, he longed to say aloud in the seminar room. And went home to poor Charlotte.

Tall Clara, with her angular movements, would have been considered freakish in any century but her own. Martha was out of period.

Martha only showed her magic when she wore plain frocks in plain shapes attainable by peasant or princess at any time since women first wore dresses. High fashion and brilliant colours were cruel to her shortness and her heavy build, robbing her of her primitive meaning. With a wide round neckline, or the deep V in which he had first seen her—any basic headhole—the unity of her head and strong throat was breathtaking, as if they were moulded from a single piece of clay. It was Martha whom Rembrandt and Degas had painted, half-draped, intimate, unselfconscious. Martha was at her most accomplished physically when she had no clothes on at all. She had the proportions of nudity. Never embarrassed or embarrassing.

It was when she was dressed up that she became squat and ordinary, especially now that the tiny waist was less tiny. Must face that.

She is my treasure, thought Leo. No one understands what I understand or knows what I know about Martha, the Old Master's darling.

Alice and Clara, to name but two, knew other things about Martha, which Leo did not see or consider important. Alice and Clara asked themselves and each other whether Leo, whose inspired egotism they had recognized the first evening they met him and enjoyed ever since, really appreciated Martha as she deserved.

Alice is a Leonardo, thought Leo, his eyes closed. With enjoyment he rehearsed telling her this, imagining her covert pleasure, her curved smile, her downward look. In his sleepy mind, Alice and Emmeline had become confused.

Christa the au pair girl had youth and bounce, and that's all she had. By the time she was thirty-five she would be all flesh and no form. But youth was alluring in itself. Thinking of Christa made Leo think of his granddaughter Agnes. If you pushed at the flesh on Agnes's little arm it plumped up, the skin as delicate and unmarked as fresh damp mushroom-skin. No pores or hairs.

In Washington, late in the evening, he had emphasized a point he was making—about meaning and essence—by putting his hand on Mrs. Flassinger's lean brown forearm, where it emerged from its sheath of gauzy greenish stuff woven with gold threads. Half caressing, he pushed at her flesh with his thumb, as he liked to do with Agnes. He kept talking while both she and he kept their eyes on his hand on her arm and on the inquisitive, digging thumb. Her arm did not plump up in response to pressure. Her dry skin collapsed into creases and furrows. The ridges in between were flaking in diamond patterns.

Cracks in sun-baked mud, seen from the aeroplane. Had the tissue of Martha's arms dried out, shrivelled, like that? He thought not. He flexed his right thumb experimentally.

Leo had large mobile thumbs, markedly waisted, with heavy joints and big nails. His nails were so coarse and horny that nail-scissors would not cut them. Martha had bought him some heavy-duty clippers. Lately he had found it hard to reach his toenails. He was growing stiff. Martha cut them for him with the clippers. She said it was like paring the hooves of a horse.

Leo, thinking about women, fell into a deep, jet-lagged sleep.

* * *

Martha meanwhile was washing the kitchen floor, which was covered in the pitted, irregular quarry-tiles that had been put down when the house was first built. Leo liked them, and had roared his disapproval when she suggested replacing them with easy-care vinyl. Mostly Martha used a sponge-mop on a long handle, but when the floor was too dirty for the mop to make much impression she filled a bucket with hot water and went down on her knees with a scrubbing brush and a floorcloth.

Under the worktop where the electric kettle stood, granules of instant coffee were trodden into the tiles, melted into gleaming blobs as hard as varnish. She scraped at them with her fingernails. From corners she harvested wads of dust woven into grey webs with Mungo's fallen hairs. In the cracks between the tiles, where the grouting had worn away, she scrubbed at the top layer of a gluey black deposit of dirt. When the floor was freshly washed and still shining wet and red, it looked lovely.

Martha sat back on her heels, cloth in hand. She surveyed the kitchen floor with happiness.

Mungo, whom she had banished into the back garden while this was going on, pushed open the back door and pranced in on a shaft of sunlight, his muddy paws tracking across the clean floor. Martha swore at Mungo and lunged at him with her wet cloth.

She was laughing as she began to wipe the floor all over again. How was it that Mungo got away with murder? He was noisy, irresponsible, clumsy, destructive, undisciplined and demanding. He was Martha's familiar. She loved him unconditionally.

While she was wiping the floor for the second time, Mungo lolloped noisily from the kitchen to the sitting-room, rucking up the rugs and sending them slipping in all directions, his feet scrabbling on the parquet floor beneath. He made a bee-line for Leo, as if noticing him for the first time since his return from America. He leapt on to Leo's lap and pressed his whiskery face and wet nose passionately against Leo, knocking off Leo's glasses and awakening him.

Leo let out a bellow of outrage. Martha, realizing what must have happened, ran in wiping her hands on her trousers. She apologized to Leo, fussed over him, kissed him, picked up his spectacles, and suggested that he should go up and have a proper rest on the bed. Her solicitude was not feigned. Her loyalty and commitment crumbled only in dreams that she did not remember the next morning. But she was undisturbed by Leo's fury.

9

✳✳✳✳✳

"BEING IN BED IN THE AFTERNOON," said Harry, "is like being ill when I was little. I keep expecting my mum to come in with Lucozade and a thermometer."

"Aunt Margaret didn't give me Lucozade. She said it was too sweet. She squeezed oranges for me. Well, she did once."

They stared at the door. Neither mother nor aunt put her face in. The lovers lay flat on their backs and Clara showed Harry the game of Lonely Hands. It was what she and her younger brother had played in bed years ago. They stretched their bare arms up straight and waved their hands about in the air, sadly intoning, "Lonely hands . . . lonely hands . . ." Ten fingers and ten more searched around in space like frantic insects. Then the two pairs of hands found each other, clutching and holding fast. The relief was enormous.

"Being in bed in the afternoon," said Harry, "makes one altogether childish. So does being in love. Same thing. That was a very childish game. No one would believe it."

"Unless they read it in a book," said Clara. Her room was full of books—one long wall shelved floor to ceiling, and every shelf crammed.

"Have you read all those?"

Clara could tell from that question that Harry was not really a reader. Someone who read a lot would know that no one reads as much as all that.

"No." She was thinking about what he had said. He had said, "in love."

Clara had inherited the books, most of them biographies, from her father. He had not died; he had gone off to Brazil. He gave her brother his forks and spoons, and most of his furniture. She got the books, a table, two high-backed chairs, and a huge piece of furniture referred to as the armoire. All these things had belonged to her father's father, who had been a doctor in Eastbourne. Apart from the bed in which they lay— bought from Jones Bros. in the Holloway Road—these inherited objects were all the furniture that there was in the room.

Clara liked her room. She wanted Harry to say something appreciative about it. It had been a day nursery when the high Edwardian house was new and a family home. There were still bars across the two sash windows to stop Edwardian tots from falling out into the front garden. There was in those days a tall wire fireguard with a brass rail along the top, to stop the children from burning to death in the coal fire. Clara had filled the empty grate with a jar of feathers dyed green. In the old days the nursery had been distempered in cream and green; Clara had painted it pinkish brown. The old day nursery was the whole of her living quarters, apart from the night nursery across the landing, divided into two to make her kitchen and bathroom.

"When they were doing the conversion I kept coming round to see how it was getting along. The whole house was full of sawing and drilling, bare wires and plaster dust everywhere. I used to see grey figures at every turn of the stairs as I came up, leaning over the banisters and slipping away on the landings. Well, I thought I saw them. They were the ghosts of unmarried daughters in long grey dresses. They were anxious about what was being done to their house. They were waiting for Papa to come home. They had nothing else to wait for."

"Will Papa ever come home?"

"It doesn't matter because the daughters have given up and gone. At least I don't see them any more. Waiting is a demanding occupation. I think they got tired and drifted away. I waited for you like that this afternoon. I pretended I was reading about Tolstoy but I was waiting, hunched up like a sick cat."

"Did you go and lean over the banisters like a ghost daughter?"

"I did that too. In case I'd missed your knocking. The bell doesn't always work."

Clara got out of bed and opened the armoire. It was a massive mahogany construction, red and glossy, with barley-sugar columns up each side, fat ball-feet and knobs as big as fists. She opened its doors to show Harry how nicely an old-fashioned gentleman, such as the ghost daughters' Papa, would have organized his clothes. To the left was a deep high cavity for hanging up suits. On the right were shallow wooden shelves that pulled out like trays. Underneath the cupboard section were two profound drawers. Every garment that Clara possessed could be accommodated in the armoire. In Eastbourne it had dominated her grandfather's room, filling the small space with its bulk and its rich mahogany odour.

"He probably couldn't smell it," said Harry. "Children notice how everything smells."

It had been in Eastbourne, in her grandfather's room, that Clara had been told the facts of life. Not by him, of course, nor by her father, but by Aunt Margaret. Why the two of them were in there, or what had precipitated the conversation, Clara could not remember. But the armoire with its knobs and carvings and its pungency had become mixed up in her mind with the extraordinary information that she was given.

"And it's the most wonderful feeling in the whole world," her aunt had said at the end of her little speech.

Clara had been even more astonished by this than by what had gone before. Not for the obvious reasons (Aunt Margaret was unmarried and of an apparently unsmirched chastity) but because it was hard, at the age of ten, to take all this quite seriously.

Clara climbed back into bed with Harry. The left-hand door of the armoire, imperfectly fastened, swung wide with a creak.

They did not get up until it was past the time that they

were expected at Leo and Martha's house. They were radiantly late.

Martha Ulm, relaxed at the head of her own kitchen table, laughed and laughed and laughed when Leo, during a silence, declaimed:

"I think continually of those who were truly great."

It had to be explained to Martha that this was the first line of a famous poem by Stephen Spender. Or, amended Anthony Arklow-Holland, the famous first line of a poem by Stephen Spender.

"Is it not meant to be funny?" enquired Martha in her flat north-country voice.

She was assured it was not. She laughed again.

"Imagine him," she said, "imagine him sitting there and thinking continually—continually, mind, not just now and then—of those who were truly great—truly great, not just a bit great. And worrying and wondering what they had got that he hadn't."

Anthony was nettled. "It's a fine line," he said, tapping Martha's hand, "and a good poem. Greatness is not a joke. Aspiration to greatness is not dishonourable." He looked at Leo for help.

"Martha does not believe in heroes," said Leo. "She did once. Life has disillusioned her."

There was a silence. Alice broke the tension.

"I think continually of those who are truly *rich,*" she said. (That's probably true, thought Clara.) Everyone laughed in relief.

"I think continually of those who are truly *late,*" boomed Leo, with meaning looks at Clara and Harry.

The evening was back on course. They were old friends, they were accustomed to being happy together.

Martha, as she went to the fridge for the lemon mousse (which had separated out, fluff on the top and stiff jelly underneath), wished she were quicker at expressing what she thought. She did not think she was less intelligent than any of the others, Leo apart. Leo was right that she did not believe in heroes. Did hero-worship have something to do with religion? Did hero-worshippers feel that if there were a special category of people who were altogether different in kind, their own littleness was excusable and inevitable?

Some people were cleverer, luckier, more gifted by nature or circumstances than others, just as some were more ambitious and determined. But, really, they weren't different in kind from anyone else. Martha remembered the Pharisee in the Bible who thanked God he was not as other men. But no one was all-round wonderful. A great national leader could be beastly in private. Did specific greatness cancel out general beastliness?

Martha might have been interested if she had known what Clara had been reading in Henri Troyat's *Tolstoy* while she waited for Harry. Tolstoy, "who claimed to be so broadminded, was extremely old-fashioned when it came to women. A champion of freedom outside the house, he applied the principles of tyranny under his roof. According to him, a wife should abandon all interest in her appearance, turn her back on the 'futilities of society' and devote herself to running the household, educating her children and distracting her husband."

Clara did not know what Martha was thinking as she held the bowl of mousse between her hands. Martha did not know what Clara had been reading. So they could not help each other. This often happens.

Martha had no children to educate. She did not conceive. It was a grief to her so sore that she covered it over. She knew that Leo was immensely relieved.

There are no grown-ups, thought Martha, spooning the mousse into bowls. The talk around the table was animated, political. There was going to be a general election. Martha had views and did not remain silent. Yet she felt as she spoke that she and all the others were aping their elders and betters. It was parents and uncles who talked politics loudly over mealtables. Yet she was already older than her mother was when she herself was born. Leo had every right to voice his opinions and be authoritative. But all the statesmen, politicians, generals and decision-makers of the world, Martha saw as she circulated the cream and the sponge fingers, were boys who had outgrown their football shorts, whose skin had coarsened, whose hair had dried out and thinned. (Not Leo's. His floppy white forelock gleamed.)

Martha's vision did not reassure her. Not in the way that hero-worshipping reassured the worshippers. The school sneak, the bully, the swot, the cheat, the captain of games, the liar, the mummy's boy, the poser, the swank, the delinquent—there they all were with their hands in the biscuit tin, their eyes on the winning post, their fingers on the button. For comfort, people believe that certain figures are magically otherwise. The doctor, the priest, the poet, the leader. Someone after all must know what's going on. Someone must be in charge.

No one is in charge.

Women don't grow up either. We are just better at pretending, so that the men who need mothering will love us. But who supports the girl children? We cling, thought Martha, and we play house, we try to make home the whole world. I'm not a real artist. I am an illustrator.

Clara, that afternoon, had read in *Tolstoy:* "Was he going to disintegrate completely—mind, will, talent—in this paralysing conjugal atmosphere?"

Martha licked the serving-spoon. What was she worrying about? The room was full of happiness. It was time to move into the sitting-room and be comfortable.

The room was full of happiness. Even Clara felt it, who was inclined to be cynical and to find fault. Leo's claret, supplied like Ferdie's by Tom Bollard, had something to do with it. Anthony Arklow-Holland, put in charge of supplies by Martha, opened bottle after bottle.

Clara no longer listened to what Leo was saying. Conversation was excitedly general for the first hour after supper, but Leo's interventions grew longer and more insistent as the night advanced and the others grew sleepy, or lost the thread, or just surrendered as Clara did to the mere flow of words, the deep, self-caressing voice.

It was still light when they arrived. Now the room was dark except where candles flickered on the table among the wine bottles. The log fire, burning low, shot out spasms of flame. Faces glowed, eyes were highlighted. Hands shone pale round dim wineglasses.

Clara, relaxed among cushions, her head against Harry's knee, let her eyes wander over the rugs hanging on the walls. We are medieval tonight. Leo is the bard. We are the lucky ones of the world. We have enough to eat, there is no war in our country, and Harry and I have each other and all this. It's the sort of night that will be remembered—in diaries and memoirs like the ones in my grandfather's books. Leo's biography. Might someone write the life of Leo Ulm?

Amused by her thought, Clara raised herself on an elbow and looked at each face in turn. Harry, behind her, put a proprietory hand on her shoulder. Well, it wouldn't be Harry, who never even read Leo's books.

But Harry was shrewd. Before she brought him to meet Leo and Martha for the first time, he idly picked up a book by Leo in her room and read a page or two. During dinner he brought up a point from the passage he had skimmed and questioned Leo's reasoning. He did it in a flatteringly concerned way, prefacing his query by saying: "I was rereading *In the Beginning* and it seemed to me that . . ."

Leo had pointed his cigar at Harry and thundered, "It's all in chapter four. I dealt with the problem in detail and I'll be most surprised if you can fault the argument."

Anthony had cut in smoothly with a direct quotation from chapter four and the moment dissolved in gratification (Leo's and Anthony's).

Anthony might well be the one to write a book about Leo. Or conceivably Alice. Not Martha. She couldn't write. She would be a "source," like Charlotte, except poor Charlotte might die before Leo.

They would all be sources. Clara saw herself as an elderly woman being interviewed by an eager young person with a notebook and a tape-recorder. "Yes, I remember that particular evening. I was there with Harry, before we were married."

But would she marry him?

"And Anthony Arklow-Holland, and Alice, Leo's daughter-in-law. No, his son wasn't there, he was in the country . . . No, it wasn't that Leo and Ferdie didn't get on exactly. They just seemed unrelated, they weren't like father and son . . . Leo read to us before we went home from *In the Beginning*. The passage about Ruskin and the waterfall from chapter ten."

Even as she constructed that scene, Clara imagined herself in the morning, alone in the thin air of her own room, saying out loud in her thin voice as she stood holding in front of her a pair of crumpled French knickers, trying to tell front from back, "Leo is sometimes the most frightful bore. Also, he's a monster."

Leo behaves like the God she was taught about at Redbrook House, always having to be reassured and praised to the skies and loved. Why was the Christian God so insecure? No one ever presumed to love and reassure a pagan god. It wasn't on the menu. You tried to keep on the right side of a pagan god, and placate him with the odd blood sacrifice. It just shows that no one ever thought that the Christian God was godlike. They thought of him as some people think of Leo, or of their own special bigwig, only a bit more powerful and difficult to manage. But just as vain and just as demanding—oh, and adorable, sometimes, just a little baby in a manger. O Come, Let Us Adore Him.

Knowing Leo was a monster, Clara adored him. She would still like to have—or to have had—an affair with him. She was ashamed of this. His attraction for her was partly because of his being "permanently energized," as Harry had once put it. But there was something else too.

It was as if she could fall in love only from a position of hostility. When Clara thought back over the men she had felt violently passionate about—the most recent, before Harry, being an irresistibly moody Finn—it was always the same story. They were men whom, in her right mind, she would have found grossly incompatible. The urgency of her passion was in direct ratio to the incompatibility.

The men she liked, the ones who became and remained her friends, were cheerful, practical, companionable people. Maybe, thought Clara, in a rare moment of unassisted clear-sightedness, the ordinary differences between men and women are not enough for me. These impossible men are my rough trade. Maybe I've been trying to get my own back, too, on all those pairs of cavalry-twill trousers and their honking rejections. Not to mention Father.

Harry was not like that. She was going straight, with Harry. It had been extremely difficult to start with. She seemed to find it easier to love her enemies than her friends.

She must tell him to go for cavalry-twill trousers after all. She needed a prick to kick against.

In the room full of happiness the French knickers slithered agreeably against Clara's velvet skirt as she sank back into the cushions. Leo was coming to the end of whatever he was telling them, letting fall the last notes of his aria. The voice slowed, dipped, ceased. In the silence Martha leaned over to Alice and said in her blunt way:

"I went and got that staple-gun I was telling you about. It's lethal, it thuds staples through wood, walls, anything. I covered the bedroom chair this afternoon, just with staples and a bit of Copydex. Never had to use the sewing-machine once."

"Brilliant," said Alice. "You must show me, after." She twined the ends of her long dark hair round her fingers, not looking up at Martha. She said, "Leo, we should all go home. But will you read to us a bit first?"

"My capable wife," said Leo heavily, "can do absolutely everything. I can only talk, and write. Perhaps she will make us some more coffee."

Martha rose at once and left the room. Leo stretched behind

him and pulled a few books out of the shelves. "What shall I read? You choose, Alice."

Alice, who had been sitting on the floor at his feet, by the fire, knelt bolt upright and looked into Leo's down-bent eyes. She looked about twelve because of her small slimness, her straight back, her sheet of hair. Watching her, Clara remembered Alice ten years ago, when they were sharing the flat. Alice came home from work, had a bath and, in her dressing-gown, settled herself at the telephone with a tumbler of ice-cubes and vodka. "I'm going to do some twilight barking, like a dog. I'm going to ring up everyone I love and make sure that they still love me." Which of course they did.

"The bit about authority?" Alice asked tentatively, trying to guess what Leo wanted. "Or the bit about the Greek boys?"

"I don't feel Greek tonight," said Leo. "Tonight I am Gothic. I think the waterfall passage from chapter ten."

He riffled through the pages of the book on his knee, cracked the spine and began to read.

"What about waiting for Martha?" interrupted Clara from her nest of cushions.

"She's heard it before," said Leo.

So had they all. The spell of the night was weakening. Leo had only been reading for a moment or two when Martha, at her most stolid and bun-like, came back into the room with a loaded tray. No one except Anthony rose to help her. Although Martha was as unobtrusive as possible, the trickling of coffee and the tinkling of spoons on china, the whispered questions about black or white, seemed more distracting than if she had been less careful. Leo had stopped enjoying himself.

"Do you have to do that now?" he asked Martha, his finger marking the word where he had stopped reading.

"You did ask me to make coffee," replied Martha in a reasonable voice.

It was chilly in the room. Clara, stretching out a hand to touch a radiator, found it cold. The central heating had clicked off. It was late. Leo had been reading badly, which was not usual.

He did not look well. He was too red, patchily. Clara felt guilty about imagining him dead. What if, by imagining a world in which Leo was just a legend and a memory, she hastened his death?

As they stumbled away down the front garden, Harry muttered to her, "That Adiantum doesn't look too healthy. In the hall."

He was talking about a maidenhair fern, flaking to death among the Ulms' coats and scarves.

10

Driving away in Harry's car from the evening at the Ulms, he and Clara had a post-mortem on the party which had so definitely died.

Harry relayed to Clara what he had said to other people. Clara reported to Harry what other people had said to her.

Clara was interested in this compulsion of males to repeat their own remarks rather than what they had learned from others. Every man she had ever gone out with had done it. Harry, unique in her experience in many ways, conformed in this respect. It must be in the gonads. Only by the deftest of interventions did she manage to fast-forward him through a re-run of his lecture to Martha on reinsurance.

Driving up Clapham High Street, they sang their favourite arias from *The Marriage of Figaro:*

Susanna, Susanna,
Quanta pena mi costi!

They settled down, after some circling, to discuss Anthony Arklow-Holland. Clara, mollified by singing, grew loquacious on the subject of Anthony, who had been present on the evening when Clara had first taken Harry to the Ulms.

"We've met before," Anthony had said when Martha introduced him to Harry.

"Yes, of course. I remember."

"At the Reform. You must come and lunch with me there one day."

Clara had been surprised, as she always was when she found that the separate atoms of her life had been fusing behind her back. She asked Harry now for his version of the Reform Club encounter.

"I'd been asked to some guest dinner by Bratsby." Bratsby was Harry's immediate superior at the Pru. Clara heard a great deal about Bratsby. Too much, even.

"On my other side was this man Anthony. He seemed a bit pale and inexperienced to be a Reform Club type, but he was a member all right. He had—well, he still has—these extraordinary old-fashioned good manners. Courteous is the word. I decided he was what they call a Young Fogey. But he's likeable, isn't he? You can't not like him. He says he lives in West Drayton."

"You know where West Drayton is? Just by Heathrow Airport. A sort of spoiled village, not really a village any more at all. It's where the flight controllers work from and there's a long-stay car-park. It must be a pretty noisy place to live in. I don't think he has a job at all, that's the other mysterious thing. Would you say he was gay?"

"Could be."

Clara had thought so too at first. "But now I think he's not anything at all. Doesn't want to do anything with anyone. There's lots of people like that, only when you're very young you can't believe it. If you never had done anything, and you got to Anthony's age—what would you think he was, thirty or so?—it would be hard to begin, and you wouldn't want to risk it."

"I couldn't guess how old he is. He's the sort of person who'll look exactly the same till he's about sixty-five, then he'll suddenly be old. But not really any different—still neat, still amiable."

"Why," said Clara, "are we going towards Elephant and Castle? That's a ridiculous way to go back. Never mind, we can go over Blackfriars Bridge . . . What did Anthony want to talk about when you met him at the club?"

"He made it easy, you know how he does—was interested in whatever came up. Pictures and books are what turn him on, presumably. Judging from tonight."

"And the people who paint and write them. Provided they're old and famous enough."

Harry resisted. He was silent. She was being what she called honest and analytical and he called uncharitable. Having started she wanted to go on.

"No, listen . . ." And Clara told him what she knew about Anthony Arklow-Holland, and in spite of himself Harry listened.

Anthony made himself conspicuously pleasant to almost everyone. But his social life was spent with people twice his age. Most of these were women—old writers, old artists, old mistresses and widows of distinguished men. He called them his Old Bats. They were people whose work or whose circle he knew about and admired. Most of his friendships, Clara suspected, started by Anthony writing fan letters.

"Fan letters" is hardly the term for those well-informed, appreciative, wistful and witty notes sent out under the Reform Club letter-heading. They always elicited friendly replies.

Anthony's good manners, Clara told Harry, were old-fashioned in more than the obvious ways. He "called" on his aged acquaintances formally and regularly, for tea—or gin. He was reliable and reassuring. He wore dark suits with a touch of frivolity in the matter of socks. He was clean, enthusiastic and articulate. There was nothing about him to threaten the older generation, since his values and his references seemed the same as theirs.

The old talked freely to him. What Anthony did not know from his reading about the byzantine social and sexual intricacies of literary and artistic circles in the 1920s and 1930s, he soon learned at first hand from late-afternoon reminiscences.

"You could say," said Clara, "that Anthony is becoming a repository. A human reference library."

"Of cultural trivia," replied Harry. "What exactly is he getting out of it?"

"He's a romantic snob. He likes knowing famous arty people not just because they are famous but because he thinks they are important. Fame is glamorous, you can't deny it. If his Old Bats have lovely London houses, or country places stuffed with relics from their past, then he likes that a lot too. It's funny, before the war rich people used to take up artists and writers much more than they do now."

"The upper classes don't read. They sell their pictures; they don't buy new ones. If they've got any money they are in the City making more."

"How is it that one never can find Blackfriars Bridge coming from Elephant and Castle?" asked Clara, as Harry swung arbitrarily to the left. "We'll have to go over Westminster Bridge now. It doesn't matter. Anthony's not just a snob, only a culture snob. He'd be just as sweet to an old hag living in one room, provided she was the real thing in his opinion, as he would be to someone who's always popping up in *Harpers & Queen*. He's a specialist. I mean, ninety-nine per cent of the British public don't give a toss for Bloomsbury or Fitzrovia, or for stories about Lady Diana Cooper or what some drunken poet did in a game of charades in 1926."

"What's Fitzrovia exactly?"

"There you are. Ask Anthony, he'll tell you. Beautifully."

"Why do the people he latches on to have to be old? Why doesn't he make friends with people who are writing and painting now, if those are the sort of people he likes?"

"He does," said Clara, "a bit. He makes it his business to know an awful lot of people. But the oldness is the romantic part. Like the song, 'I danced with a man who danced with a girl who danced with the Prince of Wales.' It's pretty exciting to have someone gossiping to you about the brilliant people you've only read about in books, especially if the person who's talking to you is in the books herself, and went to bed with everyone. It's like touching the past. Some people dream about the future. Anthony dreams about the past."

"I can understand that," said Harry. "Just about."

"There's another reason why he gets on so well with the old, and you may not like this bit so much. It's safe. There's no sexual hazard. He can discuss love affairs without the slightest danger that he'll be expected to put out himself. He took me to tea with Isobel Henneken—do you know who I mean? She was one of Augustus John's models and she wrote a novel all about herself in the twenties which was a sensation at the time called *Playing Sardines*. I haven't read it. Anyway, she lives in an absolute tip of a flat in Redcliffe Square. She really dressed up for our visit, lots of jade beads and a Poiret dress. She showed us a truck full of couture clothes, museum-quality stuff. Anthony loved it; he appreciated everything. Very camp they were, both of them. The teacups were beautiful, so fine you could see through them—and filthy, stains inside and mouth-marks outside. She gave Anthony a little ostrich-feather thing in a jewel, which she used to wear in her hair."

"Why on earth did she do that?"

"His Old Bats give him things quite a lot because they know they'll die soon and their middle-aged children wouldn't see the point of it all like Anthony does. It's very easy to make friends with old people. The more famous they are the easier it is. They feel neglected—often there's no one to talk to who knew the people they knew or wants to hear their stories. They are lonely. The really famous ones are the loneliest, because the neighbours don't ask them in for cups of tea, assuming that they have lots of grand friends, which they haven't. Everyone they knew is dead, or senile, or living hundreds of miles away. There the Old Bats sit, brooding about the past. They are highly vulnerable to a sympathetic, sensitive person like Anthony."

"What does all this make him? A gigolo? A sponger? A leech? An exploiter of lonely old ladies? A creep? Is that what I am to think?"

"I might think that," said Clara, as they drove north up the Caledonian Road, "if I didn't know him quite well and hadn't seen him with Mrs. Henneken. His respect and concern are real. He'll discuss the past, and their grievances, for ever. When I was there he was telling Mrs. Henneken that he was trying to get Virago to reprint *Playing Sardines.* I don't suppose there's anyone around who's actually read it but him. And he'll take an interest in the fact that the hearing-aid is bust or the spectacles are wrong or the plumber hasn't come, and he'll do the ringing up to complain. He's Isobel Henneken's last attachment, I could see that she really loves him, and he'll never let her down."

"Last attachments expect a quid pro quo," remarked Harry. "Several thousand quid in fact, in the form of a legacy."

"People are unfair to last attachments. They hang in there when everyone else is fed up. Relations who can't be bothered to visit more than once a year and who can't be approached about broken hearing-aids or wrong spectacles bang on and on about how calculating the last attachment is, alienating affections and all that. But a last attachment earns that affection. Old ladies can be difficult and boring and even disgusting, even when they're famous. I won't hear a word against Anthony in this respect. He not only makes life for his Old Bats nicer, he makes it possible. If he likes them and respects them, they feel better about themselves. They depend on him for that, don't you see?"

"I don't see where Leo fits into all this. Leo isn't an Old Bat."

"They don't have to be women—it's just that most of them are."

"But Leo's not old enough. Is he an investment for Anthony?"

"They are fond of one another. I don't know what else to say about it. Leo needs an audience and lots of reassurance. Anthony has no ties and can be available when Leo wants."

"Leo's got Martha."

And Leo's got Alice, Clara nearly said but didn't. Anxious to avoid one betrayal, she fell flat into another. "And Martha's got Anthony."

"Has she? What? What do you mean?"

Suddenly protective of Anthony (and of Martha) after her long outburst, Clara decided against telling Harry one other thing she had learned, that very evening. There was a moment just after supper when Leo was talking to Alice about the research she was doing for him, and Harry was telling Martha about reinsurance, when she found herself sitting on the sofa with Anthony. For something to say, she asked him why he had become a member of the Reform Club.

"I find it useful, and pleasant," Anthony said, his hands folded neatly between his knees.

Hesitantly, he told her he had a man friend, a much older friend, who put him up for membership and paid his subscriptions and bar bills.

"You are an amazing person," said Clara. "Who is this mysterious elderly benefactor? Do we know him?"

"He prefers to do good by stealth," Anthony replied, turning his quiet brown eyes on her. "Like most nice people."

Clara felt she could do some good to Anthony by stealth, or by default, if she did not add this information to the dossier she seemed to have given Harry.

Nor did she choose to tell Harry that Anthony once revealed another and less serene side of his nature. If you are always as controlled as Anthony is, Clara supposed, the forces banked down inside must be under dreadful pressure and must erupt frighteningly if the lid is lifted.

It was at a party given by Alice and Ferdie in the Fulham house. Anthony, who had drunk a lot, was being indiscreet in an amusing way about a weekend he had spent at a house in the country where Princess Diana was a fellow guest. It was quite a good story.

One of Ferdie's banking friends, who had had even more to drink than Anthony, went for him in a violent fit of maudlin royalist piety. A flood of abuse was poured over Anthony's head, in terms not unlike what Harry had been suggesting to Clara just now. Anthony Arklow-Holland, bellowed the banker, was an arse-licker, a star-fucker, a wanker, a creep, a social climber, a scrounger, a bastard and a shitty little snob. What's more, he dined out on the results.

Anthony went stark mad. He did the classic B-movie thing of breaking a wine bottle on the edge of the table and, white-faced, advanced on his enemy, who was twice his weight as well as twice as drunk.

Alice whispered to Clara that she thought Anthony was about to kill the banker. Alice wanted to ring the police, but dared not stir for fear that Anthony would move if anyone else did. So they all froze; and Anthony took another step forward.

Leo saved the day by simply saying, "Anthony! That's enough"—as if to a child or a dog. He stepped forward, holding Anthony's crazed eyes with his own, and took the broken bottle from him. Anthony slumped into a chair, covering his face with his long hands, shivering.

Leo and Martha announced they would take him home and put him to bed in their house. The party broke up. Clara, while she was putting on her coat, saw Martha tying Leo's scarf round his neck and kissing him, her eyes huge.

"You're a great man," said Martha to Leo, gratitude and anxiety in her face.

Clara did not want to tell Harry about any of this. If she married him—would she marry him?—there would always be stories that for one reason or another she would not tell him. There would always be things she knew that he did not. Did this matter?

Harry's car came to a halt in Clara's rundown street. Digging into her silence, Harry asked:

"But if Anthony doesn't have a job, what does he live on? That suit he was wearing tonight didn't come from Marks & Spencer."

"I don't know. I honestly don't know."

Part of what Clara knew about Anthony Arklow-Holland was that there were a great many things about him that she did not know. They all knew a few things, no one knew all, or the same ones. No one therefore had power over Anthony.

"I didn't really like the way you talked about him," said Harry. "You're too beady. No one's safe with you. I don't feel safe with you."

"You're not meant to feel safe with me. You've got the Pru

for that. I expect I only do it because I'm short-sighted. I have to think about people close up instead of seeing them in context and from a decent distance. I can't see figures in a landscape. I've probably got it all wrong anyway."

They were both tired. She got out of the car, went round to the kerb and kissed Harry goodnight through the open window.

"I'll ring you from the office in the morning," he said.

11

✳✱✳✱✳

A COUPLE OF WEEKS after the dinner-party, Leo, sorting through the mail in the hall at home, found a letter with a Paris postmark. It was from Emmeline Bernay. The letter was palely typed on squared paper with rounded corners. The paper had been torn from an exercise book.

Mon cher Leo,
    I shall write to you in the language of Shakespeare, as one says. I write with the typewriter because typewriters are not sentimental. I want to talk to you very much and I miss you all the time. But, with apologies to Flaubert, Madame Bovary ce n'est pas moi. You need not be afraid.

Her English seemed better in writing than when she spoke, because one could not hear her French accent. The next paragraph was about buying fruit in the Sunday morning market in the rue de Seine. The one after that was about the lectures she was preparing and the seminars she had to give. There was rather a lot about the lectures and seminars. Leo skimmed to the end.

Please, write to me. I think of you all the time, and remember us together. Come to Paris to visit me. Shall I come to London and visit you?
                                        Yours sincerely,
                                        Emmeline

She never had an English lover before, nor an American one, noted Leo, or she would know different and better ways of signing off. In spite of all the detailed information about her obligations as a university teacher, her letter seemed to him as naïve as a schoolgirl's. Everyone is the same on this level. Rich man, poor man, the educated and the simple, the wise woman and the silly girl, they all meet at the common denominator of need, thought Leo. I miss you, please write to me. Eaten by primitive anxiety, the most independent and clever woman, whatever she actually says, is crying out, "When shall I see you?" It's an inherited vulnerability, like menstruation. It's the war-wound from which she may bleed to death.

Leo was pleased with the letter. He was pleased with the evidence it gave him of his ability to cast a spell. He was also bored by the letter, and a little apprehensive. He wanted to talk to someone about his inconvenient conquest. The most natural person to discuss it with would be Martha. That was unfortunately impossible.

Leo did not pose his problem in personal terms. He generalized, even in his private thoughts. This gave his ruminations a certain intellectual stature while making it possible for him to avoid a direct encounter with either his own feelings or anyone else's. Folding Emmeline's letter, he returned it to its envelope. He asked himself two questions.

Why are women—most women—more interested in a man after he has made love to them than before?

Why are men—most men—more interested in a woman before they have made love to her than after?

His hands in his pockets, Leo stood and gazed out of the sitting-room window. The house opposite was being subjected to radical gentrification.

Men have to *unload*, he thought. The rubbish doesn't care about the feelings of the skip.

Do I really think that? Well, I just thought it.

Aha, but isn't there a difference between thinking something and *really* thinking something? Leo's mind slid luxuriously away into a consideration of the general question of propositions and propositional attitudes. Time passed. Fertilizer bags of rubble were being tipped into the skip outside the house on the other side of the road.

They were certainly going all the way, over the road. Split-level everywhere, Martha said. Whatever that meant.

Leo thought about all this for a couple of days, off and on, and then he wrote to Emmeline.

Dear Emmeline,

You are, like all your sex, a cave-woman under your impressive modern exterior.

The cave-woman surrenders to the cave-man and she becomes pregnant. Even before she knows she is pregnant, even if she does not understand the link between her surrender and the baby, and even if she does not particularly like the cave-man, her every instinct compels her to bind him tightly to her. Because she is going to have to depend on a man, when the baby is born, for food and protection. He must not now go off hunting with the other cave-men for months on end. She wants him home in the evenings. He must not now enter any other woman's cave. He must stay at her side, like the wolf-dog. Sex is the only card she can play to persuade him to hang around. But she has already played that card. The cave-man has done his biological duty by copulating with her. He has no further essential interest in her, unless she is the only sexually available woman on his side of the mountain. Nature has given the man and the woman unequal and badly synchronized biological imperatives.

Leo put down his ball-point. He was uneasy. There was something wrong with this scenario. Why was he going on so about pregnancy? He did not believe that Emmeline had got herself pregnant by him, in spite of what she had said in Washington, or she would have told him about it in her letter.

Nor was this all that was wrong. His cave-man argument did not hold water. Not all men, by choice, would rise from a woman's bed and walk away without looking back. He, for example, had been determined to marry Martha, to have and to hold. He wanted to stay married to Martha. And men committed themselves to women far less adorable than Martha. Brilliant, well-placed men ruined their lives and their careers on behalf of female nonentities or female monsters, simply because they were in sexual thrall to them. Sex is half of life. If the particular sort or quality of sex that a man craves seems accessible to him only through one particular woman, he is capable of sacrificing the whole of the other half of his life to satisfy his craving. This was what the world called true love . . .

Is this all there is to it? Had Leo answered the old question, What is love? He knew he had not. His mind veered away from thinking any further along these lines. He turned to considering Emmeline.

Leo did not in principle like what he called liberated women, although he found them exciting when taken in small doses. Yet maybe, he thought, he should count himself lucky that liberated women were, on the whole, the kind of women that he nowadays met. Emmeline, for example, was self-aware. She knew what she was doing when she used her unsentimental typewriter, her unalluring writing-paper. She had not used the word "love" once in her letter.

That was to her credit. A simpler woman would be more romantic. A simpler woman would clothe herself in the supermarket tat of True Romance as if it were haute couture and say she was "in love"—a condition which justified any amount of dangerously irrational behaviour.

Perhaps there is a poem in all this. On a different piece of paper, Leo made a note of his main points and jotted down a few of his good phrases. Then he picked up his letter to Emmeline, read it through so far as it went, and continued.

But modern women, my dear Emmeline, control the means of production, as your Marxist friends would say. There need now be no baby as a result of a man and a woman coming together for their mutual pleasure. Women are released from the long bondage to men who are not worthy of them, but on whom they become fixated in spite of their rational intelligences and even when a baby is, quite genuinely, the last thing they want from him. If women cannot respond to the order of release they will continue to suffer, like Madame Bovary. But, as you say, not you, Emmeline. You are a fine person. As I told you, you are better than your politics.

I think of our brief time together with immense gratitude and unclouded delight.

That was better. He added underneath the two lines he had composed on the aeroplane:

> *The man who said that women had no souls*
> *Was speaking truth, but not the truth he knew.*

Their application to what had gone before was, he acknowledged, hazy. But he would never finish the poem, and did not want the lines to go to waste, even though they took the discussion into uncharted metaphysical waters. The lines expressed something which he believed but could not put into conversational words, or not without bringing obloquy on himself. It had all been perfectly well understood by H. G. Wells, in a book of his letters Leo had read by chance twenty-five years before and never forgotten. Something about "the essential secondariness of women."

He signed his letter, "Yours ever, Leo," hoping that she would not take this unfamiliar (to her) formula literally. He addressed and stamped the letter. He surprised Martha after dinner that evening by offering to take Mungo for a walk round the block—having first ascertained that she was too absorbed in her work to offer to accompany him. Martha was working on a set of water-colour illustrations for a folk-tale called *The Fisherman's Wife.*

At the corner of the road he posted the letter, then took Emmeline's from his pocket, tore it into shreds and threw the shreds into a hedge. He hauled Mungo out of the gutter, where he was chewing paper in which chips had been wrapped, and dragged him home. He thought of the days when it had been Martha's letters he had torn to shreds and disposed of, when he was deceiving poor Charlotte.

After her second husband Andy died, Charlotte hit the menopause. It was like being in a small boat in a rough sea. "The change," it had been called in her youth. Something discussed in quiet voices by bulky grey women. Something not discussed at all with men or with children. "She's going through the change," they would murmur, voices threaded through with significance. "You have to make allowances."

Andy, returning once from chairing the appointments committee at the local school—the one Agnes and the Bollard children now attended—had told her that the best-qualified person for a deputy headship had been turned down on account of her age. Dr. Lomax, the GP, gave the committee a briefing about the implications of placing menopausal women in posts of responsibility.

"They are just not reliable, poor things. They are at the mercy of hormones and chemicals roaring through the system."

Andy was embarrassed as he reported this and looked at Charlotte as a schoolboy looks at his mother when telling her something disturbing that the other boys have said in break. Charlotte could not say the easy thing, she could not say anything, she knew little about it then. She felt obscurely angry and was unable to place her anger.

What happened to Charlotte at fifty was that her internal thermostat went haywire. She had heard of hot flushes but this was a dry boiling. She did not sweat at all, while under her skin a furnace blazed. Lying in bed in her unheated room on a freezing night, she threw aside the bedclothes and felt the icy air on her flesh like a cooling breeze.

The extreme of heat did not affect her by day or recur many

times. But her personal central heating, adjusted to a somewhat more reasonable setting, continued in operation. Charlotte, who had shivered every winter of her life in the high, wide-open spaces which were hall, drawing-room and dining-room at Belwood, was chilly no more. She no longer wrapped her head and neck in thick scarves when walking in winter. She might note that the air was cold, or less cold. It troubled her about as much as it troubled Martha's dog. (Charlotte does not know Martha's dog.)

There were more exotic manifestations, later. One early summer night at the cottage, watching *Newsnight*, Charlotte's body exploded into brilliance. Her skin was luminous, her hair ecstatic, the points of her breasts were diamonds shedding arrows of light. Power showered from her fingertips.

So this, thought Charlotte, longing for Leo, is the menopause. Glory. The best-kept secret in the world. My last discovery but one.

Her last discovery but two, as it turned out.

Mansell had been the gardener at Belwood for years. He and she had grown older in parallel. For the last ten years of her time at Belwood he was the only gardener, after having commanded, in her girlhood, an outside staff of four. Charlotte knew his appearance as intimately and unthinkingly as she knew the irregularities in the slate slabs on the floor of the back hall at Belwood.

Soon after Ferdie married and Charlotte moved to the cottage, in the summer of her electric storm during *Newsnight*, Mansell came over with lettuces for her from the kitchen garden at the big house. It was a steamy July day, sunless. She was outside, dead-heading pansies. Mansell piled the lettuces on the sundial and watched her working. She agreed with him that it was too sultry a day for serious gardening.

"There's rust on them hollyhocks," said Mansell.

Again Charlotte agreed, trying to remember the name of the chemical recommended for dealing with rust on hollyhocks. She straightened up and went into the cottage with the lettuces, telling Mansell she was going to make tea if he would like a cup. He followed her into the kitchen in his socks, leaving his boots in the porch.

Upstairs on the bed there had been no sense of outrage, hardly of surprise. Charlotte felt like one of Mansell's pot-plants, root-bound and dry, loosened and reviving under his hands. They had never spoken intimately in all the years. She knew his hands even better than his face—large fine hands with earth deeply ground into the creases of his palms and curved, yellow nails. They did not disgust her.

She did not speak. He said only, "I have thought about this since I saw you on the steps when you and him come back from the honeymoon. You were wearing such a little hat."

He meant her first honeymoon, with Leo.

It was a terminal act of love and ended quietly. She did not mind the lack of fireworks and hoped that he did not mind either. They did not talk about it.

Downstairs she said, "Mancozeb."

For the first time Mansell looked awkward. He was at a loss. He thought she was giving him some kind of pet-name.

"Geoff," he said. "It's Geoffrey, really."

"Mancozeb. It's the brand-name for the stuff you spray on hollyhocks to get rid of the rust. You have to keep it up, though—do it once a fortnight. I'm not sure that it's worth the bother. It might be better to get new plants. The books say they shouldn't be treated as perennials anyway."

She did not spray the hollyhocks and she did not replace them. Year after year the crinkled young leaves unfurled, and by midsummer were a mess of disease dangling from the high stems. The rust did not seem to affect the flowers themselves.

Mansell never came into the cottage again. When he brought her vegetables from the garden over the lake he came late in the evening, after she had drawn the curtains, and left them on the back step. She found them like messages in the morning.

Otherwise nothing had changed.

"Good morning, Mansell."

"Morning, ma'am. Not too bad a day for the time of year.

I'll be setting the onions for Mr. Ferdie this week, if it keeps fine."

Perhaps nothing had happened. Perhaps it was her own electric hallucination. More likely, her last moment of health and sanity.

Ferdie and Alice must never know about it. They would be appalled. Worse still, they would laugh. Alice would certainly laugh. "God, I just don't *believe* it! Lady Chatterley!" Alice would laugh and laugh.

The one person she would like to tell was Leo. He would be interested, and he would not condemn her. But too much time had passed, and never a sign from Leo. She told him in her head, composing letters she would never now write, let alone post.

Ten days after posting his letter to Emmeline, Leo had another letter from her. The envelope was very fat. Leo's heart sank. She was succumbing to the fatal female disease. How was it that women—even poor Charlotte, in the very first years of the separation—were so appallingly ready to pour out their souls (their not-souls) on paper? Why could they not keep their thoughts and feelings to themselves?

Leo's adult life had been punctuated by one-sided correspondences with girls. The more one-sided they were, the more copious they became. He had developed a dread of thick letters addressed to him in a feminine hand and marked "Personal." They used to flop into his in-tray in the Department like maimed seabirds. At least they flopped unscrutinized. Maybe he had been unwise to take early retirement. But then he would not have had the Lump Sum, which was such a comfort to him. Leo imagined the Lump Sum as a golden pile of semi-molten coins. The Lump Sum was in a high interest deposit account in the building society.

Gingerly, on his way to the tube, Leo opened Emmeline's letter. This time she had not typed. The squared paper was the same—five sheets of it, closely covered on both sides with spiky French handwriting. Nor had she written in the language of Shakespeare.

Leo scanned the first few hectic-looking lines of French and gave up. He squashed the letter back into the envelope and, meaning to have another go at it later, stuffed the envelope into his mackintosh pocket. He immediately forgot all about it.

12

CLARA WORE HER NEW CONTACT LENSES out of doors for the first time. She saw so clearly that she was afraid she would bump into things. She walked down her familiar street delicately, as if after a long illness. She bought a newspaper at the corner shop and took a series of buses across London to Martha's house, looking at everything with her naked brilliant eyes.

"Everything glitters," she told Martha. "Such hard edges."

She accepted a mug of coffee, noting the archaeological quality of a chip on its rim and a fleck of blue paint on Martha's thumb. It was not necessary to be bombarded with so much visual information. It left no energy for anything else.

Martha pushed Mungo off the sofa and sat down in the warmth he left. "It's not as if you didn't have glasses before. I can't quite see what you're going on about."

"I couldn't meet Mr. Gupta's eyes, in the shop. It's as if he sees me as dreadfully clearly as I see him."

Clara could not bring herself to meet Martha's gaze either for more than a second. It was not just the itchy feeling that she had something in her eyes—which she had.

The optician opened a briefcase and, behind the shelter of its raised lid, popped an Amplex into his mouth before tenderly bending over her to insert the transparent flakes. His own liquid dark eyes searched hers. The telephone rang in the tiny cell where this was taking place and he excused himself, stood up and answered it. Clara listened to him fielding a volley of passionate reproach. From the passionate meekness of his responses she guessed he was talking to his mother. My son the ophthalmic optician. My boy the optometrist. He puts things in girls' eyes.

"In a week or so," he told her, "you won't feel them at all." The lenses, he said, were gas-permeable. Clara imagined jets of blue flame spurting from her eyes out of tiny holes in the lenses, reducing everything she looked at to a heap of ashes.

Hygiene was all-important. The lenses must be cleaned daily with this special fluid. She must always wash her hands before touching them. There was a danger of infection. You could go blind.

Clara could not look for long at Martha because if Martha saw her as clearly as she was seeing Martha, it was more than she could cope with.

Clara was an unselfconscious person because she believed she was invisible. She never thought that anyone noticed when she came into a room, or whether she was there at all. This enabled her to behave with flagrant naturalness. It made her appear self-confident and gave her a reputation for arrogance.

When she was not wearing her glasses, short sight precluded her from reading the expressions on people's faces, and often from recognizing them at all. She forgot that everyone else did not inhabit her own foggy world. She knew her friends by their shapes, their attitudes, their ways of walking. When she wore her old and too weak glasses, she saw adequately. But the glasses themselves were an insulating layer between herself and other people. She was still, in her own mind, on the outside looking in, and invisible. She knew what she looked like in glasses, and was not enchanted by the picture. So she cancelled herself out. Glassed in or not, she was unseen.

Now she was visible, a materialized ghost, the object of scrutiny. This was unnerving.

"You've got it the wrong way round," said Martha. "I'm seeing you exactly the way I've always seen you. You don't look any different. It's us that should worry, if you're seeing us properly for the first time ever."

It was true that Clara could see the imperfections in Martha's skin, the fine lines at the corners of her mouth, as never before.

"I mustn't stay. I must go home and take the lenses out. I'm not allowed to wear them for very long at a time yet. You have to build up, more hours each day. How's Leo?"

"I hardly see him. He's signed up with Channel Four for another series. And he's been summoned to Downing Street. To help with Mrs. Thatcher's election speeches. Well, not Downing Street exactly. A man rang up from Conservative Central Office."

"But he can't—he's never been a Conservative."

"That doesn't seem to matter. They didn't even ask. They've got Leo, and some professor from Cambridge, and that man who writes plays, can't remember his name."

"Jeffrey Archer."

"Not Jeffrey Archer, another one. They all huddle together in an upper room in Smith Square and drink bottles of Fleurie and think up the sorts of things she might say."

Clara was shocked. She was also impressed, and irritated with herself for being so. She longed to ask if Leo was getting paid for this.

"He's not exactly writing her speeches," Martha said. "They are giving her what Leo calls nodules. No, that's wrong. Modules. Ideas, little blocks of argument or rhetoric, I don't know. I think they are meant to be sort of raising the tone."

"What does he say about her?"

"You'll have to ask him yourself."

Martha rounded up the two coffee mugs, the milk carton, the biscuit packet, within the circle of her arms, all at once the discreet wife of an important person. Clara's visit was not altogether welcome to Martha. She had twenty illustrations to do for *The Fisherman's Wife* and not much time to do it in. Her deadline was 15 June. So was Mrs. Thatcher's; the general election was on 15 June.

This is the story of *The Fisherman's Wife* as Martha told it to Clara:

Once upon a time there was a poor fisherman who lived with his wife in a derelict shack on the shore. One day the fisherman caught a great flounder and spared its life, throwing it back into the sea. It was a magical flounder, and in gratitude it promised the fisherman to grant all his wishes. The fisherman's wife, hearing about this, told her husband to go straight to the flounder and ask him to change their shack into a comfortable cottage. The fisherman called up the flounder from the deep and told it that his wife wanted a cottage.

"Go home," said the flounder. "The cottage is there."

And so it was, with roses around the door. The fisherman was delighted. But his wife was not satisfied. Within a week, she told her husband to ask the flounder to change the cottage into a manor house. Rather unwillingly, he did so.

"Go home," said the flounder. "The manor house is there."

And so it was—beautifully furnished (in Martha's illustrations) with fine eighteenth-century furniture and oil-paintings of ancestors. This was as far as Martha had got, but it was not the end of the story. She closed up her portfolio and quickly told Clara the rest of it.

The fisherman's wife was never satisfied. She sent her husband back to the flounder again and again, though he grew more and more anxious and unwilling. The fisherman's wife asked for a mansion, and then a palace, and got them. She wanted to be king, and she became king. She wanted to be emperor, and she became emperor. She wanted to be Pope, and she became Pope and sat on a throne wearing the triple crown.

By this time the fisherman, perpetually scuttling between his demanding wife and the magic flounder, was having a nervous breakdown. It was always stormy weather now when he went down to the water's edge. The flounder, in dreadful agitation, churned the waves into whirlpools.

One day the fisherman's wife told her husband that she wanted to be God. She didn't quite put it that way. She said she wanted to control the sunset and the sunrise, which came to much the same thing. The fisherman was horrified and tried to dissuade her. But his wife, the Pope, insisted. So he crept down to the beach, called up the flounder as he had done so many times before, and timidly told it what his wife now wanted.

The thunder cracked, the lightning flashed. The flounder leapt up out of the roaring, boiling sea.

"Go home . . . ," it said, as it had said so many times before. But this was the last time.

The fisherman went home and found his wife sitting once more in her rags in the poor shack they had started out with. The rain poured down, seeping in between the ill-fitting planks and sheets of corrugated iron, soaking the dirty unmade bed on which they must sleep that night and every night until they died.

"It's an old story," said Martha. "Too early for corrugated iron, or for eighteenth-century furniture. But I like anachronisms."

"What's it trying to say?" asked Clara. "That one shouldn't try to improve one's circumstances, or have ambitions or aspirations? That one can ask so much, and no more—not be greedy? That *women* shouldn't ask at all? It would be quite a different story if it had been the fisherman who wanted all those things, and not his wife."

"It's just a story," said Martha.

"I think it's an anti-woman story," insisted Clara. "The fisherman's wife wanted to be king, not queen. She wanted to be emperor, not empress. That's where she got across the flounder and brought on the thunderstorms."

"It's just a story," said Martha.

"You could say it was not her fault. It was her husband's fault too. Why is he such a wimp?"

"It's just a story," said Martha.

"Or it's the flounder's fault. No one should promise everything to anyone. It can't be done. OK, he was magic. But it's still his fault."

The promise of love. The promise of being known, accepted, made real, aggrandised. Harry, can I trust you? Will it always be my birthday, every day? Of course not, don't be silly.

"What's a flounder like, anyway? It's such a peculiar word. Floundering. The flounder floundered."

Martha's publishers, Trotter Books, were in Camden Town. After a visit to them she had passed two very good fish shops on her way back to the tube station. In one of them there was a flounder. She could not believe it—but there it was, labelled in blue felt-pen, "Flounder." It was a flat fish not unlike a plaice, but with an uglier face, its underlip jutting out in an unpleasant way. It was hard to imagine it as having magical powers.

"I'm not going to show the flounder. Just the churning waters. Then children can imagine what they like."

Clara had forgotten that it was a story for children.

"You could write a proper book about that story."

"It's going to be a proper book. But it's just a story."

Martha was irritated by Clara, but her peculiar interest was stimulating. Martha longed to start her picture of the mansion, which was going to be early-nineteenth-century Gothic. She did not press Clara to stay.

Clara rode home on the top of a bus through the hectically detailed panorama of central London.

Inserting and extracting the lenses was still an ordeal. She was becoming unnaturally intimate with her eyeballs. It was a relief to relapse into her old haze, and invisibility. But tonight she was having dinner with Harry. She'd put them in again for that.

The contact lenses took up a great deal of her attention. She had time on her hands since she lost her job. After her experience on the canal walk her aspirations were both greater and more vague. She read a great many biographies from the collection dumped on her by her father, and she went to bed an awful lot with Harry. She also acquired the contact lenses. She would have done neither of these things had she not been unemployed. She would not have had the time.

Martha, after Clara left, felt unspecifically aggrieved. She needed to do something to defuse the grievance, whatever it was. She would sort out the deep-freeze. It was in a sorry state. When she opened it to replace the ice-cubes, there were tinklings and small crashes as bits of ice and runaway frozen peas fell through the racks of wire mesh to the bottom. Right at the back was a hideous bone that the butcher had given her for Mungo. She never passed it on to him because bones had a bad effect on his manners and character. It must have been there for nearly a year. There were open bags with a handful of petrified beige chips in each. There was half a shepherd's pie, uncovered, grey with frost and fatigue. She would have the whole lot out, throw away the tired stuff and restock. A nice trip to Sainsbury's at Nine Elms.

First she had to pull out the drip tray. It was so long since she had done this that the frozen drips filled the tray and reared up in icebergs. She could not pull the tray out. It was wedged. The icebergs snagged on the electric coil. When she pulled at the tray the coil seemed more ready to come away than the icebergs.

She switched the freezer off at the wall, left the door open, and went back to her drawing for an hour.

The tray would come out now. Its burden of ice made it heavy. She upturned the tray into the sink. The ice, moulded into a solid rectangle two inches thick, detached itself in one piece with a crash. It was too big to fit into the sink; it would take ages to melt, and the water would be everywhere.

Martha picked up the slab. As she carried it into the back garden it occurred to her that ice was the perfect murder weapon. It was hard and heavy. When the deed was done, all you would have to do was shove it behind a bush, and after a few hours the murder weapon would no longer exist. How often had this been done? If not, why not?

Of course the ice-tray was not the ideal mould. It was too broad, the wrong shape for an offensive weapon. A fish kettle would be better.

Leo came home after lunch. During the afternoon the literary editor of the *Observer* telephoned Leo and asked him if he would contribute to an election feature. All that was required was a few words, up to 150 words to be precise, saying which way he was going to vote and why.

"I don't think I can do that," replied Leo.

Martha, working at the table, heard the pleasant voice on the other end of the line.

"You'll be in quite good company—John Mortimer, Harold Pinter, Margaret Drabble . . ."

"No, I'm sorry, I can't do it."

Martha noticed that her drawings of the fisherman's wife, as the election approached, were acquiring a distinct look of the Prime Minister. The fisherman himself was not like Denis Thatcher. He was like Leo. A flustered, demoralized Leo. Surveying her latest effort with her head on one side, Martha decided that this development had no significance. Simply, she had been watching too much television and seeing too many political cartoons in the newspapers. And looking at Leo.

"I wonder how many people," she said to Leo, "say publicly that they intend to vote one way, and then go and do something else?"

"How are you going to vote?"

"Labour," said Martha.

"Why?"

"Because I always have."

She knew this was not a good answer.

"I didn't know you were so conservative," said Leo.

Martha was sketching in the details of the crown worn by the fisherman's wife when she became king. She had propped in front of her a book opened at a colour photograph of the Hungarian crown jewels. The crown was topped by a crooked cross. It had a puffy purple velvet filling, and strings of pearls hung down from either side of the jewelled headband.

"Leo," said Martha, flicking a highlight on to a six-sided ruby, "can you imagine any circumstances in which you would commit suicide?"

It was not quite what she meant to say. She had been thinking about murder. Sometimes Leo, I wish you were dead. Then I could get on with my work and *think* about you.

Leo raised his eyes from the papers on his knee. They had been brought round from Conservative Central Office by a messenger on a motor bike. Mungo had barked his head off at this menacing apparition in big boots and helmet. Leo looked at Martha over the tops of his reading glasses.

"I can imagine committing vicarious suicide."

"What does that mean?"

"It means I kill you."

"Leo!"

"Joke."

On the other side of London, Clara, in her bath, was reading about Tolstoy. Tolstoy said to his sons: "The most intelligent woman is less intelligent than the most stupid man." It's just a story, she thought. He was telling them a story.

13

It was the Thursday before the general election. Clara reached Marsham Street, where Harry lived, early. He had said, "Come round at about seven." It was a quarter to. There was no reason why she should not ring his entryphone buzzer straight away, but she did not feel like it.

She wanted to be with him, but not until the appointed time. The unscheduled quarter of an hour was a bonus, a free gift to her from a variously disappointing day. Like a nun, she would go into retreat for a bit.

Her retreat was a pub down Dean Bradley Street. Clara bought herself a small whisky. It was very small indeed. She filled the glass up with ice and water to make it last and carried it to an unoccupied table against the wall. An evening paper lay on a neighboring chair. "POLL CUTS THATCHER'S LEAD" was the headline. It looked as if she might not get back in after all.

Clara was sitting next to a public telephone. She could not help overhearing the tail-end of a conversation between a moustached man and, presumably, his news editor.

"Tebbit has said," the reporter muttered, cupping the mouthpiece with his hand, his eyes flickering over Clara suspiciously, "off the record, you understand, he's said that he'd rather be called an adulterer than . . ."—but a burst of masculine laughter from the bar smothered the next words.

Clara wanted to know exactly what it was that Tebbit had

said. She shifted her position so that her ears were better placed
for listening, and picked up the newspaper so as not to seem
to be listening at all.

"He said he'd rather be called an *adulterer*—geddit?"

The reporter hung up and, with another sour glance at Clara,
returned to his table.

Clara sipped her watery whisky and gazed over at the bar.
Half a dozen men sprawled on the stools or stood, bottoms
jutting, in poses against the bar. The women they were with,
carefully dressed and coiffed, stood in attendance like guardian angels, talking not to the men but to one another. The
women's fever-quick eyes missed nothing that was going on
between the men who, from time to time, put out heavy hands
to fondle a rump, grip a nape, ruffle a blond topknot.

The girls' time will come when enough pints have been
sunk, enough laughs laughed, enough conversational counters
exchanged about football, the job, the car, the election. Each
woman, bridling complacently, will eventually be claimed by
a male arm. Pinioned, she will plunge out into the dark street,
high heels clacking, one of a couple. After noisy goodnights
she will proceed with her man to the real and private business
of their night out.

Confident of this the girls bide their time, secure—almost—
in assessing one another's outfits, picking imaginary threads
from the shoulders of their escorts' leisure-wear with their long
nails, chatting with animation among themselves when they
can manage it, lapsing into silence when inspiration fails.

I couldn't live like that, I couldn't be like those women.
They do what they do so bloody well.

Clara thought of the assumptions of herself and her friends.
We all take sexual equality for granted. No, not quite for
granted. We are pretty quick to spot any lapses into chauvin-
ism, any evidence of reactionary machismo. We jump down
the poor blokes' throats. What bores we must be. We're like
touchy Jews, on the lookout for slights. They can't even make
jokes about ugly women when we are around.

But we have to be right, said Clara to herself, remembering

the armies of grey women waiting, leaning over banisters at the sound of a key in the door, self-effacing women devoting themselves to unintelligent, uninteresting men, servicing gross bodies and petty destinies, bolstering egos, exhausting themselves and repressing their varied capabilities in order—in order to what?

In order to be loved. Simple as that. Simple as that? Yes.

Would I become a devoted woman, for the sake of being loved? For a day, for a week—but for ever?

A man approached the table next to Clara's, his eyes fixed on the brimming pint he was carrying. The man was heavily built and not tall. His coarse hair was dark, his eyes bright, his chin unshaven. He walked with a bow-legged roll as if what he carried between his short thick thighs had to be accommodated at every step. It seemed to Clara as if his private parts must hang halfway to the floor were it not for the supporting tightness of his jeans.

The man glanced at Clara. He sat down, took a newspaper out of his back pocket and began to read it, tightly folded as it was into a small thick wad. He sat with his legs wide apart. He rested his elbows on his knees. He took a pull at his pint.

I don't exist as a woman for a man like that. I'm too thin. Too tall. Wrong kind of voice, wrong words. Wrong hair. Wrong clothes. Well, he might like my legs, I know he would like my legs.

Clara's legs astounded her when she saw them in a full-length mirror. The slim shafts of the ankles, the long hard line of her thighs, like a principal boy in a pantomime. But she was wearing Marks & Spencer rugby pants and tennis shoes. Not his style at all.

Clara watched the short dark man. He turned over the wad of newspaper and read whatever was on the other side. She and he would have nothing to say for each other and nothing to say to each other. The peasants have been taught to read and they can't be untaught, thought Clara, meaning not the man and men like him, but herself and women like her. She watched the man.

Time was up. Her retreat was over. She collected up her belongings. Pushing open the door of the pub she ran slap-bang into Leo Ulm.

Clara was so surprised that she couldn't think of anything to say. Leo put a hand on her front and pushed her back into the pub.

"You can't go now I'm here. Are you alone? How extraordinary. What a piece of luck."

The surprise encounter was so like the daydreams that Clara used to manufacture (before Harry) that she could not quite believe in what was happening. Back at her old table she watched Leo at the bar, his pale forelock shining under the garish bulbs, as he ordered double whiskies for them both. As he carried the drinks back to the table she saw that he wore around his neck a chain of steel beads on which hung a laminated ID card, with his photograph.

"It's my accreditation, so I can get in and out of Central Office—in Smith Square, just round the corner from here. The security there is like Fort Knox. I just had to get out for a minute. They've all got the jitters. Looks like she may not make it after all. My God, heads will roll. She's already sharpening the knives."

"Better keep your voice down. This place is full of reporters."

"I mustn't talk about it anyway."

Leo ate peanuts from a plastic bag, popping them in his mouth one by one, watching Clara. He was excited by his nearness to the main event—and looked so exactly like the photograph of himself dangling on his chest that Clara fancied his real face as yet another image, dangling on the chest of another and huger Leo, and so on upwards and outwards until one came face to face with the real Leo that filled the whole world.

You cannot talk to someone who fills the world. Conversation between them did not flow. Clara did not know how to shift the fatal blockage. She had never been quite alone with Leo before. In company, they always argued and joked easily and agreeably. Alone together they were like two non-connecting bits of a jigsaw—part of the same picture, but kept apart by whoever it was that was trying to do the puzzle. Clara wished she had left the pub five minutes earlier, and not met him.

"I must go. I have to be somewhere. I'm late already." She smiled at Leo, feeling better already as a result of this paltry initiative.

"I should get back too."

They left the pub together and stood for a moment in the narrow street. They always kissed on parting—at his house, at Alice's house, anywhere. That was normal. Tonight he held her close and kissed her on the mouth. Oh God.

Leo, if you were dead I could think of you in peace and with pride, and love Harry with all my heart. Leo, I want you to be in the past, so that I can start in on my future.

Leo strode into Conservative Central Office in Smith Square, past the spotlit caravan outside, through which all visitors, however official, should pass and be searched and vetted, past the policemen on the door, past the Sloane blondes on the information desk, the loitering journalists, the security officers, the ringing telephones, the bust of Winston Churchill glaring willy-nilly at the unsleeping television screen, up the curling stairs to the holy of holies and a night of quick tempers, long knives, fast food, slow burns, short drinks and another whole week of the same to be lived through.

Awkward girl, Clara. I was really pleased to see her. Wouldn't have minded. Nowhere to go though, not round here. And I don't think she fancies me. Can't win them all. Like Edwina Currie. Quite, but not quite. Funny how you can never scratch just where it itches.

Martha, who knew she could hope to see little of Leo until after the election, lay on the sofa in Clapham with Mungo, gazing into his ecstatic goatish eye. Domesticity afforded a wealth of murder weapons. Her staple-gun, for example. She flipped Mungo's ears. You could staple someone's ears to the floorboards. You'd have to get that person on the floor first, and hold him down. Or you could staple him to the wall through the webs of his fingers and toes.

She never had these bizarre thoughts before she had a staple-gun, before she had heard the sweet thud of metal entering wood at the pressure of her index finger. It's not that the means justify the ends. The means define the ends.

Ban the bomb, thought Martha, and picked up the telephone for a comfortable late-evening gossip with Anthony Arklow-Holland.

After covering the events of the day, Anthony's and hers, Martha found herself saying:

"No, it's OK, I'm not really lonely. It's really much sort of easier when he's out all the time."

She began to cry, and could not stop. She felt as if her marriage—hers and Leo's—was an empty train rocketing noisily through the night without a driver, lights blazing, and that she and he were left behind in the dark on the platform. On different platforms, cold and cheerless, like Darlington. Through the tears she tried to explain this to Anthony. He lost her when she got to the Darlington part. He did not know the north of England.

"I only know I don't like unmanned stations," said Anthony. "I like station-masters, and porters, and waiting-rooms with a coal fire, like in *Brief Encounter*. Would you like me to come round? Just to cheer you up?"

"Yes," sobbed Martha.

It was only when she had put the telephone down that she remembered it was hardly a matter of "coming round," not from West Drayton, not at nine o'clock in the evening. She imagined Anthony throwing some explanation at his mum, who would be watching the news, and belting up the M4 at top speed.

She was glad he was coming.

* * *

In the centre of Harry's dining-table was a plant with dark purple flowers.

"African violets," said Clara, pleased that she could identify them.

"Saintpaulia," said Harry. "They do come from Africa though. East Africa. Named for Baron Walter von Saint Paul Illaire. Died 1910 or thereabouts."

"You sound like Anthony in one of his *Burke's Peerage* moods."

"You were terribly late. I was worried something had happened to you. Or that you . . . I mean, I couldn't bear it if . . ."

"We always called them African violets at home," said Clara. "Everyone does. It's affected not to."

Harry had cooked two trout. The flavour was delicate but they required a lot of careful dissecting. Clara did not manage hers well. The flesh and the fine bones got mashed together. She cast guilty glances at Harry's plate. He had removed the backbone of his fish in its entirety along with the connected small bones and laid the skeleton on his side-plate.

Clara was discouraged, preoccupied and not even hungry. She hid the mess she had made of the evening under a lettuce leaf. She drank two glasses of wine very fast. On top of the whiskies, the wine made her truculent.

After eating, lying on the settee with Harry, she became worse than truculent. She was possessed by the devil. Blame Martha's story, blame the man in the pub, blame Leo. A serpent awoke and uncoiled in the pit of her belly. It worked upwards through her chest, constricting her breathing. It poured poison out through her mouth.

The trouble started when Harry was telling her a story about Bratsby, his departmental head at the Prudential, the man who sometimes took him to dinner at the Reform. Harry found Bratsby admirable in his way and inexhaustibly amusing. He frequently had a new Bratsby anecdote to tell Clara, bringing it to her confidently like a treat to be shared.

This evening Clara reacted to Bratsby as if he were a stale item which no sane person would want to spend time on.

Amiably enough Harry changed the subject: the election. Clara's serpent dismissed the election as dreary, at least when discussed by Harry Ashe. Harry, thinking Clara was upset, asked her what the matter was. Peck, peck, peck, with her sharp little beak. Harry was patient.

It was like being patient with a demolition machine. As everything he said, and by implication everything he was ("You *would* say that"), became devalued and belittled, he lost heart and withdrew into himself. He removed his arm from round her shoulders and sat forward, miserably.

Clara's tone of voice had hardly altered. It was becoming, if anything, more sweetly controlled with every drop of poison that dripped from her.

After half an hour of this Harry was left in no doubt that the kind of person he was, the kind of values he held, the kind of job he had, the kind of ambitions he cherished, the people he found worthwhile, the background from which he came and the way he pronounced certain words were all so wrong and pathetic that he could not expect Clara to take him seriously at all.

Clara, watching her demolition job from behind green leaves, was astonished by how quickly a man could be brought low. The serpent inside her hummed in gratification. From afar, she was frightened. She had held up a mirror reflecting Harry's passivity, softness, pretentiousness, naïvety, uncertainty, social inadequacy and inexperience of the world. Love called these things gentleness, modesty, aspiration, generosity, simplicity, humility. These are the traditional attributes of women. Is the new man an old woman? Is the new woman an unregenerate man? It hardly matters. Traditional women and traditional men are also capable of ripping out each other's souls and exposing them on bare hillsides. Whoever I am, whoever you are, I need to be ratified by my reflection in your eyes. Clara was frightened and she was right to be frightened because she had done what no human being should do to another. Even in the sex war there are rules of engagement. She was a war criminal.

Harry and Clara got up awkwardly from the settee. They tucked shirts into trousers, their backs to one another. The serpent had not quite finished yet. The victim had to surrender and be seen to surrender. Clara turned to Harry and put her arms round his waist from the back. She rubbed her forehead against his shoulder. She said in a cajoling, little-girl voice:

"But I do love you . . . what are you doing tomorrow? Can we have lunch?"

Harry whipped round to face her, white-lipped. As he began to stammer and to speak, the serpent in Clara recoiled, leaving her to face him alone. The serpent began to speak through Harry.

"You are inhuman, Clara. How can you possibly expect me to be ordinary, to answer your lovey-dovey talk, after what you've been like tonight?"

He began to pace up and down his small room, up and down. Up and down, making lost jerky gestures with his hands.

"I've never put you down like that, have I? When you told me about losing the job, when you were depressed, didn't I do everything I could to build you up and make you feel good and give you confidence? Do you think that has been fun—for me? Do you think you are perfect, beyond criticism? You're always being cutting and destructive, not just today. The very opposite of loving. You watch and tease and mock. Do you want to have me as a pet? Why on earth did I think I wanted to marry you? Suicide . . . I'd be tied down, tied up, humbled, obedient to a marvellous know-all *you*. A mortgage-payer, a slave, a cripple . . . What about *my* freedom, *my* beliefs, standards, problems, *my* dreams? Are they all to be disallowed if they're not passed by you? There are more interesting things in life than just being with you, Clara. There are lots of things you don't know about yourself because people are too polite to tell you. You are boring, often. Sometimes you smell horrible. When you have your period. You stink. You're so *conceited*. And literal-minded, absolutely humourless."

He stopped pacing and spoke not to her but to the wall.

"I've listened to you and listened to you, Clara, and tried to understand you. But you're just an opinionated, self-obsessed, inconsiderate person. You don't really like sex with me either, you just want to swallow me up, you use sex to get me where you want, at your feet so that you can kick me. Women like you go on about being sexist, but you are a sadistic sexist yourself. You think you're an intelligent liberated woman. People are so *nice*, I've been so *nice*, everyone takes you at your own valuation. But you're as silly and as limited and as limiting—to me—in your own grim way as the fluffiest sort of scatterbrained female. That sort are usually kind, at least. You're not kind. You diminish everything you touch, you make everything petty, because you're petty yourself. You have no vision, you can't transcend, you're all on the surface. You're always acting. You're a manipulator, a ball-breaker, a destroyer. You haven't the least idea what it is to love someone."

And more. On and on. His words hit her like stones. She turned herself into a piece of wood so as not to feel them.

Feel nothing, now. Nothing at all. Later, you won't be able to help it, but it can be put off if you keep quite still.

Clara crouched on the rug, her back to the wall, her eyes glued to the willow-leaf pattern of the settee's upholstery. Curving stems with syncopated leaves in two shades of green, intertwining and overlapping. Nothing but endlessly repeated willow-leaves. Cling to the pattern, be it, see nothing else.

They had never had a row before, not like this. Their disagreements were tempered by jokes, punctuated by kisses. *Kisses.* You have to be joking.

It was the end of the world.

Harry turned to look at her for the first time. He said, in a drenched monotone:

"Get up. Get out. Go away."

His long legs buckled at the knees. He slumped on the settee. The willow-leaves wavered and sagged.

Clara went.

14

✕✕✕✕✕

HARRY WAS CRYING. Was he really crying? Clara closed his flat door behind her and ran down the five flights of stairs to the street. On the corner of Marsham Street and Horseferry Road she picked up a taxi, and told the driver her address without looking at him.

In the back of the cab her mind haemorrhaged. She tried to hold on to not-feeling, but grief and panic crept up on her in a tide of tar and blood. She shuddered. She was in shock. She felt something: she felt sick.

As the cab lurched and juddered northwards she realized that she was actually going to be sick. Cold sweat made her clammy all over. Her mouth filled with saliva. Sitting bolt upright, lips tightly closed, she cast her eyes round in despair. "Thank You For Not Smoking" said a sticker on the glass partition. Clara inclined her head and vomited on the taxi floor a little to the left of her left foot.

When the cab stopped in her street, on the opposite side of the road from her door, she got out and thrust a five-pound note into the driver's window. But he had turned on the light in the back and was looking round, perhaps to make sure she had not left anything. She had left something. When he saw the pool of sick he let out such a torrent of rage and contempt that Clara did not even try to apologize. She hardly heard his words, though she understood that she had lost him a night's takings since he would now have to go home to wherever it was that he lived and clean the mess up. She shoved all the notes in her purse at him, turned and ran.

Crossing the road, she lost her footing. Her ankle turned over, failed to support her. She sprawled on the edge of the wet pavement, her handbag scattering its contents into the gutter. Collecting up key-ring, comb, purse, receipts, lipstick, loose coins, address book, Lillets, she began to weep. Humiliation. Self-pity. It was only a few yards more, but she feared the space between herself and the safety of her flat.

Squatting in the gutter, she remembered the awful things that some people believe. Women only get raped if they are brooding about the possibility of rape. Rapists smell the fear. People only commit suicide if someone, secretly, wishes them dead. They smell the wish. People only get murdered if they have cast themselves in the role of victim. They connive with a passing murderer.

Unraped, unmurdered, with a firm hold on life, Clara had thought smart smug thoughts. Nothing will happen to me. I am in control. There are eggs and tomatoes in the fridge, a brown loaf in the breadbin, and the bathroom is clean.

I can take the odd risk. I go into strange pubs on my own. I smile at strangers on the street for the hell of it, sit on benches with winos, imagine myself living as they do, indulge in dangerous conversations and divulge dangerous secrets in order to elicit them from others. I am not really frightened of fierce dogs or bent policemen or gangs of black boys or the dark because if I were I would have to be afraid of rape and murder and my own black darkness.

Clara sat in the gutter. Footsteps passed, discretion and disapproval in their even tread. They passed by on the other side. They even passed by on the same side. Clara got up, braved the last few yards and let herself into the house.

On the news, President Reagan gibbered and stammered and clutched at a skeletal woman in a red dress who smiled up at him. Coloured balloons soared over their heads. Shivering with fatigue, Clara sat on the edge of her chair and stared at a close-up of the old man with the rouged cheeks uttering disconnected phrases while the female skull beside him smiled. Reagan was impersonating greatness.

He was not even frightening. Nancy was frightening. Fatuously supportive and reassuring, director, stage-manager, prompter and audience all in one. She was a wonderful wife. She was devoted to him. Those were the phrases. What right had anyone to exact such support, such reassurance, such devotion? What right had anyone to supply it, shackling the beloved, fooling him, condemning him to infantilism?

The smiling skull frightened Clara, but not as much as Clara frightened herself. She stood and looked at herself in the mirror over the fireplace, at her eyes in dark sockets and her hair in strings, and saw the witch, the bitch, the ball-breaker, the destroyer, the destroyed.

She also saw, propped against the mirror, the invitation card. Christ, it's tonight. She'd been going to ask Harry if he wanted to come with her. I don't know the neighbours really, but we say hello when we put the rubbish out and I promised I'd go.

Clara took a bath, washed her hair and put on a white dress that had been lucky. It had a frill that went all round the neck, fell crosswise over the bosom to the hem and continued all round the bottom of the skirt.

By the time she arrived it was after eleven and the party was already in an advanced stage of ripeness. Clara stood, and moved on, and moved around, smiled conciliatingly into the faces of strangers, refilled her glass, stood, smiled.

"Are you all right?" a man asked.

"Do I look as if I weren't?" she replied brightly.

She spoke to mouths, not looking eyes. Red mouths of women, capped teeth flecked with spit. Brownish mouths of men, stubble-edged, opening and shutting, thick lips and thin. All the girls were dressed up. All the men were dressed down.

Clara spotted an actor she had admired on the stage. He was sitting on a sofa talking to a red-haired girl. Both leaned their heads back on the sofa. They looked as if they knew each other well. Clara thought she would go over and tell him how good she thought he was. People like to be told how good they are at what they do. She stood in front of the sofa and said what she had planned to say.

"How nice," said the actor, not altering his position, fingering his designer stubble with a ringed hand. "How very nice of you."

Clara did not know what to do next so she sat down. There was no room for three on the sofa so she sat on the floor. The actor and the red-haired girl continued to chat together quietly. Clara could not hear what they were saying but she looked up into their faces, following each speaker with her eyes, as if she were part of their conversation—which was what she hoped to be.

After a while the actor said to his friend, in a slightly louder voice so Clara would hear:

"Why is this nice girl sitting at my feet? Do you think there is anything we ought to be doing for her?"

Humiliated, Clara got up. In a gap between dancing bodies she saw the dark space of another sofa. She wormed through the gap and sank down. From here she could not possibly hear what anyone was saying, and could not make sense of anything that she did hear.

She realized that someone had come to sit beside her on the sofa and that he was playing with the frill on her skirt. She turned her head and looked into a jolly red face with horn-rimmed glasses. It was the banker who had gone for Anthony Arklow-Holland that night at Alice's house. Or someone just like him.

Below the big face was a big waistcoat. He was dressed up, not down, and he looked hot.

"Don't I know you from somewhere?" the banker said.

"No," said Clara. "Absolutely not."

The big face came closer.

"Do you kiss?"

"Do I kiss? Do I *kiss?*" she answered, with a fury that she did not quite intend.

So the banker kissed her. Mouth again, why do mouths want mouths?

Then the waistcoat and all that went with it swivelled round, and the head with the mouth was lying in her lap. Red hands removed the horn-rims and stowed them in the waistcoat pocket. Pinstriped arms came up and locked themselves round her neck. It was very sticky and not comfortable. It occurred to Clara that "Do you kiss?" really meant "Do you fuck?"

I can't handle this. I must get out.

Clara leapt to her feet, tipping all that was on her lap on to the floor. The banker tumbled away among high heels and sandals and brogues and trainers all with angled legs sticking out of them. One of his hands still gripped the white frill of her dress which ripped as he rolled and struggled underfoot, unravelling itself with a splitting noise from the hemline and up the front and round her neck, then tangling in the legs and feet.

Clara stood up in a dress as straight as an arm, reduced to a shift. Clothed in white samite, mystic, wonderful. No, not really. In desperation she tore the last of the frill right off, and the room was full of laughter, open mouths turned towards her, tongues and gums wet and gleaming, hawkings and gurglings coming out of the dark holes of mouths.

Time to go home.

Clara did not go to bed. She telephoned 222-9000. Just on the off-chance. Conservative Central Office. They were there all night, in the last hours before battle was joined.

Leo was still there. He came to the telephone. The awkwardness of their early-evening encounter had evaporated.

Leo thought quickly and told her to meet him at a hotel in Piccadilly. He couldn't remember the name.

"The Ritz."

Not the Ritz. The hotel he meant was on the other side of the road, much nearer Piccadilly Circus. "It's the sort of place you don't see anyone you know. I'll nip down there straight away in a taxi and—er—book a room for us. That's what we want, isn't it?"

"Yes . . ."

"Bring some sort of a bag, for luggage, so it doesn't look as if we are coming in off the street."

All Clara's tiredness and nausea disappeared. She washed, and drenched both her armpits with hairspray ("Improved Hold, Extra Body"), before realizing that she had picked up the wrong can. She changed from the skin out. She put on her newest knickers, eau-de-nil with green scalloped edges, and a flowered dress from an Indian shop. She brushed her hair—lucky she'd washed it already—and rang for a minicab. She stuffed her damp towel and her dressing-gown in an airline bag and waited. It was 11:30.

Leo, with a briefcase, was waiting for her in the foyer. She saw his white-blond mane over the heads of a swarm of Japanese tourists who had just been decanted from a coach outside. He greeted her casually. He was "acting naturally."

"Hi," she said, unnaturally.

He already had the key to the room. The people at the reception desk were busy sorting out the Japanese.

"Shall we just go up?"

"What did you write in the register?"

"Mr. and Mrs. Edward Heath. Of Bexhill-on-Sea."

The portals of the lift were gold, and so were the columnar ashtrays on each side. The inside of the lift was lined with mirrors, and a Chopin piano concerto from hidden speakers sprayed into the enclosed space like air-freshener. They stood side by side. Clara watched Leo in the opposite mirror, and so did Leo. They got out at the third floor, and walked along a wide corridor. The walls were papered with sprays of flowers on a blue-grey ground, in panels. The leaves of the flowers were striped like ribbons. On the floor were blue rugs with a chequer pattern of garlands. They passed doors and doors framed in bright blue paint, each with a gilt knocker in the shape of a ring.

Leo unlocked the door of room 319.

"Goodness," said Clara.

There was a vast bed, bigger than kingsize, with a blue counterpane. In the window was a round table, with two upholstered bucket chairs. There was a trouser-press, something that Clara had never seen except on advertisements in the tube (which is how she knew what it was). There was a wardrobe thing not unlike Grandfather's armoire; Leo had already thrown it open and discovered the bar.

"Do you want a drink?"

"Yes. No. No, thank you."

Leo poured something into a glass for himself while Clara investigated the bathroom. Beige tiles, orange shower curtain, Hermès toiletries on the washbasin, white bathrobes behind the door, a hair-dryer.

"Leo, how much does all this cost?"

He answered her from the bedroom. "A hundred and eighty pounds."

Goodness.

She wondered whether he would want to undress her, but he did not. When she went back into the bedroom he was undressing himself in a business-like manner, his back to her. She undid the buttons on her dress, watching him out of the corner of her eye.

"I'll put it on expenses," he said. "They owe me one."

Clara was relieved, and also disappointed.

He turned to her and smiled.

Leo had a pale bulky body, with grey-fair fur on his chest.

He had a very small cock.

Clara suppressed her surprise. I mean, everyone knows size doesn't make any difference to anything.

Pretty interesting, though. LEO ULM HAS A VERY SMALL COCK.

Leo pulled back the counterpane, revealing the fact that it was not one huge double bed but two zipped twins. He got under the covers and lay watching her, his hands behind his head, as she finished undressing.

She, in turn, faced him and smiled. It was like a dream. Slow motion, then freeze-frame, the eternal now. She was about to get into bed with Leo.

She climbed in beside him and they turned on their sides, their faces close. She put out a hand to remove his glasses, but he pushed her hand away.

Oh.

They kissed. His free hand stroked the tops of her legs under the covers.

Clara was excited, but it was not the excitement of desire. It was just excitement. Leo's fingers were not doing quite the right things. He was just scrabbling around, as if his mind were not on it. But she wanted everything to happen now. The little cock was as bold as brass.

Everything was happening now. She put her arms round Leo's bare body and rocked him, and the longing of months, the frustration, the uncertainty, stirred and shifted, ready to be washed away for ever. She wanted to tell Leo how much she had loved him.

Instead, she coughed. She coughed again, and again. There was a demonic tickle in her throat.

Leo raised himself on his elbows, his spectacles slipping down his nose. He waited patiently for her to stop coughing so that he could go on.

Clara coughed. She clenched the muscles of her throat to stop herself coughing, but that only made it worse.

She coughed him right out.

With the air of a practical man determined to ignite a recalcitrant gas boiler, Leo attempted to start again and go on from where he had left off.

It is impossible to make love to someone who is in the throes of an uncontrollable coughing fit.

The little cock, discouraged, lost its brassiness. Leo rolled away and lay on his back, his face stony, one arm shielding his eyes. Clara half fell out of bed, bent double with her coughing, and staggered naked to the bathroom. She closed the door behind her and abandoned herself utterly to the demands of her cough.

Afterwards, she dried her streaming eyes, washed her face and opened the door into the bedroom. Leo was fully dressed, shoes and all. He was sitting on the edge of the giant bed looking gloomily at his knees.

They had not spoken one word to each other since they got into bed.

"I've rung for a taxi for you," said Leo.
"Perhaps it was the hairspray under my arms," said Clara.
Leo stared.

It had been a fiasco, but it had happened. Leo and Clara had been to bed together.

What did he think? What does he think of me now?

Clara knew that if she were a girl in a story, either she or Leo would tell Martha about it, and there would be big dramatic scenes. Or Martha would discover about it somehow by other means. And there would be big dramatic scenes.

But I am a girl in a story, to all intents and purposes, except to myself. To anyone who knows me I'm only a bit more real than someone in a soap opera. Provided they've got a colour set. They see me in three dimensions instead of two, that's the only difference. People who have only seen Leo on television think they know him, after all. They forget that he doesn't know them too. That song—

I did but see you passing by
And still I love you till I die.

What crap. But it's all there is. Knowing people is like switching channels. Zap, zap, with the remote control. See you soon, maybe next Thursday. And he, she, whoever it is, won't want to sit through the video of absolutely everything you've done between now and next Thursday either. Edit yourself, or you'll get wiped.

So no one, least of all Martha, need know about me and Leo. There will be no dramatic scenes. I know he won't tell her, and I certainly shan't.

But Lord, I would so love to tell someone. I don't know if I can bear not to. I want to tell my story.

The person Clara really wanted to tell was Harry, but unfortunately that was impossible.

15

✾✾✾✾✾

CLARA MADE AN EFFORT to take herself in hand. In the days that followed she bought all the serious newspapers and sent off for the application forms for various jobs for which she was not qualified. She read the *Guardian*'s Creative and Media page and wrote off about two more jobs for which she was qualified but which she did not really want. She was still convalescent from Leo. She was missing Harry badly. She went shopping for summer clothes in Regent Street, and on impulse jumped on a Hoppa bus on its way to Parliament Hill Fields. A long healthy walk across the Fields and over Hampstead Heath might help her to regain her calm.

For the first time, on this walk, she was happy about her contact lenses. A tree was not just a tree but a constellation of shifty leaf-shapes. Undersides of copper-beech canopies gleamed with shoals of greenish sheeny fish-leaves.

It was a grey, windless afternoon. There were few people about on the further reaches of the Heath. She might have been walking in a vast private park. Jogging men, women with dogs, boys with balls—they were there, but always disappearing between trees, over the crest of slopes, into hidden side-paths, engulfed by the landscape as soon as glimpsed. The only person Clara came within six feet of was a young man in a blue windcheater leaning against railings which protected a marsh. Away over his shoulder, on the marsh, coots uttered their eerie cry.

Mildly interested in sighting the coots, Clara paused and, before moving on, briefly met the young man's eye. It was uncomfortable. She still had not got the hang of this eye-contact business. If it was hard to look directly at someone, it was equally hard to disentangle one's gaze again after the appropriate interval. Yet not to meet the man's eye at all would have seemed discourteous.

Clara turned sharply right off the hard footpath, plunging into a muddy gully and up again the other side into a wide grassy space edged by trees. On the far side of the gully she turned back.

Why did she turn?

The man stood on the high bank she had left, under the trees. Maybe he was watching her. Maybe he was just standing there, thinking his own thoughts, minding his own business.

There is something ridiculous about women who constantly imagine that they are being followed by strange men.

Clara walked on again, determined to forget the incident, such as it was, and not let it spoil her afternoon. Three minutes or so passed. There was no one else in sight, and no sound except the swish of her shoes in the uncut grass. She might have been in the depths of the country.

Her eye was caught by a movement off to her left. Unthinkingly she turned her head to see what it was. In the shelter of the trees that bordered the meadow the man in the blue jacket was walking along in a bouncy, self-conscious way, exactly parallel to her. This time he was definitely watching her.

Against her will, Clara tensed up. Nothing bad had happened, nothing bad was going to happen. But one should be watchful, take no silly risks. That was only common sense. She was exposed in the middle of the field. Was that good or bad? There was still no one else in sight, only the man.

She stopped, he stopped. She moved on, he moved on.

He was young and clean, or cleanish. She tried to recall his expression when their eyes had met, and could not. He was strutting along now briskly on the verge of the woods, ensuring by his antic walk that she would keep glancing at him.

She turned her head towards him again. He faced her squarely, stuck his thumbs into the elastic waistband of his trousers and pulled them down to his knees.

Clara associated the word "flasher" with the sorry, tramp-like figure who emerged from the bushes one wet November day long ago when she was walking home from her first school, a day school, the one before Redbrook House. It had been a matter of dank tweed trousers, a grubby fumbling, a pale pulpy showing. She ran home as fast as she could. She did not tell her aunt. She told her friends at school the next day. They had giggled together, appalled but not really frightened.

Tracksuit bottoms give new scope to indecent exposure.

If Clara had not been wearing her contact lenses his performance would have been wasted. She might not have noticed anything odd about an undifferentiated fellow walker apparently going her way. Short sight would have wrapped her in safety.

As it was she saw the dark stripes of his body hair, his white belly and his jaunty, upstanding penis with clinical clarity.

So what? He was made as other men and Clara had seen a fair number of men. It was not the sight of his nakedness that frightened her. Her fear was less specific. She did not like what was happening. She did not know what would happen next.

She had very few choices. She could turn and go back the way she had come, to the more frequented part of the Heath, or she could go on. She could walk, or she could run. Or she could stand still and do nothing.

She did not want to be chased, and she did not want him to come any closer. She walked on, fast, trying to remember from her previous walks what was on the other side of the upward-sloping meadow. Every time she checked on the flasher with a sidelong glance he faced about and pulled down his trousers. They were close enough to have spoken to each other without shouting very loudly, but the match was played out in silence.

A tarmac path appeared, across the top of the slope. Reaching it, Clara saw with relief a woman walking towards her with two black labradors. She looked back one last time as she hurried to meet the woman and saw the blue of the man's jacket between the trees as he ran away back in the direction from which they had come.

"I shouldn't go down that way if I were you," said Clara to the woman. "There's a young man making a nuisance of himself."

"What a bore, what a pity," said the woman. "It's usually so peaceful up here. But I have my dogs, I shall be all right."

She called to the two labradors and the three of them ambled off down the field, relaxed and confident. Clara felt ashamed of herself; and for the first time in her long acquaintance with Martha's Mungo, she saw the point of him.

Watchful and still tense, Clara made her way by a different route back through Parliament Hill Fields. Her principal feeling was resentment. How foul it was that she could not walk in broad daylight, in a public place, without such a thing happening.

Back among people and voices, down by the running-track and the swimming pool, she glanced behind her up the hill. There on a bench, far away near the summit, sat someone in a blue jacket. An invisible thread seemed taut between herself and the motionless figure.

It was probably someone else. Lots of people wear blue and she had already forgotten the precise blue of her flasher's windcheater.

When she got home she deadlocked her flat door and went straight into the bathroom to take out her contact lenses. Feeling comfortable behind her smeary, smudged old spectacles, she turned on the television and watched *Blue Peter*. Then she lay on her bed with Elizabeth Longford's life of the Duke of Wellington.

Part of her mind took in that she was reading about his long and halfhearted engagement to a girl who grew plain waiting for him, while another part of her mind bombarded her with self-reproach. The way she had behaved on the Heath was quite idiotic. The man may have been unbalanced, but he was most probably not dangerous. Hadn't she read that flashers were very seldom rapists?

Why had she behaved like a frightened rabbit? What would have happened if, the first time he pulled his trousers down, she had turned towards him and walked firmly in his direction? Would he not have become the frightened rabbit, and fled?

What would have happened if she had called to him, "What the hell do you think you are doing? Stop it at once or I shall report you to the police!"

But she had done nothing like that. She had behaved irrationally, a prey not to the man so much as to all the buried terrors of nightmares. Someone coming to get you. Someone waiting to pounce out at you. Someone holding you down, stifling your screams. If she'd been a few degrees more frightened she might have crouched mindlessly down in the grass and waited for the worst to happen, breaking into a last desperate dash to escape only when it was safely-dangerously too late. That's what young rabbits did. They crouched in the grass waiting—for their mothers to rescue them, or for death. And sure as I'm sitting here it wouldn't be mother. Clara's knowledge of being hunted was as old as the world. All it took to activate the knowledge was to be, just once, hunted. Awful people who perversely say that women connive with their rapists exploit an arcane truth which they are the last to understand.

Clara had stripped naked for Harry the first time they made love. He was courteous and timid. He was anxious not to offend her by any gesture or act of his. Come and get me, she had been saying without saying it. How can you resist? It ended as she had intended, with Harry hunting her down against the bookshelves with an impersonal passion that left them both shaken.

She tried to read. The Duke of Wellington, she read, was a reluctant Prime Minister. The same could not be said of the present Prime Minister, fighting for a third term.

Clara put down the book, turned off the TV, and without premeditation dialled Harry's home number. He had just got in. He came round straight away.

Clara did not tell Harry about the flasher—there was too

much else to say to each other, and not about national politics. He stayed all night.

The general election was next day. For the record, Leo claimed that he was kept so busy that he did not vote at all.

Martha, in Clapham, voted Labour, and the Conservative candidate got in.

Clara (Islington North) voted Labour, and the Labour candidate got in.

Harry, in Westminster, voted SDP, and the Conservative candidate got in.

Alice and Ferdie, in Sussex, voted for the Alliance. The Conservative candidate romped home. Irene, who cleaned the house for Alice and Ferdie at Belwood, and her husband who managed the garage, and both the Bollards, all voted Conservative. So did Anthony Arklow-Holland.

Charlotte did not vote.

In spite of the wobbly polls, the Conservatives were returned with a large parliamentary majority. A fortnight or so later, scabs were growing over the raw hopes of the 58 per cent of the electorate who had voted for other parties. Except for people who were professionally involved in post-mortems, it was as if nothing had happened, as if the election had never been. Those who were doing well looked forward to doing better. Those who were doing badly envisaged things getting worse.

Leo found himself for the first time in his life on the side of the big battalions, or assumed to be. His name, though he did not know it, was being added to lists of the great and the good, people who, in the government's opinion, could be trusted to fill public office, head commissions, join the policy unit, sit on committees and boards of inquiry. He was invited to a royal garden party (with his wife) later in the summer.

16

THE FOLLOWING WEEKEND Alice woke at Belwood to a clear blue sky. By mid-morning the temperature was over eighty degrees. Agnes had her inflatable paddling pool out on the grass. Squatting beside it, she floated poppy petals for boats, squinting at their scarlet silkiness.

Christa, in a pink bikini, sprawled sunbathing in a deckchair, her thighs squashed sideways and spread. Ferdie sat facing her on a bench in the shade. A stranger would have said that he was staring at Christa lasciviously. A Braille book lay untouched on his knee.

Alice went slowly with Ferdie down the garden and away round the house to a twisting grass path. It ran between high banked-up beds thick with tall foxgloves, Canterbury bells, white lilies and delphiniums, backed by towering thickets of shrub roses. Agnes came running behind her parents, barefoot, squeaking with excitement.

"It's like the jungle," she said. "There could be *tigers.*"

The glittering spires of flowers were way above her head, above all their heads, the colours brilliant against the blue. The sunken green path between the flowers was so narrow that they had to walk in single file. Alice pushed aside stray festoons and paused every now and then to pull out a piece of groundsel or a sticky thread of goose-grass with her left hand; her right hand was stretched behind her, holding Ferdie's.

"It's shamefully overplanted this year," said Alice. "I can't think what Mansell was thinking of. But at least there's almost no room for weeds."

Alice, accustomed to finding cause for complaint, found the flowery path so heartbreakingly lovely that she had to criticize it in order to be able to bear it. She pulled down an overhanging branch, snapped off a dead-white rose and held it under Ferdie's nose.

"Smell that. Blanc Double de Coubert. Our favourite. Actually it smells like the most expensive kind of soap, doesn't it?"

Were it not for the loaded, scented warmth, they could have been in an alley littered with cigarette butts and used condoms for all Ferdie knew. Ferdie listened to voices, not words. He caught Alice's entranced, embarrassed pleasure in her paradise. He ran his hand along her shoulder, cupped the back of her head, pulled her face down to his and kissed her long and hard. This too Alice bore in the only way she could. She gave a little neigh.

"There're nettles somewhere in this lot," she exclaimed. "My leg's being stung."

Agnes, a complacent chaperone, was fitting the bells of foxgloves on her fingers. White on the right hand, pink on the left.

"We must go back. Leo and Martha will be here soon. I've got to think out what we're going to eat. Shall we have it in the garden?"

Martha was an intruder in the house that had belonged to Leo's first wife, and to Leo. She resented coming away from London for the weekend on her own account, because she had failed to meet her deadline with the illustrations for *The Fisherman's Wife*. She longed to be at her drawing-board. She wanted to praise the garden but did not, fearful of sounding either condescending or proprietory. The proximity of Charlotte oppressed her. The light that shone in the dusk from the cottage on the far side of the lake glinted like a malign eye.

Martha averted her gaze from Charlotte's house and focused on the flower-bed that bordered the terrace, where miniature dark violas were mixed with alchemilla. The violas did not lie sprawling along the ground as they did in Martha's garden. Using the fine alchemilla stems as supports, they risked climbing. The jointed green shoots of the violas launched themselves precariously upwards and outwards like pyramids of acrobats. The faces of the little flowers surfaced everywhere, purple-black heart-shapes among the yellow-green froth of the alchemilla. Martha longed to draw this unspeakable prettiness. She knew she had the talent to capture only the prettiness, not the unspeakableness.

"Was it you," she asked Alice warily, "who had the idea of planting violas in the alchemilla?"

"It was Mother Nature's idea."

For a moment Martha thought she meant Charlotte, and shot a glance at Leo.

"The violas are self-seeded," Alice explained. "This is a very obliging garden."

Martha wondered whether Charlotte thought about her as often as she thought about Charlotte.

The two wives of Leo Ulm never met. Charlotte hardly thought about Martha at all. Leo loomed so large for her still that she had little room in her head for anyone else.

"If you think about someone else an awful lot," Martha said to the others, "do you think it means that person is thinking about you too?"

"Anyone you fantasize about," said Leo, "is fantasizing about you too."

"Absolutely not," said Alice. "We've none of us any idea how we figure in other people's fantasies, whether we're in there at all. We might have awful shocks if we knew. We might be in all the wrong fantasies."

"Like when someone says they've dreamed about you," said Ferdie. "Such awful cheek, I always think."

Without guilt or longing, Leo thought fleetingly of Emmeline. Had he made an awful fool of himself in Washington?

Had everyone noticed what had been going on? And he'd never
sent the book to that American woman. Too late now. With
guilt and longing, he looked at Alice, cool and shining in a
flounced dress of fine ink-blue linen that left her brown throat
bare.

At the moment when Leo was remembering her, Emmeline
had just reached her apartment up three flights of stairs in an
alley of the rue Monsieur le Prince, having collected her son
from his minder and picked up milk and bread, chocolate and
yoghurt from the shop on the corner. She threw down her
briefcase, fed her child and put him to bed. She took up an
exercise book from her desk and read over the poem she had
written the night before in an attempt to exorcize her obses-
sion with Leo Ulm.

If the poem had been translated into English, it might have
begun like this:

> *I would weep*
> *If I dared . . .*

Several pages of squared paper later—for it was an introspec-
tive and long poem—it might have ended thus:

> *If I dared to weep*
> *The Seine would overflow, engulfing*
> *The quays, the streets,*
> *The squares of the city,*
> *Drowning you, washing you away.*

The translator could have rejected a literal translation in free
verse in favour of a paraphrase or adaptation of the original,
making of Emmeline's poem an English one in the style of
Meredith, or Browning, or Eliot. The poem was never translated into English. Emmeline did not send it to Leo or show
it to anyone else. When the exercise book was used up she

consigned it, as she had many others, to a drawer of her bureau. Her son will come across her cache of notebooks when he is going through her things after her death. He will not be a literary man, he will have a chain of dry-cleaning shops, and he won't make head nor tail of his mother's scribblings. In spite of her successful career and, in her own circle, her popularity, Emmeline will never be famous enough for the personal papers she leaves to be of interest to anyone outside the family. They will be of no interest to her son and he will throw them away.

The poem may be thrown away already. No one knows one way or another. It wasn't a very good poem anyway. Love poems by non-poets seldom are; they are insufficiently porous, without moist spaces in them where a reader's experience may take root. Emmeline was a young woman with a sophisticated imagination but her poem was no exception to this unkind rule.

Emmeline picked up a few dropped stitches in the matted knitting of her poem and pushed the book away. The writing had served its purpose. Her depression was outside of her, in the book, instead of inside her.

Perhaps she will recover, if she has the courage to stop dreaming the dreams that feed the pain. She had already passed out of the acute stage of unrequited love at its most consuming, when she went over and over every scrap of conversation she had had with Leo, reinterpreting his idlest words, pinpointing her own mistakes—the greatest of which, she knew, was talking to him about herself. She should have kept silent. But she was able now to think about a flowered dress she had seen and wanted in René Derhy's window in the rue Saint André des Arts without imagining wearing it to win Leo back.

At Belwood, Alice in her blue-black flounces said, "Someone's going to have to go and pick Christa up. She's missed the last bus or she'd be back by now. I don't want her staying out all night."

"I'll go," said Leo, slapping his pockets for his car keys, hoping that Alice would say she would come with him. After a second's hesitation, she smiled and shook her head.

"That's very good of you, Dad," said Ferdie firmly.

So ill-matched were father and son that each seemed to mock the other whenever their relationship was verbally acknowledged. Ferdie was not like a son. Leo was not like a dad.

"She's in Brighton," said Alice. "I'll write the address down for you and draw a map. It's in Kemptown. Clancy's house— the boyfriend."

The house, at the end of a terrace in a narrow, sloping Victorian street, looked at least as respectable as its neighbours. Leo rang the bell and waited. The door was opened by a youth with platinum-blond hair cut just like Christa's, a single earring, and a surprisingly sweet smile.

"I've come to collect Christa. I'm Leo Ulm, Alice's father-in-law."

"Oh. Yeah. I've seen you on the telly. You'd better come in."

The narrow hallway was carpeted with odd squares in different patterns, unified by dust and caked mud. Through a half-open door on the right Leo glimpsed a double mattress on bare boards littered with someone's belongings: hi-fi, socks, records, paperbacks, a guitar, shoes, a squash racket. The door on the left of the hall was closed. Behind it, someone was playing Debussy.

Clancy led him into the kitchen at the back of the house. It was a long time since Leo had been in a student house and he had forgotten how the penniless young lived. There were three thin people already in the narrow kitchen: a carroty-haired girl stirring something on an unstable gas cooker, another girl and a young man sitting at the table smoking roll-ups and drinking tea.

"This is Mary, Barry, Camilla," said Clancy. "He's come for Christa. We'd better wait until she's finished her practice."

Christa played well. Leo remarked on it.

"Yeah. She's def."

"She's *deaf*? I'd no idea. That makes it all the more remarkable."

"She's def—def-initive." Clancy looked at him with contempt.

The plangent cadences of the music penetrated the wall between the rooms.

"Would you like a cup of tea?"

Leo said that would be very nice. The carroty girl took a mug from the crowd of mugs on the wooden draining-board, rinsed it under the single tap at the chipped white sink and gave it to Clancy, who filled it from a pot on the table. They both moved as if they were tired. Leo, feeling bulky, sat down on a spare chair and sipped the weak tepid tea. The piano music saturating the air absolved him from making conversation. He wanted to ask the students what books they were reading, who their heroes were, but he felt too lethargic. The young people seemed passive, pale, their limp T-shirts rendered a uniform pink-grey by the impersonal sluicing of laundrettes. They looked at him with neutral eyes. Four overflowing plastic rubbish bags slumped against a wall stained with the smudged black chrysanthemums of damp. The slipping dripping notes of the piano enfolded the kitchen. The images of its underwater occupants blurred and wavered.

Leo, drowning in sleepiness, roused himself with a jolt as the piano music changed. Christa was playing Gershwin now—pert, jerky, suggestive.

"That's the sign that she's finished practising," said Clancy. "We can go into the front room now."

The front room. A phrase from Leo's northern youth. The front rooms of decent Manchester households in the late forties and fifties, dustless and airless. Dark-patterned settee and armchairs with cotton lace antimacassars, nets and velour curtains across the bay window, polished side-board with doyleys, china ornaments, framed photographs of young men in uniform, a clock on the mantelpiece, a coal fire laid in the grate, brass fire-irons, and of course the piano, an upright, with the wedding photograph on top.

Clancy opened the door of the front room for Leo and stood back.

The front room was uncarpeted and empty except for Christa, the piano and an audience of bicycles stacked and propped all anyhow against each other in the bay window, their front wheels and handlebars twisted at unnatural angles—dislocated, broken-necked, antlered bicycles, the pedals hanging loose like hurt hooves.

Christa, her back to the door, played on. She sat very straight, the nape of her neck under her blond spikes of hair vulnerable to the bicycles and to Leo. Looking at her, he was pleased that he would be driving her home to Belwood alone through the midsummer Sussex lanes, and no longer tired at all.

Clancy read his changed mood. Leo felt Clancy's hostility. For the first time Leo was glad of his own weight and authority in the house of nervy young creatures.

"Your friends look as if they don't get enough to eat," he remarked to Christa as he turned the car in the narrow street.

"They don't," she said. "All the time they make soup. They have not enough grant. It's the cuts, Clancy says. Is that the right word?"

"Ah, yes, the cuts." The cuts were an issue in Leo's world also, but affected it less tangibly. How out of touch he was these days with the student body. What would the Prime Minister say, if faced with the kids in the Kemptown kitchen? She was suddenly present for him, the green and brown bracelet of semi-precious stones, the pearl necklace and earrings, the bright brooch on the patterned lapel, the voice:

"Get that washing-up done and put away for a start. Put out those rubbish bags. Scrub the floor."

Then what? Perhaps that was enough to earn grace. Leo remembered George Herbert's poem: Who sweeps a room as for Thy sake, Prime Minister, makes that and the action fine.

* * *

Later that evening Emmeline in Paris had a visit from a short dark man whose name does not matter and whose mistress she had been, intermittently, for a number of years. He had an antiquarian book business which he ran from a first floor near the Odéon. He was the father of her son. His self-absorbed, vigorous love-making temporarily knocked her into submission—not to him but to life as it has to be lived.

Around them the city moaned—in French—and turned over in its sleep. In dark bedrooms, people insisted on telling their lovers the stories of their lives. None of the other people was listening properly—they too were preoccupied with their own histories, so the stories were mostly lost. Hell is where all the stories of the world lie crying to be heard. Emmeline's story is not properly told. This is not fair, but it's quite usual. Beyond Paris, beyond Europe, the earth's millions ate, copulated, suffered, slept. All would die—of flood, drought, blast, radiation, exposure, fire, infection, starvation, torture, disease, old age, or, to save time, since it was going to happen anyway, by their own hand.

The illuminations were extinguished long ago in Charlotte. The electric dazzle that had drawn Mansell all the way from the kitchen garden to her bed spluttered and died, a November firework. There was no light shining from her now and it would not come again. Illness robbed her of the post-menopausal energy and freedom that were due to her.

"I look so tired tonight," she thought as she looked in the mirror into her own eyes. They seemed smaller, sunk between bones veiled by crumpled, brown-mauve skin as thin as cling-wrap. She wasn't really tired. She slept well enough. This was just the way she looked now, every day. The fungus of her death, which had shrivelled in the blaze of her Indian summer, plumped up again in the dark. It unfurled its foul bracts.

Looking out from the cottage over the lake to Belwood, Charlotte could have sworn she saw Leo standing on the terrace, his hands in his pockets as usual.

But she no longer believed the evidence of her own eyes.

She had seen Leo so often and he was never there. Her hallucinations were getting worse. She could not resist testing herself, even though the test hurt and frightened her. It's always best to know the worst, isn't it? When the noises started in her head, around bedtime, she walked in a deliberate way to her front door and opened it.

She only opened it halfway. The horror this side of the house was different from at the back.

It was dark outside. The house was in flames, the fire leaping at angles from every brilliant window. She could hear rafters and beams splitting and crashing. The garden was lit up by the blaze, every blade of grass casting its shadow, with clots of huddled darkness here and there that were the shapes of people. Cows and pigs lay dead on the grass too, their legs stretched stiffly in the air. The smell was sickening. Behind the roar of the fire's wind was a sizzling sound, as pieces of material and of bodies fell in the lake. Then the sounds of the fire were blotted out by the roaring of trucks and tanks. The convoy rolled round the lake, over the brick bridge, advancing on her cottage. Strings of headlights flashed in pairs as the vehicles drew up at the end of her garden, the wheels churning through flower-beds. Charlotte heard the thud and scrunch of boots on gravel. She saw the giant shadows of men and the glint of the headlights on thin steel. More and more of them came, jumping heavily down from the trucks. They were marching towards the door. She waited for them.

"They shall not . . ." she said aloud.

As the first faceless one loomed up in the light from the porch, his bayonet preceding him, Charlotte slammed the door.

All was quiet. Charlotte held her breath, listening. Nothing. She tightened the cord of her dressing-gown and looked out the small window of the hallway. Nothing. Some lights still on in the house beyond the lake. An ugly, malformed moon. The ducks, alarmed by something or by nothing, erupted in an offbeat quacking, and as suddenly subsided.

Charlotte locked the front door, turned out the downstairs light and, cold with exhaustion, went up to bed. The wet night wind made whips of the trees. Upstairs Charlotte slept and dreamed of Leo.

In the big bedroom at Belwood, Alice rejected Ferdie's sexual advances, as she usually did.

"I'm sorry, I just can't. No, I don't know why."

"My cherry tree . . ."

Ferdie moaned with frustration, sightless. She too, staring into the darkness, after he slept.

The young cannot get enough of each other. Christa, having checked that Agnes was asleep, crept barefoot down the back staircase, out of the kitchen door, and ran through the scented darkness to meet Clancy, who was waiting with his bicycle at the end of the drive. Untormented, they went to lie down as usual in the soft uncut grass under the trees. Life for life's sake.

In the spare room, next door to Alice and Ferdie, Leo made love to Martha with more enthusiasm than usual. Sleeping with Mungo was like sharing a bed with an outsize sheep. The senior Ulms' matrimonial bed, in Leo's opinion, too often resembled an overcrowded railway carriage packed with peasants and livestock. The animal was spending the weekend with a neighbour in Clapham.

Leo lay on his back, spectacles still on his nose, luxuriously swishing his legs around on an un-hairy, un-gritty spaciousness of clean undersheet. Martha slept. Leo did not feel sleepy. He felt the house that had been his home for years, where he was now his disappointing son's guest, lying open to him in the darkness in welcome. And the garden . . .

Leo crept out of bed, found his slippers, and went silently down the curling main staircase and out of the unlocked front door. In the garden his way was made clear by a lopsided moon.

His way wasn't made as clear as all that. He stumbled on a stick in the rough grass. Feeling foolish, he picked up the stick and made for the drive. Better, smoother, safer. He'd walk as far as the gate.

Leo didn't get as far as the gate. He saw, in the dappled

moonlight, a white bum, a quantity of arms and legs, and two heads of light hair. He stepped off the drive into the long grass and stood over whoever it was. He stood there unnoticed for some time. Recognizing the owners of the bum, the limbs and the yellow hair, he brought the stick down on the bum as hard as he possibly could. It was Christa's, not Clancy's.

The lovers sprang to their feet and stood together glaring at him, their hands by their sides, not bothering to try to hide their nudity. Leo noted Christa's mature shape, Clancy's thin legs and narrow, hairless chest. Christa was taller than he was. But it was Clancy who stepped forward, grabbed the lapels of Leo's striped pyjamas and raised his other fist in menace.

"You fucking bastard," said Clancy. "I'll get you for this one day, you old fart. Get the hell out of here or I'll smash your fucking face in."

Leo's rage and outrage deprived him of speech. He found it hard to get his breath. His heartbeat altered in a way that made him cough. He came out in a sweat.

Stumbling and gasping, he dropped the stick and made off back towards the house. He lost one slipper. As he reached the gravel sweep by the front door Christa caught up with him, still naked, clutching her jeans and sweatshirt against her chest.

"Dr. Ulm! Leo! Please?" She caught him by the arm. He looked down into her face, monochrome in the moonlight.

"Please don't tell Alice. She would send me home perhaps. Please?"

Leo said nothing. He shook her hand from his arm and went into the house. He crept upstairs and into bed beside Martha. He was shivering.

He did not tell Martha. He did not tell Alice. Christa, in the morning, was conspicuously busy and co-operative, keeping Agnes happy and out of the adults' way, and helping Alice with Sunday lunch. As she sat down with the family for the meal Christa caught Leo's eye for a second, wriggled on her chair and rolled her own eyes upwards in a parody of pain, making of her sore bottom a conspiracy between the two of them, in which there was a reference to the possibility of blackmail.

Leo pushed his parted lips forward in a monkey-like kissing movement—an unknowing reflex response—and, more knowingly, smiled his irresistible crooked smile at her across the roast potatoes. Christa's victory was complete.

Leo did not see it that way. He suspected he had made a conquest.

Christa's pubic hair had been a black wedge in the moonlight. It contrasted strangely with the bleached yellow hair on her head. Leo thought about this, afterwards. It pleased him. Fair pubic hair had always seemed somehow nauseating to him, all wrong (poor Emmeline), he could not say why. The dark triangle was central, basic, satisfactory.

His missing slipper reappeared in the spare bedroom before it was time to pack up. For their different reasons, Martha and Leo were both pleased to be going back to London.

17

Leo, in the morning, in Clapham, was in a hurry.

"We're going to Canterbury today to do an OB as a trailer for the new series."

Having come to television late in life he enjoyed using its jargon. OB, he explained to Martha, means outside broadcast, as opposed to filming in the studio. Leo paced up and down devouring a piece of toast piled high with strawberry jam. Martha's handbag lay open on one of the chairs at the kitchen table. As Leo wheeled round to talk to her, gesticulating, a blob of jam dropped off the toast and fell into the bag.

"I'd like to do something for the boys, and for Meg. Give them something. They're really so good to me. So *generous.*"

"That's a nice idea," said Martha, meaning it. She was not critical of Leo, but she examined him constantly, from as far inside as she could get, as if his soul were her own. ("I can't call my soul my own.") She worried that he was becoming increasingly testy, increasingly self-absorbed. She was not sure whether distinction, achievement and advancing years made self-absorption inevitable. She was not sure whether exceptionally gifted and busy people had the right to be self-absorbed at the expense of others. She was not sure whether self-absorption might not be a necessary condition for the attainment of distinction and achievement. Simply she meant what she said—that it was a nice idea for Leo to do something for the production team of *Homo Sapiens.* Loving Leo, she made no judgements. But it was good that for once he was going to put himself out.

Half her mind was already on her day's work. Trotter Books were getting agitated about the non-delivery of *The Fisherman's Wife*. She was up to the Pope part. Really she ought to go to the library and find some pictures of papal gear. She couldn't just make it up. There was an intermediate picture she wanted to do first, a small one for a page-heading, of the fisherman slouching off down to the shoreline in silhouette against an evening sky. She saw in her mind's eye a rose-red wash shading to grey-pink. The rose-red, a colour she adored, must be intense but not too bright. Hard to mix, hard to fix.

"I thought, a good dinner," said Leo, licking jam from his fingers. "Something really special. We ought to be back from Canterbury by eight, eight thirty."

"Nice idea. Where will you take them?"

"I thought I'd just bring them back here. Much jollier at home. There'll be five of them, and you and me. Is that OK with you?"

"Why didn't you tell him to piss off?" asked Alice, who dropped in unannounced around lunchtime.

She sat at the kitchen table drinking Perrier from an opened bottle she found on Martha's draining-board. Martha, at the table, was painting away as if her life depended on it. Her life depended on it.

"Can you imagine telling Leo to piss off? I couldn't—could you?"

Alice blushed. Martha studied the blush dispassionately. It gave her a new idea for her background wash. Alice's blush did not rise from her neck evenly but patchily, in deltas and archipelagos of deepening colour.

She jiggled her paintbrush in the water-jar and closed her paint box. It was not good. She would have had to stop working soon anyway, while she was still skating on the surface of things. If she became engrossed it would make her feel ill to break off. She had this dinner to work out. And now Alice.

"There is pleasure in service," she said to Alice. "I'm doing what Leo requires me to do, and doing it as well as possible."

"Balls," said Alice, rolling her eyes.

"It's not balls. It really does please me to be able to do what is needed, to be what Leo wants me to be, and to fit in my own work too. It makes me feel proud. And it makes the work doubly exciting, never a drag—it's like having a lover I keep wanting to rush off to."

Alice drained the dregs of the wine bottle into her tumbler. "I think it's neurotic. A sort of megalomania. It's so like you not even to have a cleaning lady, when Leo could afford to pay for five cleaning ladies. You just want to do everything yourself, control everything."

"It doesn't feel like being in control to me," said Martha mildly. "It feels like responding to outside pressures from minute to minute."

"You deceive yourself. You always have. You're not shamelessly smug like Helen Bollard—ask Clara about her—but that's because you *are* deceiving yourself. You're just a dictator in little, even though you're so nice and we love you. Nothing can happen in this house without your knowing about it. If I were to move those . . . those cups on the dresser, for example, by a couple of inches, you'd notice and feel threatened. You decide when the sheets are changed, when things go to the cleaners, every last petty thing. You never delegate. No wonder you're tired."

"None of that's irreversible. If I had to work for someone else I'd adjust perfectly well."

"Nonsense. If you were to go and work in some office now you'd go mad, you'd drive them mad. You're unemployable—you're so used to doing everything in your own way, in your own time, unobserved, uncriticized. That's the point—no one can say you're doing things wrong, because everything here is yours, and you made the rules. You're an absolute monarch and woe betide anyone who questions your authority."

Martha was puzzled by Alice's vehemence. "It doesn't feel like that to me. Why are you going on about it? You're being daft."

Because I'm bloody envious, Alice did not say. Because, Alice thought, I have Irene to look after Belwood and Christa to look after Agnes, and I am Ferdie's cherry tree and all that, and I don't want to be a domestic masochist like Martha—but I don't have the grit to be good. I don't even have the grit to be wicked, and try and take Leo from my darling Martha. He wouldn't, anyway. He doesn't want me *enough*. I could kill him for that, for wanting me just a bit.

Half of Martha's mind was on tonight's dinner. The whole of her mind was rarely on any one thing at a time. She went to the fridge and took out a glass bowl, in the bottom of which lay the remains of yesterday's salad. There was quite a lot left. Lettuce leaves and slabs of avocado, after their night's immersion in French dressing, glistened darkly. They were well on the way to a return to primeval slime. Martha hooked up a limp shred with her fingers and ate it. Delicious. But it would not do. She scooped the slithery green corruption out into the garbage bucket.

"You make me sound so bossy," she said to Alice. "Like I said, I just respond to each next thing. I don't actually make any decisions at all."

"You just made one," said Alice. "A decision. I watched you. You decided to throw away the salad. You didn't have to consult anyone, you just did it. Confidently. There's absolutely no difference in kind, only in scale, between you deciding just like that to throw away a salad and a general deciding to attack, or an emperor deciding to behead."

"It's a nice thought. But scale must count for something."

"Not philosophically."

"For a student of philosophy," said Martha, "you have very little idea of process. How one thing leads to another, all the time, backwards and forwards. You just see states. And you seem to me to be *in* a bit of a state, today."

Martha picked up her bag from the chair and fumbled inside

it for a tissue to wipe her oily fingers. Her purse was sticky and so was her diary. Withdrawing her hand in disgust, she found a red gelatinous mess on her index finger—a blob of raw flesh, torn from something that had been alive. Frightened, she held the repulsive mass on her finger close to her face to study it. It smelt of strawberries.

After Alice left, Martha up-ended her bag on the table and with a damp cloth wiped the jam off everything that had been in it. She fished from its dusty depths various loose coins and put them back in the wiped purse. Nothing more valuable than a five-pence piece. How is it that the coins at the bottom of bags are never, but never, pounds?

Martha went to the freezer and took from it two chickens for the dinner-party. She laid them on the right of the sink. Next to them was her electric drill, plugged in, a large-bore bit in place. Earlier in the week she had started making holes in the wall to put up a new shelf, and had been interrupted.

She picked up the drill by its bright blue handle and pressed the trigger. The drill thrummed in her hand. She applied the juddering thing to a chicken and felt the bit driving deep into its deep-frozen flesh. She withdrew her tool and attacked the other chicken. She stood back and looked at what she had done. The chickens looked funny with holes bored through them.

Clara meanwhile had been lunching with Harry and Anthony Arklow-Holland at the Groucho Club, of which Anthony was a member. (And who pays that subscription? wondered Clara, remembering the Reform story.)

After lunch Anthony stayed on in the club to see someone else, and Harry and Clara parted lovingly in Dean Street— Harry to return to the office, Clara to visit Isobel Henneken. She liked Anthony's Old Bat, and had taken to calling in at Redcliffe Square on afternoons when she knew Anthony could not be there.

Mrs. Henneken was wearing a rust-coloured brocade kaftan,

a lot of carved jade ("museum quality," as Clara liked to say), three pairs of spectacles on cords swinging round her neck, and pink-and-brown-checked bedroom slippers (jumble-sale quality). She reclined on a stained and saggy sofa; Clara perched on a rickety gilt chair. The tea-tray lay on the floor between them. They discussed the problem of whether or not Mrs. Henneken should write her memoirs.

"But what would I put *in*, Clara darling? And what would I leave *out?* Or more to the point, *who?*"

"What does Anthony think?"

"Our darling Anthony is part of the problem. There's the little matter of his *father* . . ."

This was pretty interesting. None of Anthony's friends knew anything at all about his family.

"I shouldn't really go into it. But if you're going to *help* me with my memoirs you'll have to know a few things. Are you *discreet?*"

"An oyster," said Clara. "A positive oyster."

"Between ourselves, then. I had a little *go* with Anthony's father, during the war."

"Was that before he married Anthony's mother?"

Mrs. Henneken cackled. "He was *married* all right, but he was never married to Anthony's mother. A fool, but not *such* a fool. When are you going to pour that tea?"

Clara got down on the dusty carpet and poured. It appeared that Mrs. Henneken had forgotten to put any tea in the pot. Clara passed her hostess a green-and-gold-lustre teacup of hot water, which she took and sipped without comment, to Clara's relief. She didn't want to break Mrs. Henneken's train of thought. She wanted to encourage her to go on, but not to seem too avid. She poured out some hot water for herself into the second cup, a translucent porcelain bowl painted with garlands.

"Is Anthony's mother still alive?"

"Of course she is. It's who he lives with, in that dreadful little flat near Heathrow. Poor old Maeve Arklow. Such a pretty girl. She came from Waterford—the only part of Ireland where the accent is ugly. *Such* a pity. In Sligo now, when I used to stay at Westport . . ."

"What about the 'Holland' bit?"

"That's just darling Anthony's nonsense. Arklow's where the crockery is made in Ireland. The peasants there call crockery 'delf'—from Delft, do you see? That's what Maeve always called it. Delft is in Holland. Anthony just made it up, like a crossword clue, and added it on. Very convincing as a name, really."

"How did you come to know his mother?"

"I told you, darling. You must *listen*. She took him off me. Little bitch. She came over just after the war and got a job as a chambermaid at the Ritz. *Such* lovely bed-linen they had there, even in the fifties, don't you remember?"

"Not really, no."

"That's where she met him. He used to come up from the country when he was bored and stay at the Ritz for a few weeks. Of course when she got pregnant she had to leave. He never knew anything about it—not till after, when Anthony was quite a big boy."

Clara took a deep breath, and asked calmly, "Who was he, who *is* he, Anthony's father?"

Mrs. Henneken played with her jade. "Darling, I can't *bring* myself to say it out loud. Come over here to me."

Clara crossed to the sofa and was overwhelmed by the unwashed sweet-and-sour aroma of Isobel Henneken, who whispered a name in her ear.

"No!" Clara sat back on her heels, incredulous.

The Old Bat's eyes held hers in a long and meaningful communion. When it comes to gossip, it is equally blessed to give and to receive.

"And it's he who . . . pays all the bills, and everything?"

Mrs. Henneken nodded solemnly.

"And is it he who put Anthony up for the Reform Club, and all that?"

Mrs. Henneken was irritated by Clara's naïvety. "Of course not, darling. Do have *some* sense. That's just a dogsbody, a family lawyer, I don't know. Give me some more tea. Ought you to add a little hot water to the pot? Isn't it getting too strong?"

Obediently, Clara poured hot water from the tarnished silver jug into the hot water in the teapot, and filled Mrs. Henneken's cup. There was one more bit of the story she wanted to know.

"How did they get to know each other again, Anthony's parents?"

"I wouldn't call them his *parents*. That gives quite the wrong impression. There is his father—and there is his mother." Mrs. Henneken held up her mottled left hand, and her mottled right hand, and stared theatrically at Clara through the space between.

"Sorry. Yes, I see."

"When Anthony was old enough to go to school she worked as a cleaner at the airport. You know, pushing a gloomy mop around all day. It was handy for where she lived. Then when they brought in all the Pakistanis she packed it in, she couldn't take that, there they were in their nylon saris and their cardigans and she couldn't even pass the time of day with them. No English, you see."

"And Anthony's father?"

"It was too extraordinary, really. He was stalking through the airport to the VIP lounge with all his aides and secretaries, and there was old Maeve with her mop, and they had an eye-meet, and they both *knew*. So she dumped the mop and followed him into the VIP lounge, and I don't know what happened there, he didn't tell me, but they came to an arrangement, and Anthony went to a different school, and to Cambridge—Selwyn, was it, one of those *unreal* colleges—and had the allowance, and Bob's your uncle. Only he has to stay with his mother because *she* got nothing out of it, and he can't chuck her and he can't bring her into London—darling, she's the most fearful old bag now, and she *drinks*—so really he's a very good boy."

"Who else knows about this?"

"Darling Anthony doesn't—I mean he doesn't know who his father is, and *I'm* not going to cause trouble by telling him. I'm a *double* oyster."

"So no one else knows?"

"Well, I did tell someone. I shouldn't have but I was all worked up—it was just after *he* had told me about meeting Maeve again. I told Leo Ulm. You don't know Leo? You do?"

"Yes, I know him quite well. I see him often."

"So hard to tell with the young these days. You seem to know nobody. Nobody who *is* anybody. That's why darling Anthony's such a *joy*. So you know darling Leo. You've no *idea* what a lovely, lovely thing he was as a young man. Sonya took him up in a big way, in the late sixties that would be. You didn't know Sonya? No, I thought not. I met him at Sonya's. I had a little *go* with Leo, even though I was a bit older than him even then. I suspect Sonya had a *little* go with Leo too . . . He was married to that plain *buff*-coloured girl with the place in Sussex, but sitting rather loose in the saddle."

"Yes. Charlotte. I know her too."

"Was that her name?"

"Does Anthony know that Leo knows?"

"No . . . but he knows that Leo knows something. I think he likes to imagine that Leo might actually be his father, poor darling . . . You *are* going to help me with my tiny memoirs now, aren't you?"

"I'd love to. Really. But we'll have to see."

Holding her delicate teacup in one hand, Clara ran a finger of her other hand round the stained rim. It was more than a stain; it was a deposit. Food-slime and membrane-scum from the inside of someone's lip, from various people's lips, hardened on. Clara turned the cup right round so that the handle faced the other way. It was just as bad on this side. If she wanted a clean drink of water, let alone tea, she had arrived at Mrs. Henneken's a decade or so too late.

But it was only when she was walking up the Old Brompton Road towards South Kensington tube station that it occurred to Clara that everything Isobel Henneken had told her might be a pack of lies—or at least a distortion. She longed to love and admire female survivors and all Old Bats, but recognized that some of them at least might be poisonous. Poor Charlotte. Poor Maeve Arklow. Poor Anthony, confused and filled with fantasies. Poor wife of Anthony's alleged father, another grey woman waiting, in this case a grey lady. And Leo? What a repository of fantasies *he* was.

It was nearly ten that evening before Martha heard Leo's key in the door. He and his younger companions came thumping through the house to the kitchen.

"Darling," said Leo. "Here we are. I think you probably know everyone—Nick, Nick, Tony, Nick—and of course Meg."

"Mary, darling!" cried one of the Nicks, or Tony, bustling forward and throwing his arms around her. "It's been ages! You're looking *wonderful!*"

"Martha," said Martha, who was quite certain she had never met him before in her life. Nick, or Tony, stepped backwards straight into Mungo's water-bowl. The bowl overturned, shooting water all over the floor and sousing his white Reeboks.

"First thing you have to learn in a strange kitchen—where the dog-bowls are! I must say, I'd never have guessed the middle of the room."

"We can eat now in about five minutes," said Martha, sounding even more Yorkshire than usual, raising the heat under a saucepan. "Leo, why don't you take everyone into the other room and give them a drink?"

They had all had some drinks already, to judge from their jubilation. Nick, Nick, Tony and Nick—all youthful, well spoken, slim, cord-trousered, with good teeth and hair—went off with Leo.

Meg stayed in the kitchen with Martha. She was older than the men—quite a bit older, Martha realized, on closer inspection. Her hair was pulled up and back into a jaunty pony-tail and she was as slim as a reed. But there were deep vertical lines between her eyebrows and creases beside her nose. Her jawline was no longer pure; her cheeks were beginning to pouch. She was still weighed down with books, maps, other people's jackets, two clip-boards and a straining plastic carrier bag.

"I can't stay," said Meg.

"You look tired out," said Martha. "Dump all those things on the floor and sit down."

"Anything I can do to help?"

"No—yes, you could chop that parsley. The whole lot. Thank-you, that's lovely."

Meg was so patently loaded with responsibility that Martha assumed she must be the series producer at least. Meg put her right.

"I'm the production assistant. I'm frightfully lucky to be on *Homo Sapiens*—everyone wants to work with Leo."

From the sitting-room came a deep rumble-rumble-rumble, punctuated by cries of appreciation and amazement from the young men. Martha guessed he was telling them about what he did in 1968; it was his party-piece.

"What do *they* all do then, if you're the production assistant?"

"Well, Nick in the red shirt is the producer, Nick in the leather thing is the director, Tony—the one in the black sweater—is the editor, and Nick in the pink T-shirt is the assistant director."

"They all look about fifteen years old to me."

Meg sighed. "And they're getting younger all the time. Like policemen."

Martha, glancing sharply at Meg again as she bent over the parsley, decided she must be years older than herself, somewhere in her mid-forties probably.

"What does the production assistant do exactly?"

Meg looked up and beamed. She loved her job. It transpired that she had risen at six that morning to get into the office early from where she lived in Sevenoaks, checked on the transport—a hired Ford Sierra—for the trip to Canterbury, telephoned all the Nicks and Tony to make sure they were up and ready, checked that the crew—sound man, electrician, cameraman and their complement of assistants—were all set with their own transport arranged, picked up photocopies of scripts and schedule, booked lunch for everyone at a hotel in Canterbury, done a load of paperwork, driven Leo, the Nicks and Tony to Canterbury, found somewhere to park, got everyone together outside the cathedral, kept a log of the takes and attended to the timing, dissuaded the cameraman from telling the director how to direct, bought aspirins for Leo's headache—"Did Leo have a headache?"—hunted for take-away coffees and carried them back for miles on a cardboard tray, disposed of the tray and cups afterwards, rearranged lunch at a different venue, cancelled the first booking, lost the crew, got everyone together again for the afternoon shoot, organized that, found the petty cash for a round of drinks when it was over, driven everyone all the way back to London . . .

"Goodness. And will you become a director or a producer too, when you grow up?"

If Meg heard the irony in Martha's voice she ignored it. "Well, it happens sometimes. Not very likely, not for me. Not at this stage in the game. But I'm really very lucky. It's a marvellous job."

"Dinner-time!" shouted Martha. Leo and the young men reappeared in a stampede. Mungo cowered in face of the massive opposition and slunk away to lie by the cooker.

"I can't stay," said Meg. "I've got to get home. I'll be late as it is, and my mother isn't very well."

She said this hurriedly as if the anxiety of a sick, dependent mother was not something she expected anyone else to be interested in. Nor were they. Nick, Nick, Tony and Nick barely raised their eyes to her as she gathered up all her paraphernalia and prepared to leave. They were too busy capping each other's anecdotes. Leo half rose clumsily from the chair in which he had just sat down, but Meg waved him back and he relapsed gratefully.

"But you haven't even had a drink!" called the pink-T-shirted Nick, even more baby-faced than the rest and not yet inured to media manners.

"That's all right," said Meg, baring her teeth in gallant memory of what must have been, years ago, a broad and lovely smile. "Bye, boys."

Martha saw Meg out. She was still muttering, as she scuttled off into the dark, about the budget and about taking the Sierra back tonight before she caught her train at Charing Cross, so as to avoid paying another day's car hire.

"Meg seems to be under rather a lot of strain," Martha remarked to the red shirt on her right, during the soup.

"Nonsense," said Nick. "She adores every minute of it. Running everything, being indispensable. It's getting people like Meg to move over that's the difficult part."

"Move over?"

"You have to give younger people a chance. Let them get a foot on the ladder."

Martha grimaced. She saw that there was no hope for Meg. The more she hurried and scurried, the heavier the burdens she carried, the more the young men would avert their eyes from her. The axe would fall, and then there would be just Sevenoaks and mother. And then, no mother.

Well, we shall all die.

It was past two o'clock in the morning before Martha saw the last of Nick, Nick, Tony and Nick. They had eaten heartily, finishing all the chicken. Martha masked each helping in thick parsley sauce so as to conceal the strange holes in every slice. No one could have foreseen, that night, that the new series of *Homo Sapiens* would never be made.

18

IT WAS TUESDAY, 21 JULY, the Ulms—Leo and Martha—were going to the Queen's garden party. It was pouring with rain. Serious, dispassionate rain.

Martha stood in front of the bedroom mirror with a comb and a can of hairspray, trying to push her freshly washed and still damp hair into a shape. She ran the fingers of her right hand through soft and now sticky hair, she ran the fingers of her left hand through small seashells, light and dry, in the china bowl on her dressing-table. Sapphire sea, deep-green umbrella pines, hot white rocks and sand. It was the first time she and Leo went away together. She was overwhelmed—by her love and his love, by the inordinate beauty, by the scent of oleanders, by being alone with him all day and all night. On the beach she began collecting shells with a peculiar concentration. She went about it as if everything depended on her doing it properly. It was not the collecting so much as the choosing which shells to pick up and which to reject, for the shells were everywhere. She was very particular. She wanted only the smallest and most perfect ones, minuscule fan-shapes, pure chalky white or inlaid with rose and mauve, like fingernails.

Leo, impressed by her concentration, padded after her in his swimming trunks and offered his contributions.

"Is this a good one? And this one?"

"Yes," she said consideringly, scrutinizing the mother-of-pearl slivers in his upturned palm. And sometimes, "No."

At which he was crestfallen, but did not argue. When it came to seashells Martha had the last word. Realizing this, she saw the chink through which survival shone. Leo knew more people, more facts, more of literature and history and even art than she did or ever would. But if she said "No" there was nothing he could do about it.

They walked back through the midday heat to the hotel, to the cube-shaped white room with the flying gauze curtains misting the blue of the sea. Siesta. She said "Yes" to everything he wanted, wanting it too, aware that "No" was, after all, possible.

But she had never said "No" to Leo very often, about anything. The dusty seashells trickled through her fingers, light and dry, clicking and whispering.

On the sheet of paper enclosed with the invitation was printed in bold type, "Guests arriving (and departing) by chauffeur-driven cars at the Grand Entrance must expect considerable delay." The Constitution Hill and Grosvenor Place entrances were, it was stressed, "convenient for those arriving or leaving by public transport."

Leo, reading over her shoulder, said, "It sounds like instructions for entering the Kingdom of Heaven."

It was to be public transport for the Ulms. This fact and the rain reinforced Martha's natural inclination not to dress up. She put on a cream summer suit with a green cotton sweater and her chain-store pearls, all six strands. Leo made a meal of his own preparations, struggling into his morning suit, groaning—"Oh God, oh God"—losing and finding and losing studs and links, smoothing his grey top hat with his discarded pyjama bottoms, cleaning his shoes and smearing shoe-polish over the bathroom carpet. He breathed hard and seemed to find everything an effort. Mungo, disturbed by their disturbance, scrabbled frantically at Martha's legs, laddering her tights.

Once they were ready to leave, there was another setback. She could not find the umbrella. They couldn't possibly go anywhere in this weather without an umbrella. She dragged on boots and a mackintosh and took the car to Clapham High Street. There she bought a suavely masculine black umbrella, one that would not disgrace Leo.

When at last they joined the stream of people and umbrellas at Grosvenor Gate, her spirits rose. "Let's enjoy it," she whispered to Leo, taking his arm.

They emerged on to the broad lawn of Buckingham Palace. A band, sheltered by a bandstand from the rain, was playing a selection from *My Fair Lady*. Hundreds of people were already mincing and milling about on the grass between the lake and the broad backside of the palace, elevated on its high terrace.

"Not unlike Belwood in some ways," said Leo. "Only bigger, and not so pretty."

A sour swirl of wind blew the new umbrella inside out. A spoke sprang away from its mooring, and then another, as Leo strove to regain control. The umbrella was useless.

"How much did you pay for it?" he enquired tetchily.

"About a fiver."

"There you are then."

Furtively, they deposited the dislocated corpse of the umbrella behind one of the Queen's trees and proceeded without protection. Within minutes Martha's hair was in streaming rat's-tails and her shoulders wet through.

Anglican church dignitaries wearing fancy dress in shades of purple and scarlet boomed greetings to one another, sauntering around with their wives scampering behind them holding down sodden British Home Stores hats. Excited comments were audible from less exotic persons enjoying a unique day out, in a variety of accents from southern brays to north-country rumbles.

"We see here," said Leo, "representatives from every corner of our glorious and far-flung empire—Newcastle-upon-Tyne, Gloucestershire, East Grinstead, Finsbury Park and all stops to Potters Bar."

Martha could not tell whether he was criticizing the gathering for its lack of distinction or for its elitism. In charity, she decided on the latter.

"There are *some* black people," she said.

"Indeed," said Leo.

They had not as yet seen anyone that they knew. This was very unusual for Leo and it made him edgy. Tea was being dispensed in a long veranda or pavilion bordering the lawn at right angles to lake and palace.

"Shall we go and get something now, before it gets too crowded?"

Anything to get out of the indiscriminate rain. Tables and chairs, gawky on the grass and gleaming wet, were deserted. Manoeuvring in the crammed tea-place took on the laboriousness of a medieval joust. Recalcitrant umbrellas had to be lowered and accommodated. Additional clearance and turning-room was called for by hats on heads unaccustomed to carrying wide loads. The violence natural to British people struggling to get hold of free food was hampered, though not altogether inhibited, by their accoutrements and by reverence for the provider of the tea. The rudeness was rendered polite by being perpetrated in slow motion. A hand in a nylon lace glove on the end of a blue crimplene arm drove its way across Martha's face, scraping her nose, and grasped a strawberry tart.

"I'm so sorry, *please* excuse me."

Martha, being small and without hat or umbrella, was apt for the battle. She secured two cups of tea and two plates (white with gold rims), passed the teas back to Leo and filled the plates with as many different things to eat as she could reach.

Something was happening. Like cows in a field when someone walks by, everyone turned to stare. A troop of Beefeaters were descending the palace steps, clearing a path before them. The guests, lowing and mooing, lumbered towards this event from every corner of the sodden gardens. From the mild elevation of the tea-pavilion, the Ulms watched the crowds on the lawn being herded with practised brutality into a horseshoe shape, leaving a curved ten-foot avenue between the line of guests. This was for the passage of Her Majesty.

Martha and Leo joined the people lining the grassy route at

a point where stood two Australian colonels, their khaki uniforms enlivened with generous swags of yellow-gold braid, of the kind that Martha used for her upholstery. (Only lately had she discovered the usefulness of braid for concealing staples and embarrassing joins in the material.) The larger of the colonels upheld a multicoloured golfing umbrella as if it were his regimental banner. Martha and Leo, standing as close as was decent to his proud military back, found that the umbrella covered them too.

Next to the colonels were two aged persons of indeterminate sex in wheelchairs. They were grossly handicapped physically and, it appeared, mentally. Their pale eyes rolled and did not focus. Twenty monarchs could have passed by, or none, for all the difference it made to them.

"Perhaps there will be a miracle when she comes by. Like Lourdes," Martha muttered to Leo. "A nice day out for their keepers, anyway."

She smiled happily into the radiantly smiling faces behind the wheelchairs.

Men in morning suits stood sentry at intervals all along the waiting lines of guests. They chatted to the people close to them while very obviously keeping an eye out for the arrival of the Queen.

The small figure in mango-orange, carrying her own semispherical perspex umbrella over her straw boater, appeared at the palace end of the horseshoe. It was she. Flanked by taller figures with black umbrellas, she began to walk slowly between the expectant lines.

Martha realized what the function of the elegant officials was. Certain guests and their spouses were being picked out to be presented to the Queen. They were led forward as she approached by the aide closest to them, and the chief one of all, at her side, gracefully made the introductions.

"I think they are equerries. Courtiers. Like in history books. I've always wondered what courtiers looked like and what they did."

It was going to take a very long time for the Queen to get

to the Ulms' section of the horseshoe. Her Majesty sustained quite a solid little conversation with each of the chosen ones. The gentleman official, or courtier, nearest to Martha and Leo was not taking much notice yet of what was happening up the line. He was entranced by the Australian colonels. He stood chest to chest with them, peering at their medal ribbons, enquiring with jocular condescension what they were.

"I don't recognize that one, or that," he said, poking. "And I'm a medal man myself."

The colonels explained their ribbons in matter-of-fact voices devoid of deference. They displayed no gratification at the attention they were being paid. The aide in the morning suit, unrewarded, moved on.

The aide was long-legged, thin, erect, silver-haired. His striped trousers and black tailcoat were a really splendid fit. He strolled absently past the unfortunate grotesques in the wheelchairs as if ignoring them was, in itself, the most delicate of courtesies.

Martha saw him being greeted as an old friend by a svelte middle-aged woman who kissed him on both cheeks and introduced him to—presumably—her son, a young man of about twenty-two with curly hair and a roguish smile, dressed rather more informally than even Martha thought right, in a crumpled linen suit.

The courtier talked a little more to the mother—his manners were faultless—before turning his attention to the son. The mother immediately dissociated herself from this conversation, turning away her head and smiling vaguely into the rain, self-effacingly gratified.

The Ulms couldn't hear what the boy was saying, but the courtier's tones penetrated the chattering of the crowd.

"Jolly good! ... Well done! ... That's extremely interesting ... Yup, yup ... Jolly good."

And, before reluctantly resuming his patrol of the ranks:

"Keep in touch. Let me know what you decide. I could have a word with Toby if it would help at all. Jolly good."

The two shook hands in a manly way.

Martha, sunk in the deep trance of the innocent bystander,

was not aware of Leo's fury until she removed her attention from the scene she had just witnessed and realized he was hissing words into her right ear. She'd missed the beginning.

"... establishment in action. Did you see the smooth one in the morning suit, *mesmerized* by the boy, looking into his eyes man to man, oh yes, he knows the parents, oh yes, very promising. Not quite what you'd call *gay* the one in the morning suit, not what you could call *queer*, but playing fields of Eton and all that, it's the young men that turn him on, though he's no doubt married to the sister of someone he was up at Oxford with, a stringy dumb Honourable with a face like a rock-bun and no hair on her, no tits and no bum, he'd run a mile rather than face up to a real woman, he tolerates females who are good sorts and good sports and *ladies*, they're part of the furniture especially in the country and you can pretend they haven't got cunts, and look at the young guy, he knows the score and the rules of the game by instinct, it's bred in the bone, grinning his fanciable grin, twinkling into the old sod's eyes, hands in pockets jiggling jiggling, such a charming boy, called the other 'Sir' with the right touch of irony, intimacy, camping it up in full view and no one realizes, but that lad is making his number and the old sod is loving it, it's how he made his own way, oh yes, whether it's the Guards or the City or the Foreign Office or whatever, there'll be a word dropped in the right quarter, Oh I met Olivia Something-Wonderful's boy, charming young man, needs a bit of encouragement, needs a job in fact, anything you can do for him, old boy ... And there's a note taken and a sherry poured and a call put through, no problem, it's the preferred way of recruitment, it's the way they reproduce themselves for Christ's sake, all the closet queens in high places in the church and the services and the BBC who've been charming young chaps themselves once and got up there in the same way, Well Done, Jolly Good, oh *shit*, you don't have to know anything, you just have to have the right accent and the right wonderful mummy and know how to lick tight well-bred arses with your cocky little-boy smile, oh shit oh shit oh *shit*."

"It's not all like that these days. Think of Norman Fowler."

Martha turned to look at her husband, perturbed by his outburst. His usually pale face was blotched with purple and red.

Sometimes she wondered quite why Leo had ever married Charlotte Bench-Markham. Well, she knew really. And it hadn't worked.

He was still looking horribly agitated, and a dreadful colour. "What's got into you?"

Someone over Leo's shoulder was waving at them. Two people. Isobel Henneken emerged from the tea-pavilion, making an entrance out of what was really an exit, and came weaving across the grass towards the Ulms. She was clinging to the arm of a man who held an umbrella over them both. The man turned out to be Anthony Arklow-Holland.

Mrs. Henneken was looking her best in layers of turquoise and midnight-blue chiffon, somewhat bedraggled. The swooping peacock feather in her hat was damply entangled in the hair that sprouted from beneath her hat-brim in frizzy tufts. Lumpy grey pearls swung in her elongated earlobes. She kissed both Leo and Martha; she obviously had no idea who Martha was, and Leo did not introduce her. He did not look at all pleased to see Mrs. Henneken. He was still looking blotchy. Martha smiled comfortably at Anthony.

Mrs. Henneken raised a liver-spotted hand and twiddled her fingers at a little old man who was plodding by, gift-wrapped in the dress uniform of a bygone age. He seemed not to notice the greeting.

"But it's Poopy! It *is!* Poopy Baldock, my very first earl. He adored me in 1932." She turned to Anthony. "Darling one, did I ever tell you? He opened an unlimited account for me at Woollands. Opposite Harvey Nichols, gone now. Typical of Poopy, it wasn't a very smart shop. I expect his mother got the girls' liberty-bodices there so he'd heard of it."

Martha gazed with interest at the retreating back of Lord Baldock.

"How he's *shrunk,*" said Mrs. Henneken. "But I *think*—just for old times' sake—I really ought to go and have a *word.*"

She ducked out from under Anthony's umbrella and tottered away in her high-heeled sandals in pursuit of the shrunken earl. Martha saw her accost him with a sharp tap on the shoulder. The old man turned suspiciously and, after an unflatteringly long moment, admitted Isobel Henneken under the shelter of his umbrella. She was so much taller than he was that he had to hold his arm vertically up in the air. Mrs. Henneken hung on, and the legendary lovers of 1932 disappeared into the rain.

Martha noticed that their strategic position behind the Australian colonels had been annexed. She was no longer so keen to stare at the Queen now anyway. Leo was a few yards off, talking to a professional person with a beard. The man had an umbrella, which no doubt added to his charm. The two appeared deep in discussion about, she overheard, "the cuts," and Leo was looking reasonably composed.

So Martha turned back to Anthony. She took his arm and Mrs. Henneken's place beside him under the umbrella.

"Well," she said. "I don't see why we shouldn't try to enjoy ourselves. Let's go and check out her herbaceous border."

On the same day, at the same hour, Emmeline Bernay in a topless yellow bikini was floating on her back in the Mediterranean off Castiglioncello in Tuscany. On the beach a friend, whose name was Francine, kept watch over the boy. Emmeline's upturned face stung pleasantly with salt and sun. Her eyes were closed against the blue brilliance of the sky.

To increase this bliss, Emmeline forced herself to imagine its opposite. Her imagination conjured up the picture of a long dusty road winding from nowhere to nowhere, alive with women and children painfully walking with bags and burdens, grey-faced, parched, hopeless. It was an intense vision. It only lasted a moment.

Emmeline, in the sea, was in the process of relinquishing her passion for Leo Ulm. It was draining out of her and dissolving in the uncaring ocean. Renouncing barbarism, she would think of him henceforth infrequently and with amusement. The relief was enormous. Emmeline floated, weightless.

If she had not let Leo go things might have turned out differently. It is possible that love—even unrequited, long-distance love—sustains the life of the beloved.

Love sustains the lover too. It is addictive. Emmeline would have withdrawal symptoms. When the euphoria of release passed she was leached, exhausted, empty. The sun beat down on the featureless beach, blanching the sand, bleaching the shadows, leaving only a dead heat. The child began to cry. The two young women gathered up their things and trailed back to the car.

In the gardens of Buckingham Palace the public-address system boomed out through the wind and rain, penetrating every corner. It was heard in the Mall by chauffeurs sitting in their parked cars under the dripping trees, waiting to drive home aldermen and mayors and archdeacons.

"Mrs. Leo Ulm to the St. John Ambulance tent please. Mrs. Leo Ulm. Mrs. Leo Ulm."

Leo was already on a stretcher. An ambulance was inching its way towards the disaster area along the gravel walk at the foot of the terrace. Leo was unconscious. Martha had hardly ever seen him asleep even, since he woke before her in the mornings and came to bed later in the evenings. He looked horrible.

"He's had a stroke," they told her.

Martha, terrified, climbed into the ambulance after the stretcher and the attendants. Someone passed her Leo's wallet and his spectacles. She shivered with shock in her wet clothes. Anthony, after a moment's hesitation, got into the ambulance as well, encumbered by his umbrella and Leo's grey topper. They left the palace by the Constitution Hill gate and, with the siren screaming like a deranged donkey, lurched and roared through the rush-hour traffic to Westminster Hospital. It took for ever.

When all the guests had left, the palace staff cleared up the gardens as usual. They removed the notices nailed to stakes stuck in the grass by the lake: "Ladies" one way, "Gentle-men" the other. They worked over the paths and lawns pick-ing up rubbish.

In that section of the population that gets invited to royal garden parties, decent people and crooks are represented in the same proportions as in any other. But they are, the crooks especially, of a painstaking respectability. They do not drop much litter. They bring very little litter with them to drop. Tissues, cigarette stubs, sandwich crusts, the odd earring, dry-cleaning ticket or clip-on buckle from a lady's shoe.

A young lad in the palace livery came across the Ulms' umbrella behind the tree where they had hidden it. He ap-proached it warily. It might be a bomb. In his opinion security on these occasions was not all it might be. He saw what went on and drew his own conclusions. Having decided that it could not, in the nature of umbrellas, be a bomb, he thought it might come in very handy for himself. He could do with an um-brella. The punters might telephone the palace—the number is in the book—about a lost jewel or a dropped car key, but they'd be unlikely to chase up a plain black umbrella.

But he could not even get it to open. Rigor mortis had set in. The umbrella that started the day in Clapham High Street ended it in the garbage disposal system of Buckingham Palace.

It was about 5:15 when Leo collapsed. Cameras are not allowed to be brought into Buckingham Palace gardens. A privileged *Times* photographer, stationed on the roof of the palace with the Special Branch sharpshooters, took one reel of film of the lawnful of umbrella-tops distributed in groups and pairs like cells clustering and dividing. He left straight afterwards, bored and wet, and took the film back to the picture desk at Wap-ping to be processed. He missed a small scoop. But the caption under the umbrella picture in *The Times* next day, 22 July, referred to the fact that Dr. Leo Ulm, the well-known author, philosopher and television pundit, had unfortunately been taken ill during the afternoon and was now in intensive care. The Queen had sent her best wishes for a speedy recovery.

19

THEY THOUGHT LEO WOULD DIE, but he lived. When he was strong enough he was transferred to Charing Cross Hospital in Fulham Palace Road for assessment and rehabilitation. He was paralysed down his right side. He could not speak and he could not read. Print made no sense to him at all.

But he was still Leo. He was more Leo than ever. His crooked smile, a lot crookeder, was even more heart-stopping than before. His eyes were his only agents of communication. They were eloquent: they held forth, they ranted. He loved his nurses, and they loved him. His "good" hand, his left hand, strayed appreciatively over them as they hoicked him from bed to chair, from chair to commode.

As he regained his physical strength he became troublesome, roaring wordlessly in protest against his impotence. He disappeared on voyages of exploration in his wheelchair, spinning himself along the corridors, going up and down in the lifts, ending up in Radiography or Orthopaedics or the staff canteen, where he was apprehended and, after some confusion, returned to his ward by a patient orderly.

Martha, Alice and Clara came to see him every day. It was easy for Alice, because her London house was only five minutes' drive from the hospital. It was easy for Clara, because she had nothing much else to do when Harry was at work. Martha, being his wife, had the right to be there, and the sole right to ask questions of the doctors and expect answers.

An unadmitted rivalry sprang up between the three of them as to which brought in the longest-lasting flowers, the most imaginative little gifts, the most entertaining bits of gossip—and, most crucially, which of them was quickest to understand him and read his mood. For the first time in his life, Leo was at the mercy of his emotions. He soon learned to harness them to get what he wanted. Tears welled up in his eyes—tears of anger, of gratitude, of frustration, it was not always easy to tell which.

Alice and Clara, their hearts touched by his easy tears, abandoned the attempt at verbal communication and responded to his emotionalism in kind, petting him, holding and kissing his hands, babbling endearments and comfort-words. They had him, one might say, exactly where they wanted him. Or was it he who had them where he wanted them?

Martha disapproved of all this soppiness, and told them so. She firmly believed that Leo was going to make a complete recovery; it was only a matter of time—and hard work. She behaved with him almost as she had when he was well, and in her visiting times took over where the speech therapist and physiotherapist left off. She tried to get him to talk, to recognize written words and pictures, to count, to do up buttons one-handed, anything.

He did begin to speak, incoherently.

"Emzorr . . . ," he kept saying. "Emzorr . . ."

He was trying to say "I'm sorry," which, once unscrambled, became his all-purpose conversational counter for a time. The second phrase that was restored to him through the neurological fog was "Bugger it."

Until he could do a bit better than this, there was not a lot of point in Ferdie coming to see him often. The sightless son, the speechless father, sat side by side a hundred miles apart. Hand-holding was not something that these two could do.

Harry came sometimes, and Anthony Arklow-Holland often. (Both Anthony and Leo seemed upset after these visits.) People came who were not close friends or colleagues of Leo's, some moved by straightforward sympathy, and a few professional disaster-haunters who befriended the sick and unfortunate for their own sick and unfortunate reasons. Leo, unable to pick and choose among his visitors, was at everyone's mercy. One of the Nicks came once, but not again.

The difficulty of being with Leo was that the visitor had to do absolutely all the talking. Clara saved up stories for him about whom and what she had seen and done, but her life was too uneventful for this to be enough. She found herself confiding in him, telling him about herself—her feelings, her hopes and her anxieties. He listened patiently, with his left eyebrow ironically raised. When she went on rather long, he fidgeted.

There was poetic justice in Leo's enforced transformation into a listener.

While Leo was in hospital Clara discovered that she was pregnant. After the first shock she became, to her own astonishment, deliriously excited. This unwanted, unexpected pregnancy acted like the opening of a lock-gate, freeing pent-up capacities for action and expression she did not know she had. It was as if she could relate wholeheartedly to the world—bus conductors, paper boys, people in shops, Harry—without constriction, for the first time in her life.

"We're going to have a baby," she said to Leo.

Leo's left eyebrow worked overtime. "Bugger it—BUGGER IT!" He laughed and bellowed and waved his arm about, frantically trying to ask or tell her something. He pointed at her, then at himself.

Clara laughed with him, and nearly cried. He was making a joke about her ambiguous use of the word "we."

"Oh, not you and me, darling. I wish—I wish it had been. I wish it could have been."

So, in the end, she declared herself to him.

They were delighted with one another. He passed her a grape from the bowl on his locker. This was a marked sign of favour. Leo was possessive about the fruit and other treats that people brought for him, slapping at any hand that absent-mindedly crept towards the piled-up delicacies.

But, thought Clara, if I, who am an oyster, sit here rattling away and telling him everything that is in my head, things I'd never have told him if he was well, presumably everyone else does too. He'll know so much about everyone that we'll have to watch out when he learns to talk again. He'll be dangerous.

Leo recovered his general health more quickly than the doctors expected. By the end of September—two months after his stroke—he could walk a few steps unaided, had more words at his disposal and could dress himself with his good hand. He was nearly ready to go home.

For Martha it had been a strange period. The terror and confusion of the first few days faded into the routine of hospital visiting and the new task she set herself—restoring Leo to active life, however long it took. It wasn't altogether an unhappy time for her, or for him. For the first time in their marriage, she was in the ascendancy. For the first time, he had one hundred per cent of her attention when they were together. He had the ultimate proof of her devotion to him. The sentimental attentions of Alice and Clara were delicious, but he owed his recovery to Martha's hard-edged commitment and he knew it.

But even that wasn't the whole story, for Martha. She came home late each afternoon to an empty house and thanked God surreptitiously for this island of spinsterly peace. She took Mungo for a run on the Common, ate—in Clara's way, bread and cheese and apples—and worked all evening. The atmosphere in the house, without Leo, was different. It was as if a wind had dropped. Martha finished her illustrations for *The Fisherman's Wife*, five months late, and took them into Trotter Books. Even though publication had had to be put back, they were very pleased with her. Future assignments were discussed. She was sent a cheque.

Leo was coming out of hospital on 9 October. The 16th was his birthday.

* * *

Harry had been away on a course and Clara did not want to tell him about the baby over the telephone. When he was back in London she wanted to see him as soon as possible. She could not wait till the evening. Harry had a lunch appointment the day he got back, and a valuation to do in Albemarle Street afterwards.

"I tell you what, we'll have tea. I'll meet you at that hotel in Piccadilly."

"The Ritz."

"Not the Ritz, on the other side of the road, much nearer Piccadilly Circus, it's changed its name and I can't remember what it's called but you can't miss it. The foyer will be full of Japanese businessmen, go straight through to the lounge on the left."

"I know it," said Clara.

She glanced nostalgically at the gilded doors of the lift as she made for the tea-lounge. It was like an Edwardian ballroom, heavy with plaster mouldings and gilded mirrors. The waitresses wore black dresses with white aprons. In the centre of the room a woman in evening dress was playing a harp. The melancholy twanging was backed by the discreet chatter of couples and families sitting round the edges of the room on sofas and in armchairs, having tea off white-clothed tables.

The night before, having arranged to meet Harry here, Clara dreamed she was searching for him all over London. In the dream she opened the door of a silent restaurant and saw scores of identical small round tables with white cloths on. At each table sat a single man, alone, facing her. As she stood there, each man raised his head to stare at her. No one said anything. None of the men was Harry.

Clara chose a sofa from which she could watch the door. The waitress brought a tiered pagoda of sandwiches and requested Clara to choose between five different kinds of tea. Clara asked for Earl Grey; and with the Earl Grey came Harry.

She told him about the baby. Their baby. It would be born in the spring.

"We'll have to get a little house," said Harry. The sale of

his flat in Marsham Street would give them the down-payment and some over. He spoke of mortgages, of insurance policies, of endowment policies (with profits). He could get it all fixed at the office, anything they wanted.

As he talked the balloon of his pleasure and excitement—a huge, translucent, pearl-pink balloon—swelled and swelled until it burst. He gave a howl of joy, throwing back his red head, waving his arms and stamping his feet on the floor. The Earl Grey spilled all over the white cloth. Faces turned towards them. Voices stopped. The harpist faltered in her twanging. The waitress mopped up the mess.

"I think we would like some cakes now," Clara said to her.

Harry's delight did not come as a surprise. For months, even before their great row and the reconciliation, she had felt the pressure of his singlemindedness. She had dreaded acknowledging it. She continued to turn her head away and dance out of reach. What she had been evading was not Harry but the committing of herself. To anything. She could do it now. Her cramped heart was unclenching. It still hurt a bit to let it, like tearing off a sticking-plaster.

"I love you, Harry. I want to live with you."

"Is it just because of the baby? Because you need me now?"

"I'm different because of the baby. I can't feel conditional any more."

She bit into an éclair.

"I don't just want the baby. I want everything. I want to work too. Not while he's—she's—little. I worked it all out while you were away. I thought, I could be a teacher. Then I'll be at home in the holidays. I'll do a teacher-training course when she starts school. I'll be a tough teacher, I've thought about everything. And Alice and Martha can be godmothers."

"Bratsby can be godfather."

"All right."

They neither of them had thought or spoken of marriage, this time. A baby and a house-purchase financed by an endowment policy (with profits) were quite enough to be getting along with.

* * *

The initial awkwardness of Clara's first visit to Southampton was diffused by the pink tulips she had brought. Harry's mother made a great to-do about finding the right vase, and his father poured sherry.

Clara was curious to meet Harry's parents. Mr. and Mrs. Ashe lived in a large semi-detached brick villa. On the other side of the road was the river Itchen, urban and steely as it flowed to the invisible sea.

"Are we going to tell them about the baby?" she asked in the car.

"Not this time. Let them get to know you first. This is Cobden Bridge—we're almost there."

His parents seemed very normal and fussily hospitable. Mrs. Ashe, who was a nurse, provided a massive meal on blue and white china. Clara remarked how pretty it was.

"It's Royal Copenhagen. We've always liked Royal Copenhagen."

The Royal Copenhagen plates were ceremoniously loaded by Mrs. Ashe with roast lamb, onion sauce, roast potatoes, carrots, broccoli, mint sauce and red jelly. Afterwards there were three puddings—apple charlotte, marmalade steamed sponge and a chocolate mousse. All the food had to be talked about, incessantly.

"I just hope this lamb is nice. I'm not at all sure it's as nice as the joint we had last weekend. What do you think, Robert?"

"You should have got a chicken. You can't go wrong with roast chicken."

Clara declared that the lamb was "wonderful." Mrs. Ashe took it very badly when neither she nor Harry would accept second helpings. The serving-spoons drooped from her fingers. She looked as if she might cry. Nor was she content for them to have just one of her puddings. They had to try them all, one after the other, with cream on.

"I'm afraid the sponge is a little dry. Is it too dry? It's not my usual recipe. I should have stuck to what I know."

"It's not dry at all—it's wonderful," said Clara.

They talked a little about Harry's sister, who lived in Australia with her husband and children. There were photographs of the children on the mantelpiece.

Mrs. Ashe brought in a tray of coffee. "Is it too strong for you? I didn't know how you liked it. Harry always says I make coffee too weak."

"It's wonderful," said Clara.

The table was at one end of the sitting-room. When Mr. Ashe had been passed his coffee he left the table and went to sit in an armchair by the fireplace and read the *Radio Times*. Clara looked at him over the top of her cup, trying to see Harry in him. Robert Ashe, cased in brown tweed, was tall and thin like his son, but there was a meanness about the mouth that was all his own. His eyes fixed on the *Radio Times*, Mr. Ashe extended his coffee-cup at arm's length. Cleverly spotting this, Mrs. Ashe jumped up from the table, took his cup, refilled it, carried it back to him, returned to the table and sat down—but only for a moment.

"Now you young people go and talk to Father while I get this lot cleared away."

"Nonsense, we'll help you," said Clara, beginning to stack the Royal Copenhagen pudding-bowls. To her surprise, Harry did not back her up. He pushed back his chair, stretched and walked like a somnambulist to the armchair opposite his father's.

"Well, we'll let those two have a bit of a talk, anyway," said Mrs. Ashe.

As she dried up Royal Copenhagen china in the immaculate kitchen Clara, through the open door, could hear father and son having their bit of a talk.

"Remember Terry Paine, then? He was captain when you were still taking an interest. Never really fulfilled his potential in my opinion."

"He lived near our school. We used to see him. Remember Ron Davies? He was a forward too. The crowd loved him."

"He had one of those funny haircuts. Good in the air, he was. And what about Chivers—Martin Chivers?"

"He went off to Spurs. And then abroad. Bobby Stokes was

your favourite. We were there, Dad, remember, when he scored a hat trick against Man United."

"It was his début too. Great day. Who else was playing then?"

"Bobby Stokes wasn't really any good, you know. Just lucky. Who was goalie?"

Silence.

Mrs. Ashe, who had been listening raptly, raised her head from the Fairy Liquid suds and called out:

"Wasn't it Gordon Banks? Or that Nobby Stiles?"

Mr. Ashe groaned theatrically. "Gordon Banks never played for the Saints, and neither did Nobby Stiles. You know nothing about it."

His voice was thick with derision, but Mrs. Ashe pinked and giggled, seeming to be really happy for the first time.

"Harry used to love football," she said to Clara. "Does he still follow the Saints?"

"I don't really know," said Clara. "He's never said."

Mrs. Ashe, having finished the washing-up, was setting out a tea-tray.

"I've done a walnut cake for our tea," she said, anxious again. "It's Robert's favourite. And an almond sponge—Harry might well prefer that. I didn't know what you liked of course. I do hope they'll be all right. I'm not too pleased with my oven at the moment. It's not been reliable. It's new, electric. We've always had gas before. The baking's been a bit uneven."

"I'm sure it will be wonderful," said Clara. But her automatic reassurance did not do nearly as much for Mrs. Ashe as did the glum, graceless mastication of the men. Harry managed two slices of the almond cake, ashamedly, as if against his will, and she glowed.

"He never could keep his hands off my almond sponge. And you really enjoyed the walnut, didn't you, Robert?"

She might, from the triumphant throb in her voice, have been talking about sexual pleasures, irresistible even to the most chaste and ascetic of monks, which she alone could supply.

Clara and Harry didn't talk much on the way back up the

M3 to London. They listened to the radio. Clara, overfed, slept a bit.

"Football and food . . . ?" she said, tentatively, as they approached Sunbury.

Harry, his hands on the wheel, flexed his fingers in the sketch of a gesture.

"If you want to talk," he said with difficulty, "you've got to have a topic. So, OK, football and food. It's all there is. They can't change now. It's nothing to do with us. They're all right."

"Of course they're all right. They're—wonderful." She could not resist adding, "I must say he treats her rather shabbily. And it's a miracle how both you and he are so *thin*. It's the ultimate rejection. The triumph of mind over mother."

Harry gave a short barking laugh. Clara felt remorseful, as you do when you force someone to acknowledge a quite unnecessary truth. To make up for it she put her right hand on the blade of Harry's thigh. Harry shifted a little in the driver's seat to facilitate her act of contrition, which was also an act of love.

There was a lot that was wonderful, a lot to be pleased about: Leo's return from hospital, his birthday and Clara's pregnancy. Alice and Ferdie suggested a celebration at Belwood.

Alice said to Martha, privately, "I give it three years." (Meaning Clara and Harry.)

Martha drove Leo and Clara down to Belwood on the day before the birthday. Leo was fine in the car; he had a collapsible wheelchair from which the women helped him to decant himself, with much protest, in and out of the front passenger seat. Clara sat in the back with Mungo, on his best behaviour for once. It was midweek, and Harry could not get away till the Friday night. Clara liked the way he made no fuss about separations.

Leo could walk a little, but was apt to keel over without support. Alice put a divan for him in Ferdie's study, so that he had no need to struggle with the stairs.

They were cosy in the big drawing-room that evening.

Christa played Chopin on the piano to Ferdie and Leo while
Clara and Martha got the supper. Even Ferdie was less lugu-
brious than usual. His father's helplessness shifted the balance
between them. He insisted on pushing Leo's chair into the
dining-room for supper and made a blundering black comedy
of it, crashing the wheels against the side of the door as they
went through. Agnes did not think it was funny.

"Are you all right, Grandfather?"

After supper Christa put Agnes to bed and then played the
piano again. The three women and Ferdie were tired. They
wanted to go to bed, and settle Leo in the study first. Tomorrow, his birthday, would be a tiring day for everyone. But Leo
waved them all away, making loud negative noises. He could
get himself to bed when he felt like it, he made them understand.

Mungo was restless too, and would not settle. When chided
he lay gloomily under the piano for a while, his chin on the
floor, and then came out and whined again. Martha let him
out into the garden but he wanted to come in again at once.

It was understandable. He was in a strange house. Maybe he
did not like Chopin.

In the end Martha, fed up with him, shut Mungo into the
kitchen for the night. Everyone went up to bed except Christa,
still playing, and Leo, staring into the fire, looking across the
room at the fair foreign girl at the piano, staring at the fire
again.

The great storm woke Agnes up. It was pitch dark. The roaring
of the gale made the whole house tremble. It was so loud that
Agnes did not hear the sickening creaks, splinterings and thuds
as massive beeches, oaks and chestnut trees keeled over and
crashed all around the house. She heard the wind. She heard
rain and twigs lashing the window-panes and the hectic clattering of the wooden sashes. She heard the hysterical tinkling
of broken glass, and flat crashes which were slates falling off
the roof and breaking on the terrace.

Agnes lay under her duvet on her back and was frightened. When the storm quietened she got out of bed and ran next door into Christa's room. Christa sometimes let her get into her bed when she had a bad dream.

Christa wasn't in her room. Agnes felt the bed. It was flat and cold. It still had the cover on it. Christa hadn't come to bed at all. Perhaps it was not the middle of the night yet. But Agnes felt sure it was. She did not know what to think.

Agnes considered going to her parents' room. Just then the wind began to scream again, and the thought of negotiating the long dark corridor and the landing to the other part of the house was too awful to contemplate. Agnes went back into her room and switched on the light. But nothing happened. It did not work.

She felt around for the shoebox in which she kept her farm animals. She carried it back to bed with her and lay there feeling each of the animals in turn, identifying them by their shapes in the dark. She told them not to be frightened. She slept a little, but not much.

When Agnes woke again, properly, the storm was over. She could tell from the greyness of the window that it was not time to get up yet, but it was definitely morning. What had woken her was Mungo, in the kitchen below her room. He was crying in a muffled way, as if he knew he should not bark or howl aloud as he would like to. He was scrabbling at the kitchen door.

Mungo probably wanted to go out. Agnes decided it would be public-spirited of her to go down and let him out of the back door before he woke everyone else or made a mess on the kitchen floor.

When she opened the kitchen door Mungo shot out past her and made straight down the passage and across the hall to the drawing-room.

Following Mungo, Agnes saw that the French windows into the garden were swinging wide, the glass broken in stars and tatters on the terrace and on the polished boards inside. The curtains were blotched with wet. The room was cold. Mungo was across the drawing-room, through the open French windows and over the terrace before she could say anything to him. He was haring backwards and forwards on the wet grass down by the lake like a mad dog.

Agnes stood just inside the drawing-room, shivering in her nightdress.

She saw her Grandfather Leo.

Leo was sitting facing her, in his wheelchair. He was looking at her. Something was wrong. His face was a funny colour. His eyes were not talking.

Perhaps it was because he was not wearing his glasses. Perhaps he could not see her very well. She had never seen him without his glasses on before.

Agnes padded right up to him.

He still did not look at her. There was something wrong.

Agnes turned and ran from the room, up the blue torrent of the front stairs, and into her parents' bedroom.

"Mummy, Daddy, wake up! You've got to wake up! Please . . ."

Clara slept through the storm. She awoke to footsteps and hubbub. She got up, went to the mirror and put in her contact lenses. (She had become very swift and expert at this.) Dragging on her dressing-gown she followed the sound of voices downstairs and into the chill drawing-room.

She saw Alice by Leo's wheelchair, cradling his head in her arms, crying. She saw a cushion on the floor at his feet, and beside it a broken pair of spectacles. Leo's. She saw Ferdie speaking on the telephone. She saw Agnes huddling under the piano. She saw Alice picking a thread out of Leo's glossy white hair with hopeless tenderness. She knew that Leo was dead.

20

Martha had slept badly, half roused by the storm. When Clara knocked on the door of her bedroom she was fast asleep.

There is no nice, easy, right way of waking up your best friend and telling her that her husband seems to be dead.

An ambulance came and took Leo away to Brighton General Hospital, where he was pronounced officially dead. Heart failure, they told Martha, who went with him.

Leo's wheelchair still stood in the drawing-room. Ferdie sat by the telephone, ringing for someone to come and mend the glass in the French windows; also an undertaker, the solicitor, the vicar, *The Times* and the *Independent*. And the BBC. When he was through with all that, Clara telephoned Harry.

Over a late breakfast, Agnes told her mother that Christa had not been in her bedroom when she went in to see her during the night.

"Nonsense," said Alice wearily. "She was here last thing."

"I *promise* you, Mummy. I *promise* you she wasn't there. She still isn't."

To spare Alice, who looked at the end of her rope, Clara went upstairs with Agnes to Christa's room.

Christa's room was very tidy. The bed was made.

"You see," said Agnes. "I *told* you."

Clara opened the top drawer of the chest of drawers. It was empty. On the top of the chest, anchored by a little jug with an artificial rose in it, was a folded piece of paper. Clara pushed aside the jug and opened up the paper.

I have gone to Clancy in Brighton. I do not come back to Belwood again. Dr. Ulm is sick but I do not like it what he did and I can not stay. I tell my parents. Christa.

"What does it say? Did Christa write that?"

"She says she's gone to stay with Clancy. Who's Clancy?"

"He's her friend. Her boyfriend."

Clara crumpled Christa's note into her jeans pocket and went back downstairs to the others.

"She's not there. Her bed's not been slept in and her things are gone. There's a note saying she's gone to Brighton and isn't coming back."

Alice made a despairing gesture. Clara was relieved that she did not ask to see the note. What in hell did that stuff about Dr. Ulm mean? Dr. Ulm was Leo, not Ferdie. It probably meant nothing at all. It was not the moment to bother about it anyway.

At midday a police car appeared in the drive. The officer said he was afraid he had bad news.

More bad news?

It appeared that Christa, standing with her suitcase trying to hitch a lift into Brighton in the middle of the night, had been caught by the storm and hit by a falling branch. She was spotted lying in the road, pinned down, by a postman in his van early in the morning. She was in the same hospital as they had taken Leo to. She was alive, but unconscious.

Ferdie, who had spent the whole painful morning on the telephone, returned to it and rang up Christa's parents in Geneva.

Leo's funeral was private. They told the scores of people who got in touch after seeing the announcements of his death that there would be a memorial service at St. Martin-in-the-Fields at a later date. Anthony Arklow-Holland had offered to organize this.

Since Belwood was Leo's son's home, and he had died there,

it seemed natural to have the funeral at the parish church, even if there was a certain indelicacy about laying him to rest in the same churchyard as all his ex-wife's relations. Charlotte was not coming to the funeral. She told Ferdie and Alice that, when they went over to the cottage to tell her that he had died. No, she didn't want to see Dr. Lomax. No, she didn't want to see the vicar. No, she didn't want to come over to the house. She didn't want to see anyone. So, after sitting with her over cups of tea for half an hour, they left her.

It was a small group that followed the hearse down the hill to St. Margaret's Church (C of E), where Leo and Charlotte had been married thirty-three years ago, and which he had never entered again except for Ferdie's christening until this day. Not even Ferdie and Alice knew the vicar, except to say good-morning to. He looked after three scattered, apostate parishes and did not live in Belwood village.

Clara went to the far end of the front row of pews, followed by Alice. Agnes stood between them, holding her mother's skirt. On the other side of Alice was Martha, and then Ferdie on the aisle. Anthony Arklow-Holland and Harry sat together in the front row on the other side.

Dearly Beloveds. Forasmuch as. World Without End Amen.

Clara could not take in the weighty, beautiful words. She could not look at the flower-covered box in the aisle which contained Leo. She could not see across Alice to Martha, to know how she was managing. The walls of the nave were covered with memorials to dead gentry. Clara read the one nearest to her:

Sacred to the memory of Mary Jane Bench Markham Wife of SIR JAMES BENCH MARKHAM of the County of Sussex. She departed this Life for the Heavenly Mansions 19 Jany 1783 in the 29th year of her age, a Godly Lady a Dutiful Wife a Pious Mother. Also of Helena Bench Markham Wife of the said Sir James Bench Markham who Died 5 July 1792 aged 33 years. A kindly Stepmother and a Worthy Helpmeet. Peace at the Last. Also of SIR JAMES BENCH MARKHAM Gent^{mn} and Friend of the

Poor Beloved by the Just and Feared by the Unjust. A Gentleman Nobly Made and Mourned by his children and his Friends Departed this Life 26 December 1828 in Fullness of Years and Honour. To Him the Glory Amen.

The organ panted and moaned as Mrs. Lomax, the doctor's wife, coaxed it into life. Martha had said she wanted a hymn, and she knew which one she wanted.

"Hymn number three hundred and eighty-nine," announced the vicar.

There was no choir, so it was up to them. Mrs. Lomax played the first line of the tune. Martha, Alice and Clara raised their heads and took deep breaths.

"Fight the good fight wi-ith all thy might . . ."

The three voices chimed purely together, with confidence, just like at school, chasing the familiar rippling melody up and down the scale.

> "Lay hold on li-ife and it will be
> Thy joy and crown eternally."

Agnes, sandwiched between Alice and Clara, didn't know this hymn. She looked up at their clear, absorbed faces and listened to their singing with astonishment.

Mrs. Lomax was taking the hymn at a spanking pace. (She'd left something in the oven.) The girls were not singing alone. There was a low masculine thrumming, lagging half a beat or so behind, too substantial to be emanating only from Ferdie, Anthony, Harry and the vicar.

Martha cast a glance over her shoulder and saw Tom and Helen Bollard, Geoff Mansell, Irene and her husband from the garage—and Nick, Nick, Tony and Nick, hymn books held high, doing their boyish best. (Not Meg. She was presumably "moved on" in the autumn shake-out at Channel Four.)

Outside, it was raining. Beside the new grave, Martha wept.

"Man that is born of woman hath but a short time to live, and is full of misery . . .

"... Come, ye blessed children of my Father, receive the kingdom prepared for you from the beginning of the world. . . ."

Charlotte had been knocked irrevocably off balance by the news of Leo's stroke. His death broke her.

Charlotte thought she was cowering in the back of a cave, squatting on its damp earth floor. She was keeping as far as she could from what frightened her. The pale fungus, horribly frilled, grew up against the rock wall. It was dark in the cave and the fungus gave off a glow like a visible stink. It was getting bigger all the time, unfurling fresh fans of sliminess. What if it touched her? The thought of the slightest contact with its clammy flesh made her retch.

Charlotte was inert, at bay in her refuge. Fear made her as inanimate as stone. All her strength was spent in holding herself together and maintaining her stillness. A lump of granite gets tired and tense over the centuries. It aches to abandon its principles and explode into a million million irresponsible particles. But it must not, or the whole universe would explode.

The low mouth of Charlotte's cave was stopped by a stack of fallen branches. Spots of light filtered through on to the threshold. Outside lay the dry brassy day. Charlotte thought she heard voices approaching.

They were coming to get her. Let them come. She was not going to budge. They would have to drag her out, smoke her out, cut and slice her out.

The voices seemed to be nearer. Charlotte's mind changed direction. Worse to be cornered in the cave than to die face to face with the enemy in the light. She leapt up, electrified, smashed her way through the boughs across the entrance to the cave and burst out into the light. She ran wildly down the bare hillside screaming, loosing the fragments of her terror into the wind. She ran and ran.

* * *

Charlotte ran out from the dim dining-room of her cottage where she had been huddling on the floor for the past three days and nights, ever since they came to tell her that Leo was dead. She ran round the lake, stumbling through the fallen birch trees, and across the grass to the big house.

Ferdie, Alice, Clara and Martha were in the drawing-room, talking quietly. Harry was in the kitchen. Everyone else had gone home. Empty wineglasses stood on the mantelpiece and on the piano. Agnes knelt on the floor under the piano, arranging her farm animals.

They heard Charlotte before they saw her. She came to a halt in the doorway of the drawing-room, her clothes stained and awry, her hands bleeding from the scratches of branches, her eyes staring, her breath coming in gasps. Mungo, enchanted by the stench coming off her, tried to round her up, barking.

There was a long aghast pause while Martha got Mungo under control. It took them a moment to realize who it was. Ferdie sat with his head in his hands while Clara and Alice jumped up to put their arms around Charlotte and steer her into the room. At first they thought she had been mugged. Within seconds, it was clear that the disaster was different, and more frightening. Martha just sat still, holding on to Mungo's collar, hoping that her presence would not make things worse.

But Charlotte did not focus on the usurper. Her eyes were fixed in a glaring stare on a pile of flowers that lay on the round table behind the sofa. They were florist's flowers, carnations and gladioli, sent by Isobel Henneken but delivered too late for the funeral.

Charlotte stretched out a hand and grasped a red carnation by the neck.

"Leave them," said Alice, "and come and sit down. Clara, would you go and make us all some tea? And Agnes, darling, will you help Clara and Harry with the tea?"

For once, thought Martha, it's not up to me to decide what to do. She watched as Alice took Charlotte's arm to guide her round the sofa. Charlotte shook Alice off. With her head thrown back she cried to heaven:

"Let me have just *one!* Just *one!* You can spare me *one!*"

Alice, taken aback, said quickly, "Yes, yes, of course you can have one."

She hurriedly disentangled the stalks and extricated the broken-necked carnation. Charlotte crushed the flower in her dirty, bleeding hand.

Ferdie had felt his way to the telephone and was talking to Dr. Lomax's receptionist. Charlotte drank two cups of the tea Clara brought in. She sat staring in front of her, humming a little. They waited.

When Dr. Lomax arrived, he took Charlotte into Ferdie's study and examined her on the divan bed that had been meant for Leo. He gave her an injection. After ten minutes he reappeared, and said to Ferdie:

"I'm not going to go through all the formalities necessary to have your mother admitted to a psychiatric ward. I've only been able to do a very brief examination, but she's in a bad way physically. I don't even know if it's treatable. God knows what pain she must have been in—she'd never consulted me about it. I'm taking her in for tests."

He was upset. He had known Charlotte for ever.

Ferdie went into the study to sit with his mother until the ambulance came—the second time in a week that an ambulance had been called to Belwood.

Agnes trailed out of the front door after the grown-ups. As she was climbing into the ambulance—she refused to be put on a stretcher—Charlotte turned, taking something out of her cardigan pocket.

"Your pig," she said to Agnes in her own kind voice. "I've had it for absolutely ages. I found it in the grass. I forgot to give it to you."

"Oh, good," said Agnes, taking the pig. "I'd been wondering what had happened to him."

Grandmother and granddaughter looked at one another and smiled. Charlotte did not look at anyone else, or say goodbye.

She paid no attention to Alice, who was getting into the ambulance too to accompany her to hospital.

"What's the matter with Granny?" asked Agnes as the ambulance rumbled away down the drive. "Will she be better soon? Is she sad about Grandfather and about Christa?"

"Yes, she's sad," said Clara. "She's ill, and very sad."

"Mummy should have let her have all the flowers, shouldn't she? Not just that one."

"But she only wanted the one. Just one. She *said*."

That night Clara shared her room at Belwood with Harry. He fell asleep and she did not. There were things on her mind.

It was Christa's note that started it off. She had thrown it away, and could no longer remember quite what it had said.

Leo's glasses had been on the floor. That was peculiar for a start, wasn't it? Though they could have just fallen off if he had had some sort of seizure. The glasses had been lying on the floor by a cushion. The cushion hadn't been on the floor when the rest of them went up to bed. Clara distinctly remembered Alice tidying up, folding the newspaper and plumping up cushions of sofas and chairs, everything in its place. The blue thread that Alice had picked out of Leo's hair in the awful dawn had been the same kingfisher blue as the cushion on the floor.

Charlotte, crazed by grief, might have come over from the cottage and smothered Leo with the cushion. Anthony Arklow-Holland could have driven down secretly, come in through the French windows and done it—because he was, or wasn't, Leo's son. Anthony was capable of violence. Leo could have grabbed Christa with his left hand and tried to do something to her that horrified her, and *she* could have smothered him with the blue cushion. Or the boyfriend might have come and done it. Even Martha could have done it. There are always reasons why husbands and wives might want to kill each other; it was not even worth itemizing them. Or Ferdie could have done it. He hated his father really. Alice herself could have done it—

because she could not have him, because she could not bear to see him laid low, any number of reasons. The same was true of herself. She knew she had not smothered Leo with a blue cushion. Probably no one else had either. But *something* must have happened.

The death certificate had been issued, or Leo could not have been buried. No one was asking any questions. Christa—still unconscious, they heard, in a coma—had been flown home to Switzerland.

Clara's doubts about the way Leo died would just have to become part of the furniture of her mind. Not a very nice piece of furniture. She must never drag it out into the light and dust and polish it. She must never put it up for auction. Clara wanted to get away from Belwood now as soon as possible, with Harry and their unborn baby, and not see any of these old friends for rather a long time.

Before they left next morning, she and Harry walked slowly and sadly round the garden and lake looking at the storm damage. The fallen trees looked like prehistoric members of the animal creation. Deprived of dignity they lay across the grass, across one another, hundreds of tons of saurian limbs and torsos, twisted, fractured, mutilated, defeated. Their canopies of green leaves were heads of live bright hair on cadavers.

They saw where a giant beech had torn away a chunk of the earth's surface as it fell. Walking round the root-plate, as round and green as the plastic bases of Agnes's toy farm trees, they saw the roots of the beech sticking out at right angles to the hollow from which they had been wrenched. Most of the roots, pale and tapering as parsnips, seemed shockingly inadequate for the weight of life they had been expected to support.

Elsewhere, people were already taking action. Chainsaw whined busily to chainsaw over the fields and across the Downs. At Belwood, all was mourning and stillness.

21

✳✳✳✳✳

No HEALTHY YOUNG PERSON can sustain grief and tension for an unlimited period of time. Martha was surprised how quickly she settled down to a new, dun-coloured normality. Grief was her companion. It was very nearly her only companion. She was hurt that Clara did not come round more often. She felt as if she had been dropped. Happiness makes people selfish, she supposed, or maybe Clara had only really been interested in Leo all the time.

Alice did not come much either, but Alice had problems of her own. Charlotte was dying, with painful difficulty, in hospital. Alice had not yet found a replacement for Christa, and she had to drive Ferdie in to see his mother every day.

Charlotte did not tell Ferdie that she was worried. She was worried about the way the cottage had been left. She had not tidied her chest of drawers. Charlotte had always said to herself that before the fungus rose up and engulfed her she would tidy her drawers. Then she could let herself be destroyed in peace. She couldn't bear the thought of fastidious Alice picking over the tangles of stockings and underwear, the unironed blouses, the jumble of old sweaters, the piles of down-at-heel shoes. So when Alice asked her if there was anything on her mind Charlotte could not bring herself to say anything. Alice would have offered to go and tidy the drawers, not realizing that this was exactly what Charlotte was afraid of. Besides, Charlotte knew how much Alice had to do, all this visiting, and looking after Agnes.

Martha, all on her own, had plenty to do as well, quite apart from her new commission—illustrations for an expensive children's version of *Don Quixote*. She was gradually sorting through Leo's clothes and taking bundles of his shirts and pullovers to charity shops.

Going through the pockets of his mackintosh, she extracted the usual grubby mass of bus tickets, receipts, a dirty handkerchief—and a thick envelope. It had a French stamp on it and was marked "Personal."

She took it through to the kitchen, poured herself a cup of coffee and sat down. There were five sheets of squared paper in the envelope, obviously torn out of an exercise book, with writing all over both sides of each sheet.

"Cher Léo . . ."

The whole letter was in French. Martha pushed aside a preliminary sketch of Rocinante (based on a picture in an old veterinary textbook called *Diseases of the Horse*), pulled a pad towards her and began translating the letter.

Dear Leo,
    You have made me very happy and very unhappy and your letter made me angry. I do not at all like what you wrote to me. I am twice unhappy, once because I want to be with you and once because what you wrote was . . .

Martha was not quite sure what *affolant* meant, colloquially. She went into the sitting-room and brought back the big French dictionary. She worked on the letter for two hours. Little by little she grew bolder, no longer translating word for word but running ahead of the writer and putting down what she knew must surely be meant, adding her own phrases where the original seemed inadequate. Every now and then she felt it was her own letter to Leo, until she was pulled up by an opinion which she did not share. When she reached the end and read the name "Emmeline" she let out a long slow breath.

She had never heard of Emmeline. There was no address at the top of the letter or on the envelope.

. . . what you wrote was frightful. It is not irrational or reprehensible to feel affection for those who have given us pleasure, or to express that affection. I know you are a distinguished man but I am not impressed by your arguments. It is you who are a cave-man, Leo. You really want the woman to sit yearning in the cave while you go hunting and marauding. So long as we fit your antique fantasies, you will love women. You will even idealize us and put us on a pedestal. If we won't stay up there you get scared and will not love us. Even if you don't admit it you want to be free to grab any sexual opportunity, saying that she was asking for it, or that you don't know what came over you and couldn't help yourself. The women you grab don't go on pedestals, they are just occasions for pleasure, not really people at all. Is that the category I come into? The absent and unattainable woman inspires poetry and art. The absent and attained woman is just a nuisance, if she won't absent herself properly. I think that all men want is good sex, no arguments, and to be comfortable in their home. Very reasonable, perhaps, and more economical in time and money if the same woman provides the lot. If not, the lack must be made up elsewhere. The first depressing thing is that an automaton could provide all these needs if one could be found. The second depressing thing is that all the old-fashioned axioms that I laughed at when I was eighteen still sometimes seem to sum the whole situation up. "All men are the same." "Men only want one thing." It is terrible for a woman when she is unhappy, or in some practical difficulty, and a man comforts and helps her and deals with the difficulty, and maybe allows her to cry and puts his arms round her—and just when she is thinking, here at last is a good kind person who is a man, he starts unbuttoning her shirt, and it's as if all the kindness and help was just a preliminary ruse to disguise his main aim, which is to get inside her. She is expected to be "nice" about this. That didn't happen with you and me. Because I wanted you, I followed all your cues. When I moved out of line and talked to you as if we were friends, that's when I lost you. Though you had talked to me. Not as a friend? No, just a bucket. And if a woman longs to make love with a man, and it is inconvenient for him—the second time, rarely the first time—he feels he can freeze her off and be self-righteous and, possibly, ridicule her in his mind. If I want any man as a friend for life I am a fool if I let him become my lover. Yet there are happy lovers. It's not hard, for a time, until desire becomes unequal. There are happy marriages too—I don't mean couples who just stay together. I think it depends on one being much more unselfish than the other. Sometimes, perhaps, it is the man. I think if I married I would insist on separate lives, so that we could remain lovers for longer, and then be great friends. But I'm not married. No one has ever wanted to marry me. I am too much for men, or not enough for men, I don't know which. I don't understand marriage, Leo. Is it a fortress against the world? Or a metaphysical adventure? A return to the nursery? Or an *excuse*? I know life is difficult for men too. Always being competitive, always awarding yourself and other people marks out of ten. I think perhaps younger men are not like that, the people who were born in the sixties. The men I've known have always been much older than me. I'm fighting the battles of my mother's generation, and the women of that generation—the women who are your contemporaries, Leo—lost all their battles. Why did you keep saying "I'm sorry"? It can't just be because you're English. Your "I'm sorry" is either too trivial or too dreadful to fit the case. It's either that what happened between us was so unimportant that you said "I'm sorry" as you would if you were stretching across someone to reach an ashtray. Or it was to make quite sure that I realized you were out to hurt me, the way one says "I'm sorry" to a fired employee or a child who must be punished. Either way, it's horrible.

Something in Emmeline's letter stayed in Martha's mind long afterwards, when the rest had faded. It seemed to be addressed to her.

> I don't think you understand what it was for me. To accept a lover, after long and routine faithfulness to someone else, is to lose your virginity for a second time. It is as important, and as shattering, and as exciting, as the first time.

"What would you do," Martha asked Anthony Arklow-Holland, "if you had something written down that was very important and personal? Something that does not really belong to you, but you can't give it back?"
"Will you ever want to read it again?"
"No."
"Will you ever want anyone else to read it?"
"No."
"Then burn it."

The fifth of November is carnival time in the conventional country town of Lewes. The citizens celebrate Guy Fawkes Night in an arcane and riotous seventeenth-century manner unknown elsewhere in Britain. Bonfire societies representing the different areas of the town plot and plan for weeks beforehand, deciding on a "theme," designing and building elaborate floats and making ingenious costumes. Grocers and bank clerks abandon their everyday selves and join their society's procession in extravagant disguise, winding noisily and competitively through the dark streets holding aloft flaming torches.

For the Bollard children, it was the event of the year. Alice, with an overexcited Agnes, went to one of the bonfires—higher than ever this year, because of the wood brought down by the storm—and ended up at the Old Rectory where Tom Bollard was uproariously jovial and Helen at her most earth-motherish, serving lentil soup and sausages to thirty dirty, overtired children and their parents.

Leo had loathed bonfires and fireworks, because of the accident that had blinded Ferdie.

Martha remembered this as she and Anthony built a modest bonfire in her back garden on Guy Fawkes Night. When it was fairly blazing, Martha brought out Emmeline's letter and her version of it, and threw all the sheets of paper on the fire. They watched the pages blacken and burst into flame.

It wasn't enough. Martha ran back into the house and brought out an armful of letters and papers from Leo's desk. These too she threw on the fire.

"Are you sure you know what you're doing?" asked Anthony.

"Yes. Help me. I can't do it all by myself."

Together they cleared the top of Leo's desk, the pigeon-holes, the five packed drawers beneath, two stuffed suitcases from the attic and three tall filing cabinets. They carried out hundreds of letters, notes, lectures, programmes, drafts, manuscripts, typescripts, offprints, accounts, official documents, contracts, invitations, pamphlets, and more letters, some going back thirty years, white, blue and brown envelopes, discoloured yellowish envelopes, envelopes with foreign stamps and striped airmail borders, all of them addressed to Leo Ulm. They threw the whole lot on the bonfire.

Only they could have done it. The child who builds the teetering castle of bricks is the one who is allowed to knock it down. Martha, the curator of her husband's memory, and Anthony, the walking repository of twentieth-century life and letters, could do it.

The trouble was that papers do not burn easily. They become solid fuel of a resistant kind. Corners and loose sheets curled and flared while the airless mass of the material threatened to put the bonfire out altogether. They had to unpick the heap, pushing and pulling at the layers of paper with long sticks, burning a little at a time. The air around them was full of smoke and cracks and bangs. Rockets and Roman candles from neighbouring gardens and the Common sang upwards and exploded in fans of stars and colours in the dark sky. Mungo, who like Leo hated fireworks, lay upstairs on Martha's bed.

It took them hours. At last the bonfire was a quaking red and black heap of paper ash, which the wind sent floating upwards and down again, the fragile shreds settling all over Martha and Anthony. Filthy, their hands and hair smelling of smoke, they sat on the ruined grass by the embers and lit sparklers. Holding her sparkler in front of her, waving it about vaguely, Martha told Anthony about another bonfire, long ago. Her story went a little way to explain why Leo did not love Ferdie more, and why he did not want more babies. Martha thought it might explain why she herself had never conceived—with Leo. It wasn't about Ferdie's accident, though it was Leo who had told her the story.

Charlotte had apparently insisted on having her baby—Ferdie—at home, at Belwood. She had never been in hospital and hated the idea. The local midwife settled herself in Charlotte's bedroom when labour began. She checked that all the items on the list she had given Charlotte beforehand were laid out on a clean towel on the chest of drawers. The midwife's requirements seemed horribly primitive to Leo, who had, at the last minute, to finish collecting up what was on the list. Electric kettle, torch, saucepan, cotton wool, antiseptic, scissors, clean rags, two pudding-basins, towels, quantities of newspaper and two empty fish-paste jars.

He had to go into Lewes and buy two jars of fish paste, since there was none in the house. They used the gritty, rusky stuff to make sandwiches with at lunchtime. The sandwiches were very nasty. Then Leo washed the jars and lined them up with the rest of the equipment.

"What *were* the fish-paste jars for?" asked Anthony.

Martha suspected he was nervous of what the answer might be, imagining bizarre obstetric horrors. Home confinements were hardly Anthony's field. She was telling this story to the wrong person. But she still wanted to tell it. She bumped his sparkler with her own in a friendly way.

"Just to stand thermometers and things in," she said.

"I didn't know people had babies at home in modern times."

"This was in the mid-fifties. Lots of people did—it was quite routine."

The midwife got Charlotte out of bed and spread a thick layer of newspapers between the bottom sheet and the mattress. Then she settled Charlotte back in, and sat timing her contractions. While they waited, the midwife knitted.

The sparklers went out. Martha told the rest of the story in the dark.

Ferdie was born at about eight o'clock in the evening. He arrived very quickly at the last, before Dr. Lomax had time to arrive. The midwife was quite pleased about that, since she despised the protocol which ordained that the patient's GP should be there for the interesting part.

Leo had not been present at the birth, though the midwife had indicated she could use a second pair of hands if he felt up to it. He wandered about the house feeling scared and tense, not knowing what to do with himself.

"Dr. Ulm! It's a boy!"

There wasn't much time to savour this triumph, or to say much to Charlotte, who smiled up at him and kissed him. The midwife was wrapping something up in newspaper. She was wrapping it—whatever it was—in the bustling way that they wrapped fish and chips in Leo's north-country youth—thoroughly, folding the paper over and up at the ends and then at the sides, then adding another layer of newspaper and folding again. She passed the well-wrapped bundle to Leo.

"I'd like you to get rid of this for me, Dr. Ulm, if you'd be so kind."

For a moment Leo thought it was the baby. But it couldn't be; the little purplish creature was in its new Moses basket by Charlotte's side.

"Get rid of it?"

"Haven't you got a solid-fuel boiler?"

"No, it's gas."

"Then take it outside and burn it, Dr. Ulm."

"What is it?"

"It's what we call the afterbirth."

Leo took the parcel and went out into the garden. It was almost dark. He laid the parcel down on the ground and put a match to the newspaper wrapping. It flared up, then went out.

Leo went into the kitchen and found two firelighters at the bottom of an old packet. With these, the blaze was fiercer and more convincing. The paper burned away—and its contents cooked, like the offal it was. It smelled. The umbilical cord unwound in the flames and wriggled spasmodically. The spongy afterbirth made gravy, which dripped and sizzled on the damp earth.

Leo put an end to the nightmare by finding a spade, digging a hole among the elaeagnus bushes (he didn't know it was elaeagnus, but he had shown Martha the spot) and burying the charred placenta in a shallow grave. Later he got into bed beside the sleeping Charlotte, on a clean sheet, the newspaper still in place and crackling beneath him when he turned over. He did not sleep well.

"Lucky they didn't have a dog," said Anthony, thinking squeamishly of a scrabbling Mungo.

Anthony and Martha went back into the house. She fed Mungo, while he poured stiff drinks. Anthony, after the holocaust of Leo's papers and Martha's story, conducted himself like a man who has undergone an ordeal. He clearly felt he was learning about life. Martha surveyed Leo's empty desk with guilt and satisfaction. She felt she had learned something intangible about herself and Anthony, and liked it.

"Do we have any more sparklers?" she asked him.

Alice encountered Helen Bollard, with Polly in tow, in Brighton's brightest pavilion, the new Asda superstore. They agreed that it wasn't a patch on Safeway. Their loaded trolleys nuzzled one another as they talked. Alice's news set Helen Bollard's mind racing. She could not wait to tell Tom.

Alice and Ferdie were doing the unthinkable. They were selling Belwood. Only days after the great storm had come the collapse of the stock market. Ferdie, since the Big Bang, had been playing the market with intoxicating success, and had got rid of the last of the safe stocks that his mother had made over to him. Now he was very badly down. He owed a lot of money. He had no capital left with which to start again. The storm had done serious damage to the roof at Belwood, and he was under-insured. There seemed to be no alternative to selling up, and no real objection. His mother would never be returning to the cottage, which would be sold with the rest of the property.

Agnes was the one who would miss Belwood. She would see it for the last time at an even younger age than her father, when he lost his sight. Like Ferdie she would hold it in her mind all her life with a child's vision, her paradise lost of scarlet poppies, bluebells, the cherry tree. She would miss Tracy, her best friend at school. She would forget that she was bullied by the Bollard children; she might even forget that bad things happened.

Alice did not really mind leaving Belwood a bit. She liked the idea of being in London all the time, and improving the Fulham house with the best furniture and pictures from Belwood. She thought she might do a further degree in philosophy at London University; and Agnes, if the local comprehensive was no good, might go to Queen's College in Harley Street. (Alice had not really understood that she and Ferdie had no money at all. Clara, hearing the saga in instalments from Martha, understood for the first time what a silly person Alice was.)

Helen Bollard was only half listening to what Alice was saying.

"Who's the agent?" she asked.

"Knight Frank and Rutley."

Helen did not have the nerve to say, "How much?" which was all she longed to know. It would be, perhaps, a little crude. Commiserating, sending love to Ferdie, smiling her rabbitty smile, she disentangled her trolley from Alice's and precipitated it, and Polly, towards the checkout. Then straight home to the Old Rectory, and the telephone.

Alice went home too, and had a long and serious conversation with Ferdie. He explained to her just how bad things were. His portfolio was in ruins. He had invested heavily in the Bell

Group of Australia, which had stood at over 10 Australian dollars and was now down to 1.75; and in Rotaprint, whose shares had been at 18½ and were down to 2¼. There would be no Queen's College for Agnes. Ferdie had also had shares in various insurance companies, whose prices had been adversely affected by the storm.

"Does that mean Harry Ashe will lose his job?" asked Alice, who was irritated by Clara's new serenity.

"Of course not. Those companies have vast reserves, and anyway they'll put their premiums up."

Misfortune gave Ferdie authority. He was in his element. Alice, for the first time in her life, was all at sea. But Alice would float. It's all right for *her*.

22

✻✻✻✻✻

CHARLOTTE (BENCH-MARKHAM, or Ulm, or McAndrew), only daughter of the late Brigadier and Mrs. F. R. O. Bench-Markham, had all but departed this life. Departing was hard work and she had not much energy left. If she stopped concentrating on her dying, life seeped back in its dreary way and she had to start all over again.

She lay very still. She was dying from the outside in. When she moved or was moved, chills rang through her body, as when one lies too long in bathwater that has grown cold. Sometimes she was nearly there, coming laboriously closer to the point of light at the end of the subterranean tunnel. This light was not a threat, like the brash glare outside her cave, before. At the end of the tunnel was only soft sunshine, cool grass, running water and an end.

To have arrived. If only she could. She was almost there again when a face was thrust close to hers, a kind black face asking her if she would like a little drink of water. Ingrained politeness made Charlotte struggle to reply and, in the struggle, she was dragged back from her desire yet again.

It was not a new experience. Always, the object of her desire had moved out of range. She could not now remember what or whom she had desired when she had been in life but she recognized the familiar sinking feeling of failure and disappointment. She was no longer in life but residual life was still in her, ebbing, and trickling unwillingly when forced by outside pressures.

In the end, Charlotte would get to the end, to the kingdom prepared for her from the beginning of the world.

Martha and Anthony Arklow-Holland have come to an arrangement that pleases and amuses them both. The Clapham house is too big for one person, and all the more so now that Leo's clutter has gone. Anthony will give up the flat in West Drayton and move in with her. His mother Maeve will come too. Martha understands that Maeve has no one but Anthony and that she cannot be abandoned.

Maeve Arklow is just an ageing woman who had a good time, as good times go, and fell on evil days. She is proud of her son to the point of mania. She does not drink. Isobel Henneken just made that up. It is Isobel Henneken that drinks.

(In spite of Anthony's recommendation, Virago Press, the feminist publishing house, will not be reissuing Mrs. Henneken's novel *Playing Sardines*. They wrote him a nice letter, but said they found the book "tawdry in its values, and disappointingly superficial." Clara, when she heard, remarked drily to Harry that it was evidently not enough to be conspicuous, sexually well-connected and over seventy-five to be a heroine of the feminist revolution. Though it helps.)

Martha, huddled against Mungo in the night, hopes that taking Anthony and his mother into her house will not turn out to be a mistake. What does Anthony *do* all day?

Nothing, but nothing, is going to be allowed to prevent Martha from meeting her deadline for the *Don Quixote* pictures.

Will I be his lover, his sister or just his landlady?

Whichever, Martha will be it to the best of her ability, because she always tries to meet other people's expectations. It seems the only decent thing to do. Martha hardly ever says "No."

Her preliminary sketches for Sancho Panza are based on herself—the stocky body, the straight brown hair, the capable hands.

* * *

It had been a wet, cool year, with less sunshine than average. The great storm had stripped millions of leaves from the trees before the proper time, robbing November of the gold it was owed. Autumn turned into winter without anyone noticing. There was no frost or snow, just an intensification of wetness and coolness.

In the week before Christmas there was one perfect out-of-season day. The sky over London was clear pale blue. The light was sharp and brilliant. Harry telephoned Clara in the morning and told her he thought he might have found their house. The particulars had been in his mail. He wanted her to pick up the keys at the agent's and meet him at the house during his lunch hour.

When he telephoned, Clara was lying on her bed listening for the twentieth time in a week to a recording of *The Magic Flute* by the Vienna State Opera, conducted by Karl Böhm. *The Magic Flute* had replaced *The Marriage of Figaro* in her obsessional affection. She kept meaning to tell Harry that she had been quite wrong about all Mozart's loveliest love songs being false, designed to deceive. In *The Magic Flute* the love songs were songs of real love, even if they were sometimes funny, like Papageno's and Papagena's. Well, love was sometimes funny.

She would forget to tell him again, today.

Clara took a tube to Stockwell, south of the river, and then walked. Exercise was good for her. To her relief the ponderous house-agent did not insist on accompanying her to the house; it was empty. He pointed out the street to her in his *London A–Z*. It was almost invisible as it bent round in a short semicircle off the main road. Clara's contact lenses made her longsighted; she could not read the small print.

Not hoping for too much, she walked in the roar of lorries down the featureless south London street, past unprosperous shops, selling electrical goods and videos, past a tacky men's outfitter's, a Halal butcher, a card shop, a sauna with dirty strips of blinds, a bread shop. Clara went into the bread shop and bought a filled roll. Cheese and tomato.

Just before the railway bridge, he'd said. This must be the turn now.

At the beginning of the nineteenth century this part of London, two or three miles south of the river, was not London at all. It was flat countryside, with villages linked by lanes running between market gardens, dairy farms and fields of lavender. Before dawn, horse-drawn carts creaked along the turnpike road and over the bridge into the smoky city carrying produce for its shops and markets, its taverns, lodging-houses and private mansions.

The small street into which Clara turned was a village relic, preserved by oversight and indifference. On either side of the narrow curving roadway were detached houses of old stained brick, with small-paned sash windows. Each sat behind a square front garden enclosed by wooden palings, but each house was different. One was three storeys high, another was so small that it could only contain one room downstairs and one up. Another was double-fronted, with black-grilled basement windows and stone steps up to the front door. The next had elegant Gothic windows downstairs, and a green plank door instead of a window upstairs—the old hayloft. Some of the houses had pointed timber porches, added later. They were in varying states of disrepair. There was rotting woodwork and peeling paint; cracked windows, never washed, were draped from within by crookedly hung material decomposing into cobwebby filth. In one, a new pseudo-Georgian door had replaced the original, and the wooden sashes made way for metal window-frames.

The tall house with the FOR SALE sign was on the bend of the lane. Clara pushed open the low front gate, walked up the path and fitted the key in the round-topped front door—a sequence of actions she would endlessly repeat. She was doing it for the first time.

She left the front door half open. When Harry arrived she was leaning over the curved banister-rail waiting for him. She saw his shadow on the hall floorboards before she saw him.

"There is room for the armoire," she called. "And in another bedroom there's a built-in cupboard. For keeping skeletons in."

"Do you like it?"

Clara liked the house so much that she could not think of anything sensible to say. "I like the way it smells."

She had already been in it for half an hour and seen everything that it was, and everything they would make of it, with the eye of vision. She left Harry to go round for the first time on his own, afraid of putting him off by her certainties.

She went to sit outside on the kitchen step to wait for him; she was in the shade, but it was not cold. The theatrical winter sun illuminated the further half of the back garden—rough grass which ended in a tangle of hawthorn, alders and brambles, and the railway line. A goods train went slowly by. She could hear it but not see it. The trains too would become an accompaniment to their lives, a way of knowing they were at home.

The baby moved inside her. She was getting used to that now.

"This is where we will live," she said in her head to the baby. "There's an awful lot to do to it. But we have all the time in the world."

Harry came and sat beside her on the step. They looked at each other. Clara saw that he felt the same as she did. They put their arms round each other.

Clara said, not knowing she was going to say it, "Can you imagine committing murder?"

"Yes. Yes, I can . . . Are you thinking about Leo?"

"I suppose I am."

The relief was enormous.

Harry pulled a nettle out of the crack between the step and the flagstones. He shredded the nettle, letting the fragments fall.

"I think I know what happened. But I don't think we'll talk about it. Ever. You don't need to know."

He got up abruptly and went back into the house. Clara stayed where she was.

I don't need to know. Someone knows, so the story is not screaming to be heard.

Someone must have confided in Harry, revealed what he or

she knew, confessed even. Ferdie. Alice. Anthony. *Martha.* (I don't need to know.) Clara tried to think back to occasions when Harry might have made whatever his discovery was, but she had too little evidence to go on. Had Harry, or any of the others, been to see Clancy to tell him what happened to Christa?

Clara found it extraordinary that she had so quickly suspected that Leo had been stifled with the blue cushion. The loose thread in his hair was no proof of anything. Just another loose end.

His dear face, his dear hands, rotting now like any other garbage.

But I had wished him dead, sometimes. Witches have been burned for less. Who is not guilty?

A "good story" is one that has a substantial pay-off, like *The Fisherman's Wife* or *Don Giovanni.* Children like tidy endings: the wicked giant was killed and the prince and princess lived happily ever after. But no story is ever over. A true story is one in which people decide to believe. Harry has probably got it wrong. He doesn't like loose ends, he likes to be sure. I do too—but about quite different things. It doesn't matter.

Harry reappeared at the kitchen door and said, "What a lot of people would do, you know, is to open up these small rooms and make the whole ground floor open-plan."

"No, I don't want that."

"You sure? Could be dramatic. Big box-office hit."

"But the world, the whole world, is open-plan."

We have to manage out there, in the fog, bumping into things, in danger.

"I want to put my hand on a door-knob, turn it, open the door, close it behind me, and be in a room that is just as it was when I last saw it, with our things in it, and quiet air."

"You'll be lucky. You've forgotten what children do to rooms. Toys scattered everywhere, socks, bits of paper, crayons, stains on the carpet, cushions all over the floor . . ."

"But there'll be one room where the children aren't allowed," said Clara. "Won't there? For you and me?"

"And for the house-plants," said Harry.

Slowly, as if sight-reading a piece of music, they went round the house again together, talking about it, Clara allowing her passion to show, but thinking more than she was saying.

She would clear that wilderness at the bottom of the garden and put a greenhouse there. Harry's plants would live in the greenhouse. Definitely.

Maybe that was too punitive. She was plotting to put her mad step-daughters—Obregonia, Wiggininsia, Mammillaria, Greenoria and Frailea, oh poor Frailea—in an orphanage.

They paused on the landing and looked down into the front garden and the lane.

"If we put a little table in the window here," said Clara, "it would be a good place for some of your plants, wouldn't it?

"The thing is," she said, as they came back downstairs into what would be the sitting-room, "I think I shall die if we don't get this house."

She was behaving as if the security of the house was the most important thing, more important than her alliance with Harry.

In retrospect, will he feel he has made a bad mistake? Will I?

I think that everyone else was right, I should have made myself independent first and then found out whether I wanted to be with Harry always. But at any given moment there is no real choice, only a single priority. I walk blind, just as much as Ferdie does. My vision like his illuminates only the past. Looking back, I see an infinite number of possible routes. But the person looking back is someone else, with a different priority—which may make her wise about the past, but which is forcing her, sightless, into yet another uninformed decision about today. "Now" is the blind-spot. The eternal now. We must be happy for as long as we can, and kind to each other.

Harry spoke of damp, of renewing window-frames, of modernizing the kitchen and bathroom, of heating, of the roof.

Especially the roof. Even the agent had felt compelled to mention the roof. Harry was talking about money.

"If there's so much wrong with it, then we'll just get it cheaper!" said Clara. "I think we should make an offer *now!*"

She saw in her mind's eye some other couple coming round half an hour after they left, and going straight back to the agent with the down-payment.

Harry looked at his watch. He ought to get back to the office.

On the floorboards beside the iron grate was a dusty black telephone, upright and old-fashioned. On impulse Clara picked up the receiver.

"It's connected! It's working!"

Once in a lifetime institutional inefficiency benefits the customer. Clutching the agent's particulars, Harry dialled the number.

It was the shortest day of the year. The sun was already going down, burnt orange behind low clouds. Clara the nest-builder stood waiting; all around her, dust-motes glinted in the misty rays that penetrated every flaky corner of the room. As he talked to the agent Harry looked with love and amusement at her long thin legs, her impatient bird-head on the fragile neck—and the incongruous bump that was the baby, over which her old camel coat would no longer close. Their kingdom, his and hers and their children's, had a leaky roof. It was not a heavenly kingdom. But they were both ready now to take it on.

There is a FOR SALE sign up outside the main gates of Belwood too, and advertisements in the Sunday papers, in *Country Life* and in *Country Homes and Interiors*. Belwood too has a leaky roof. Tom Bollard is trying to put Helen off it. He is unwilling even to go to the trouble of a survey, which he knows in advance will be horrendous.

Helen Bollard is a very determined person. They may buy Belwood, they may not. Meanwhile Helen has snapped up

Irene, who three mornings a week picks up after the Bollard children and trails a squeezy-mop over the kitchen floor at the Old Rectory. She calls Mr. and Mrs. B. "Sir" and "Madam" with undiagnosed sarcasm. Irene is not a snob. She respects the Bollards' prosperity. She just doesn't like them very much, and is keeping her eyes open for another job. (Helen Bollard has no idea of this.)

It is a bad time of year for selling large, dilapidated country-houses. Ferdie and Alice, since they were leaving, have not gone to the gratuitous expense of having the bodies of fallen giants cleared from the garden. Over two months have passed since the great storm. Toadstools and fungi thrive on and around the prostrate tree-trunks. The grass on their up-ended rootplates is growing, in all innocence. Exposure has weathered the torn-up roots. They seem to have acquired bark. A root is a branch that grows underground. A branch is a root that grows in the light. On last summer's whippy growth, sprawling over the grass, there are new leaf-buds, nourished by corpses. Daffodils and crocuses, prepacked in their bulbs and programmed to respond to the cool wetness of early spring, have prematurely exposed themselves under the shrubs edging the grass, where Agnes dug for her worm. Nettles are springing up there too, and everywhere. Mansell has been laid off. It's not the meek that shall inherit the earth; it's the nettles.

Charlotte's cottage, empty and deserted, unheated and unlit, has been annexed by snails and spiders. Alice did go in, as Charlotte had feared, and cleared up her things. But she hardly looked at them. Working quickly and crossly, she stuffed the contents of the chest of drawers and the wardrobe into black plastic rubbish sacks. They are still there, leaning against the bedroom wall. Not until Charlotte has died will it seem proper to dispose of her clothes. The furniture from the cottage has been sent to local auction sales. The only thing of Charlotte's that Alice wanted was a portrait of Ferdie's grandfather by de Laszlo, done in the 1920s. This now hangs over the fireplace in the pinched drawing-room in Fulham. In Charlotte's dark kitchen a tap drips, and her yellow teapot, somehow forgotten in the packing-up, still stands on the draining-board. Perhaps it was left behind because it had not been washed up. There are two teabags in it, fuzzy with green mould. The last time Charlotte made tea was for Alice and Ferdie when they came to tell her about Leo's death.

On the lake the ducks chug up and down, round and round, quacking indecisively. The mild weather confuses them, too. One laid an egg last week but lacked the confidence to build a nest. The egg lies cold in the mud on the edge of the lake.

In another month or two they will know exactly what to do. The drakes' necks will turn iridescent green. They will rape the ducks. That is their job. The ducks, when they have recovered from this indignity, will waddle off around the margins of the lake looking for somewhere to build their nests. The drakes will follow them, a few steps behind. Two drakes to each duck. Paternity is hard to ascribe in the duck world and they are taking no chances.

The ducks build down-lined nests behind the drooping hellebores, in the roots of the thickets of dogwood, in the tangles of fallen birch branches. They lay their eggs and then they sit on them. That is their job.

But not yet, not until the snow has fallen and melted and gone.

It has begun to rain again. The rain falls impartially on the lake, the ducks, the fallen trees, the deserted cottage, the big empty house, and on the pages of a child's book left out on the terrace, unidentifiable, returning to pulp. No one is watching, so it might as well not be happening. A story can't be stopped except by a joke or an epigram or a judgement, and there's no one around to make one.

A Note About the Author

Victoria Glendinning won the Duff Cooper Memorial Prize and the James Tait Black Memorial Prize for *Edith Sitwell: A Unicorn Among Lions* (1981). She reviews books for *The Times* and *The Sunday Times* (London) and for other journals in Britain and the United States. The author of several acclaimed biographies, of which the most recent is *Rebecca West*, she is now working on a life of Anthony Trollope. Victoria Glendinning lives in London and Hertfordshire, has four sons, and is married to the Irish writer Terence de Vere White.

A Note on the Type

The text of this book was composed in a digitized version of Trump Mediæval. Designed by Professor Georg Trump in the mid-1950s, Trump Mediæval was cut and cast by the C. E. Weber Type Foundry of Stuttgart, West Germany. The roman letterforms are based on classical prototypes, but Professor Trump imbued them with his own unmistakable style. The italic letterforms, unlike those of so many other typefaces, are closely related to their roman counterparts. The result is a truly contemporary type, notable for both its legibility and its versatility.

Composed by Creative Graphics, Inc.,
Allentown, Pennsylvania
Printed and bound by The Haddon Craftsmen, Inc.,
Scranton, Pennsylvania
Designed by Anthea Lingeman